FRENCH CREEK

The story of one community's survival after the Collapse of eastern America

Paul H Rowney

This is a work of fiction. Names, characters, business, events and incidents are the products of the author's imagination. Any resemblance to actual persons, living or dead, or actual events is purely coincidental.

Published by: PHR Media LLC, Nashville TN 37211, USA.

Cover design by Yeonwoo Baik
ISBN: **979-8-9869861-0-4** (KIndle)
Join our Facebook Group:
French Creek-The Book

Discuss post-apocalyptic living. How would you survive in the 19th century? What would you miss from the 21st century?
Ask the author questions about the book.
Find out more about the sequel to *French Creek*-and how to get a free copy when it's published early 2023.

Dedicated to:

My amazing, long-suffering wife Sheri, who saw too many household projects put on hold while I wrote this book. To my daughters Stephanie and Rachel for their encouragement and for being two wonderful people. To Trevor for his advice and support in reading the early drafts.

To retirement that has given me the time to write my first book. And to the residents of 'French Creek' for their unintentional inspiration.

Contents

CHAPTER 1

Billie never saw the shooter. He never heard the shot or felt the bullet as it entered his skull, instantly ending his twenty-eight years of life.

Alone in Sentry Post One, he was supposed to be on guard, protecting the French Creek community from the people who slowly crept through the moonlit Kentucky night towards his unsuspecting village. But the work was boring (there had been no intruders in over six months), and keeping his concentration proved difficult. He fell asleep, never to wake up.

Billie wouldn't be the first to die that night.

"Got 'im" said the group's leader, Hal, with a hint of self-satisfaction in his voice. He put down his rifle and turned to the rest of the group with a smile on his face. "Good shot, though I say so myself", he whispered. Not everyone thought the same.

Jane, one of the three women in the group, was not impressed. "Was that really necessary? We could have taken him out some other way, surely?"

"Best be safe than sorry, wouldn't want him creeping up behind us. Come on, let's keep moving, we've got work to do." Brooking no further argument, Hal urged the group of four men and three women quietly along the dried-up creek bed towards the village

Except for Hal they were not trained killers, or professional soldiers. Just, it appeared, a desperate, hungry, homeless group of vagrants who by necessity had become adept at the art of killing to survive. Compared to the years immediately after the Collapse, they were now a rare breed. But when they did appear, the fact they had survived so long meant they were dangerous and determined.

They crept up French Creek's almost dry riverbed, hugging the banks of overgrown vegetation that offered good cover as they advanced towards the village.

They had spent a couple days watching and waiting, seeing what defenses the Community had built to keep people like them away from the residents, the food, and their valuable, life-saving resources. Now, they made their move to take them.

From their lookout just off SR 90, Billie had been easy to spot, and the lack of attention he displayed made him easy prey. Once he was disposed of, they advanced up the river, determined to reach the village.

They were moving into the unknown, unable to reconnoiter any further from their lookout on SR 90 due to the nature of the hilly terrain. The group had no idea what awaited them—a well-fortified encampment? Or a village ripe for the taking?

Billie may have been sleeping on duty, but Pat in Sentry Post Two wasn't. The shot jolted him to high alert. He knew a hunting party had been sent out for deer, but this shot sounded different. For the first time in six months, there was someone out there with humans in their sights.

Pat was one of the few in the village with any military experience. A three year deployment in Afghanistan had ended abruptly. The whole US presence was pulled out at a few days notice, because the millions of dollars required to keep them armed and supplied each day had dried up. They were needed back in the US to keep law, order and discipline in the midst of economic chaos brought on by an unforeseeable 'perfect storm' of natural disasters. The fragile physical and economic infrastructure that had kept the country running on the edge of catastrophe for so many years, buckled then finally collapsed.

By the time Pat and his fellow soldiers were back in the United States, not even the mighty American military could keep control of millions of citizens facing starvation. Within days of his arrival at Fort Bragg, he and most of the base deserted to find their way home and protect whatever family they had left.

Five days of walking, stealing cars, and defending himself against hapless looters frustrated by the empty Wal-Mart shelves had brought him to French Creek. Like most of his fellow soldiers, he kept his Army-issued M4 rifle and stole whatever he could easily carry that could be of use in the future. One such item was the scope fitted to his rifle and the other, night vision goggles.

Now here he was, scanning down the valley from his high vantage point on what was known locally as the Indian Burial Ground, waiting for the ghostly green images produced by the goggles to come a little closer. Seeing them, he knew the shot he'd heard wasn't for a deer, but for Billie.

Flashing pinpricks of light from fireflies sporadically burst into his goggles and faded away. He brought the walkie-talkie to his mouth and clicked the send.

"Billie, do you read me? Over." Not even static returned his call.

He tried again, then a third time, then switched channels in case the idiot had forgotten the correct one for this night's watch. Nothing.

"Oh shit, no," he murmured under his breath, a nagging feeling of fear clutched at his stomach. Now fully alert his senses were heightened as he methodically scoured the dark landscape beneath, praying the lack of response from Billie was not bad news. But three years of watching out for the murderous Taliban, night-time killers of astonishing skill who could travel across open terrain and be upon you before you knew it, had fine-tuned his senses to danger. And that's what he was feeling right now. A sickening sense of trepidation. But, as the adrenaline kicked in, a sharpening of focus and calm.

There. On the third scan across the riverbed, he saw movement. The long hair of one of the female intruders poked briefly above the undergrowth. He held the goggles steady while he picked up the walkie-talkie to rouse the other sentries and the rest of the village. He saw two, then three, finally seven more bodies moving slowly parallel to him about six hundred feet away.

"Home base, do you read me? That shot was not the hunting party. We have intruders. Seven, maybe more, in the riverbed close to Marker 400. This is not a drill! Go to Code Red now!"

One of Pat's first moves upon returning was to set up a series of watch posts at intervals along the road leading into French Creek, which was about a mile from the SR 90. The three manned sentry posts looked towards the road to Albany across to the hills and the Western end of the valley. Alongside the road into French Creek, were small marker posts every two hundred yards indicating how far from the main road any visitor had traveled. They were meant as easy reference points as most of the houses and barns at the East end of the French Creek near the intersection with SR 90 had been demolished for fuel, building materials, and to offer no protection to intruders.

French Creek started as a trickle of spring water at the far East of the village and gradually gathered in size as it flowed towards the main road. At times, the banks were almost six feet deep, offering ideal cover for the group moving towards the village. Ironically, it made for an easy route into the village without being seen.

"Copy that, Pat. I'll get the reserve crew up and ready for action." The disembodied voice of Night Watch Commander Eddie South came over the airwaves into Pat's earbuds.

The other post nearer the village confirmed receiving Pat's Code Red call, and a prearranged defensive plan went into action. Though it had not been deployed for any genuine emergency in a couple of years, it was rehearsed every four weeks.

Satisfied that he had alerted the village to the danger, Pat was now concerned about the hunting party still somewhere in the woods. They were separated from the creek by a large pasture several hundred feet wide. They obviously didn't know what was happening, though hopefully they heard the solitary shot which alerted them to return to the village.

Pat's focus returned to the unwelcome party creeping along the riverbed. Pat assumed they had done some reconnaissance but probably didn't know the level of French Creek's defenses. He could have taken a shot—they were five-hundred feet away now—but the defense plan allowed a small intruder group to proceed up to Marker 600. At that point, they would have moved past Pat's hidden watch post, closer to the village, and into a welcoming committee of well-armed villagers.

The plan also sent six armed men through the woods to come up behind any intruders at Marker 200. Thus, effectively preventing them from retreating back to the main road. They had planned and trained for several different intruder scenarios. Pat hoped he'd called the right one.

He radioed into night watch command in the Baptist church, a tall building in the center of the village that allowed for better communications and defense.

"CC, let me know when Marker 200 by SR 90 is covered. Over."

"Will do." Eddie's reassuring voice, a farmer and one of the more level-headed members of the village, came through loud and clear.

"Their ETA is a few minutes, I'm guessing. Will confirm when I know. Over."

Pat kept watch as the group, all armed with a variety of rifles, shotguns, and handguns, continued to move forward, unaware they were being tracked.

The Kentucky night was cool and calm; dawn began to break through and enhanced the half-light provided by a vivid full moon. It was early fall, and the trees still provided some cover for the intruders. There was a little cloud cover, but the moon allowed reasonable visibility despite the dark. Pat figured that's why the intruders had chosen tonight to make their move.

In a few weeks, French Creek would be a torrent of flash floods and dangerous roiling currents of water. But now, after the summer season, it was dry except for occasional pools of shallow water, good only for horses and cattle to drink.

Eddie radioed to Pat that the men would be at Marker 200 in two minutes. The stillness of the early dawn was suddenly broken as he heard the hunting party come noisily out of the woods, staggering under the weight of a large deer. Thinking they were under attack, the intruders opened fire at the hunters.

Caught completely by surprise, initially, the hunters had no clue where the shots were coming from. In their panic, they started running towards the river-and the shooters- resulting in two being hit, the third diving for cover behind a fallen tree. It seemed the intruders had night scopes too.

Pat radioed Eddie.

"Tell the group going to Marker 200 to stay put when they get there. Our hunters have alerted the intruders. In five minutes, get the guys at the village barricade to move towards the intruders. I'll try and keep them pinned down. Let's gradually close the trap and send them back down to the team near the main road. Over."

"Roger that, Pat. Will do. Over."

Pat put the radio and goggles down and brought his rifle up to firing position. He looked through the scope: 390 feet. The intruders were at ninety degrees to him, still trying to put down the last hunter behind the tree, who was wisely sitting tight.

Pat aimed at the first intruder who had opened fire on the hunters. With a practiced and steady hand, he put the cross hairs on the leader's body and fired. Instantly, it slumped to the ground. The others looked confused at first, then scared as they realized an unknown firing position had opened on them. In quick succession, Pat fired twice more, hitting one of the women. Panicked, they started to run back down the riverbed, straight towards the men at Marker 200.

For a minute, there was silence. Then a stuttering of rifle and machine gunfire. After no more than two minutes it stopped as abruptly as it had started.

The echoes of the brief crackling of gunfire ricocheted around the valley before going quiet. The crickets resumed their night time chatter. The fireflies continued to dance in the dark.

CHAPTER 2

French Creek is named after the small river that runs East to West along the bottom of a typical Kentucky hollow. On either side flourishes verdant pastures and woods wrapping the hills in a dark green blanket. A small village of some one hundred homes, it was once a traditional tobacco-growing community. But following Big Tobacco's decision to stop growing the plant in the 1970s, many small farms had since fallen on hard times.

Despite the economic hardship that followed, French Creek had survived with a population hovering around one hundred and fifty. Its main income for most families was manufacturing illicit drugs, subsiding on welfare, or cash-in-hand jobs. A few outsiders tempted by the cheap houses and land, bought properties as weekend getaways or retirement homes. It was a typical bucolic rural scene with pastures running up either side of the creek for several hundred feet to the edge of the woodland-covered hills. Some of which rose gently to heights of six hundred feet or more. It was rural living at its simplest.

When the Collapse happened, the tight-knit community had no problem figuring out how to survive the catastrophe wiping out fellow Americans by the million. The rest of the country was a place most of them had never seen and had no desire to visit either. Many believed they had it coming to them. In a poor area like French Creek, self-sufficiency was second nature to many residents. As the shops and supermarkets were stripped bare of stock, they shared resources and managed to survive better than most. They realized that unless they had some leadership and organization, the long-term future of French Creek could deteriorate into chaos very quickly. So, a village council was elected to run the community. The planning of everything—security, law and order, food production, and most day-to-day activities became a communal endeavor.

It was part of the Village Council Chairman, Roger Makefield's role, to make a decision on what should happen to the surviving intruders.

Roger stood with his hands behind his back in a classic military at-ease stance. At almost six foot five, he made an imposing figure. His position as chairman was the result of his natural leadership qualities, justified by ten years in the Army, including tours of Afghanistan and Iraq, where he had risen to the rank of major before leaving the Service just before the Collapse. He was also a man not afraid to make tough or unpopular decisions if circumstances warranted them—and this was one of those times.

He wasn't an original resident of French Creek; his home was in Bowling Green, Kentucky. But he and his family had been staying with his sick sister in French Creek when the Collapse started. By the time she recovered, it made sense for him to stay. His military background, forceful character, and natural ability to lead resulted in him taking charge. He was formally made Chairman of the Village Council four years ago. He'd remained in that position since, working alongside other residents who had expertise in areas he did not.

He walked up and down the line of survivors from the group, now numbering six, staring at them with a mixture of annoyance and pity. He finally stopped and looked down at his captives.

"So you thought we'd be easy prey for food, guns, ammo? Well, you were wrong there." he asked rhetorically in a calm voice.

Roger rarely lost his temper—he didn't need to. Through sheer force of personality and physical presence, listeners got his message. With a level head, his direct approach brooked no argument. Currently, he needed to stop the relatives of Billie from carrying out some instant justice to the group standing dejectedly in front of him. He alone was the village's judge, jury, and executioner, and he didn't shirk from those responsibilities.

"We were only after some food, didn't mean any harm. We were just passing through on the way to Louisville. We heard there's still a government camp with food there," pleaded one of the women.

Next to her, another woman was lying on the floor, bandaged and unconscious. A third stood over the injured woman doing her best to offer comfort. The men stood with faces down, sullen, defeated, oozing both desperation and fear.

"That's what they all say," answered Roger. "But we just don't have the resources, or time, for people like you. We've worked too long and hard to allow scum to try and take what isn't theirs. You're damn lucky only one of you was killed and another two wounded. Surrendering quickly kept you alive."

Roger continued his lecture. "But we have a process for dealing with intruders. We no longer execute them. We'll give you a choice: prove your worth to us or leave tomorrow."

The latter was almost a death sentence as living off the land was near impossible, and most other communities reacted in the same way as French Creek: no patience or sympathy for those who wished them harm. They hadn't survived five years by being soft-hearted.

"Prove our worth? What's that mean?" asked one of the men, a wiry individual with a scruffy blonde beard. He looked as though he hadn't slept in days, eaten, or washed in weeks. A slight hint of hope crept into his voice. Roger noticed he was bleeding from a wound in his arm.

"Simple. If you have skills that can help us, then we might allow you to stay. If not, we'll give you a two-day supply of food and point you in the direction of Louisville," explained Roger, leaning back on the table, satisfied he had their attention.

The rest of the group looked on as Council Secretary Jason Miller reached for his notebook that listed skills or abilities the community needed or might need in the future. A former accountant, he was the opposite of Roger in every respect. Short and bald with John Lennon-like glasses perched on his nose, he had an almost Dickensian look to him.

Selection was based on a variety of factors: the ages and fitness of the existing workforce, their plans for long-term improvements, special skills needed to help with those projects, and any other special projects the community wanted developed.

Jason started with the first man in line.

"Okay, tell me what you did before the Collapse. Don't lie—it serves no purpose. We'll find out soon enough, and the consequences won't be good."

"I was a marketing manager and salesman in the medical industry." The man said it with little emotion, knowing full well it was hardly a valuable skill post-Collapse. Probably why he was still an itinerant wandering half-starved around the countryside.

"And you?" Jason moved on to the second.

" Retail sales," he answered in a despondent voice.

Making notes in his book, Jason moved in front of the first woman. She was tall, thin, and blonde, and carried herself with confidence and a touch of arrogance. Beneath the grime was the worn, weary look of someone who had seen and suffered like most women in the past five years.

"And you?" asked Jason.

"Jane, Jane Davidson. I was a nurse in EMS."

"Can you prove that? That's the kind of skill any community would want. If that's the case, why are you wandering around the country with this bunch of idiots? You're a desirable commodity."

"Because I stayed with my husband." She stared directly at Jason.

"And which one is he?" Jason inquired, staring back at her.

"You just killed him."

Whatever stoicism she had maintained until that moment disintegrated. Despite, or maybe due to, all the horrors she had seen and endured in the last five years, it appeared this final blow was just too much. The leader of their group was gone. She now faced an uncertain and unpleasant future if she couldn't convince this group of skeptical men and women she would be an asset to their community.

As the tears flowed and her composure evaporated, everyone in the room waited to see if Jason would alleviate her distress by allowing her into French Creek. He and the Council had seen many such histrionics over the years. People pleading for their lives, offering bribes, all promising the Earth just to be allowed to stay. But the rules were clear and for most, didn't work in their favor. Refusal meant a dangerous trek to the next village, a government camp, or death.

Showing little emotion and without looking up from the book, Jason quietly announced, "You can stay for three months on a trial basis. If you're lying or your skills do not prove to be useful, you'll be thrown out."

Jason questioned the rest of the group. The two women were sisters—Jenny and Bryanna had knowledge of growing vegetables and preserving foods (they'd run a homemade foods store in Somerset, Kentucky) so were a welcome addition. One of the men, Austin, had farming experience which French Creek could use.

The others were to be patched up, given a two-day supply of food and one gun, and escorted back up to SR 90 to an uncertain fate. Despite their begging, Jason was unmoved. They would leave as soon as possible.

Dr. Jo Brown, who'd been watching impassively from the sidelines, now moved forward and told the lucky four to follow him to Surgery to be checked out and patched up. The injured woman, Bryanna, was helped out of the Council Hall, followed by the doctor.

Arrangements were made to collect the dead and a burial detail set up to quickly dig and bury the graves. No one wanted the dangers of disease from decaying corpses causing any problems. A quick memorial service at the church on Sunday would have to suffice as a funeral for them all.

"That was some shitty day," Roger said, grimly to the rest of the Council members who had been there to watch proceedings. "Two dead, but four new members, all with needed skills. And a deer to eat. Hardly a cause for celebration, but it could have been worse. French Creek survives another day."

CHAPTER 3

It was early evening. A beautiful fall day was coming to an end, which meant school, chores, and homework were done. It was time to eat.

"What's she like? The new woman?" asked twelve year old Sandra while her mother shucked some beans for the evening meal.

"Bit upset at losing her husband. Otherwise too early to tell. Says she's a medic. Be useful if she is."

Sandra's mother, Denise, had been at the Council meeting last night when the surviving intruders were brought in. The women in French Creek always viewed female newcomers with mixed feelings. It was good to have more female company, but they were wary of how their men folk might react to a spare woman now in residence. More than one marriage had broken up when men with wandering eyes decided on a change.

Those women shunted aside had nowhere to go, which led to some awkwardness when they saw their husbands flaunting their new brides. But these break-ups happened; everyone had to accept them or leave.

An informal marriage and divorce process was established by the Council when it became obvious that all the various church denominations had differing views on both subjects. For simplicity's sake, a non-denominational marriage, divorce, and funeral service was implemented. Some even wanted to try polygamy when the number of marriageable women became too many for the number of men in the community. This was squashed, and Jason made sure the number of new community members allowed the sexes to roughly even out over the years.

"What about the men?" Sandra's interest in the opposite sex had begun to appear. Under the current laws of the community, she could be married at fifteen, allowing for more children to be born while the women were stronger and healthier.

Denise looked at her daughter. She was growing up too fast. Her body was slim and lithe and beginning to develop curves, but as a mother she was still trying to protect her from temptation and disappointment.

"Sandra, you're too young to be looking for potential husbands. I didn't really look at them anyhow. One was an engineer and another a farmer, I think. You just get your schooling and practical course work done. Then you can start husband hunting."

After the first year of the Collapse, Council decided that school would be from ages five to fifteen years, with an emphasis on practical studies covering farming, cooking, gardening, recycling, mechanics, hunting, and skills necessary for the success of the community. Academic studies were not ignored; they concentrated on a thorough understanding of math, chemistry, history, biology, physics, and medicine. To the relief of the older students, the likes of calculus, economics, and ACT tests went out the window.

The school day was from six AM to noon, allowing all children to contribute to the community's basic needs: looking after the animals, growing vegetables, cooking, household and other work chores. And it was the same for girls as boys—everyone had to have basic skills. As they grew older and left school, their aptitudes and abilities were channeled where needed.

"Oh, Mom! I was only asking. You know who I want to marry. Bobbie Johnson! He's a year older than me and a great mechanic."

"Well, we'll just have to see how it all works out. Now watch the cooking. I have to go take some food to the newcomers in prison. I'll be back soon."

Denise had to admit… the man named Austin seemed pleasant in manner and looks. It was the first time she had even considered taking an interest in another man. She had been a single mother since her husband was killed by marauders who'd attacked French Creek soon after the Collapse. After that she'd been so involved in bringing up Sandra and coping with the stresses of post-Collapse living relationships had been a low priority. Sure, some of the single (and even married) men in the community had made their intentions all too clear at times, but she wasn't interested—until, maybe, now.

Gathering up a tray of food—bread, cheese, and some fruit—she glanced in the mirror. She needed to trim her long, auburn hair. As for a little makeup? No chance—she'd be the laughingstock of the village if she started getting all glamorous just because a couple of new men appeared. She contented herself by pulling her hair into a ponytail and wiping her face clean of dirt. That was her half-hearted attempt to smarten herself up before she met Austin and the other newcomers.

The in frequently used 'prison' doubled as a quarantine and medical center, in the large Baptist church. Nurse Helen tended to Bryanna's wounds as Denise arrived with lunch.

"How's she doing?" Denise asked, nodding towards Bryanna..

Dressed in the obligatory white coat, Helen was in her mid-thirties, painfully thin, with a perpetually gaunt look about her. It belied a heart of gold and an amazing ability to heal people with the homegrown resources at her disposal. She looked up from her medicine chest containing a bewildering array of plants, leaves, and herbs.

"She should be fine. Another week or so and she can get up and about. Just gotta make sure no infections flare up. That plantain and nettle poultice seems to keep the inflammation down and the wound clean."

"Hopefully she can get some food in her to help things along. How are the others doing?"

"All behaving themselves. The two guys seem more than grateful to be here. As long as they don't cause any problems, that's all I care about."

Denise left the food and turned to leave when Austin shouted across the room. "Thanks very much for the food, Miss Denise. Really kind of you. We're all starving."

Denise turned to look at him—a transformed man, aged around thirty with short cropped, blonde hair and a beaming smile. Cleaned up and rested, he looked quite respectable. His accent gave him away as a New Yorker.

"You're welcome, sir. Enjoy," Denise replied with a coy smile.

As she opened the door to leave, Denise felt herself blushing. Really, she told herself, stop behaving like a teenage girl. All he said was thank you. Despite her self-admonishment, she found herself almost skipping back home.

CHAPTER 4

The Collapse, as it became known, had been totally unforeseen. A combination of Nature at its most ferocious and destructive in tandem with a divided country, a weakened economy, and rudderless leadership.

Like a termite-ridden house, the United States had been on the brink of Collapse for years. It just needed one small tipping point, one tiny push to cause the final disintegration. Once it did, nothing could stop the ensuing cataclysm.

The tipping point was when one of the country's thousands of historically-benign seismic fault lines shifted just three feet. It happened one October morning under a clear blue sky—a sudden slip in the Wilzetta-Whitetail fault zone. In geological terms, it wasn't a large shift. But where it happened couldn't have been worse—under the oil town of Cushing, North Dakota.

For a small town of seven thousand people, Cushing had more oil stored in its three hundred tanks than anywhere else in the World. It was probably the busiest and largest oil hub in the country. Some sixty percent of America's oil flowed through it or was stored there, amounting to a jaw-dropping 80-100 million gallons at any one time. The Department of Homeland Security designated it as a place of "critical infrastructure," meaning its destruction could cause irreparable damage to the security and economy of the United States.

And that's just what happened.

Ill-prepared for such an earthquake, Cushing's poorly constructed tanks ruptured, as did miles of pipeline around it. The damage caused a black tidal wave of oil to surge across huge swathes of the county. More importantly, it created an immediate cessation of fuel supplies across the country. Almost overnight, the price of oil rocketed, followed soon after by the worst shortages since 1973.

Wholly dependent on gas and now stranded at warehouses across the country were thousands of trucks that would normally be supplying supermarkets with their inventory. As most only carried three-day's stock on their shelves, panic-buying soon stripped them bare within twenty-four hours.

But that was just the start. Over the next four weeks, Mother Nature unleashed a series of category four and five hurricanes that blasted across Florida, Texas, and the North East coast, causing billions of dollars in damage. The disruption to millions of inhabitants—inhabitants who were already trying to cope with little fuel and shrinking supplies of food, was total. The hurricane in Texas further devastated the country's refining capacities, exacerbating the gas and oil shortage.

In the heavily-populated North East, gas and food supplies dried up within days. The government, which had relentlessly cut funding to FEMA and Homeland Security, were unable to offer any real help on the scale required. Equally devastating, the thousand-mile-wide hurricanes dumped unheard-of amounts of rainfall, causing major floods across the Eastern states from Georgia up to Maine. These successive biblical-size disasters put unheard-of strains on every part of the country's fragile infrastructure. The final countrywide crushing catastrophe was just two months later when winter storms in the North arrived with a vengeance.

Chicago, the Midwest, and North East were then hit by a series of bone-numbing cold fronts that dropped over ten feet of snow at Chicago's O'Hare airport in just two days. And there it stayed, as it did across a fifteen hundred mile frozen swathe from North Dakota to Vermont down as far south as Ohio and Pennsylvania. With fuel still in short supply and supply routes frozen until March, demand for electricity rocketed as people tried to keep warm, cook, or just survive. The power grid crumbled as it had done so many times before. Shoddy maintenance and aging infrastructure turned rolling blackouts into permanent ones. Soon fifty million Americans found themselves living without the basic life-supporting utilities they had come to expect and rely upon.

Most Eastern airports were without power, underwater, or out of action due to staff shortages as people stayed home to protect themselves, family, and their property. Ports were damaged and oil-refining capacity was reduced to a trickle.

Meanwhile, whatever rescue and relief operations FEMA and others could mount were hampered with little fuel, damaged distribution points, and paltry assistance at government, state, or local levels. They had failed to deliver after Hurricane Katrina and Ian. This disaster was 100 times the size.

By Christmas, sixty percent of the country's population was without livable supplies of power, food, and gas.

Then, as if to take advantage of its weakened populace, a particularly virulent strain of the long-forgotten COVID virus re-emerged in Baltimore and spread like an unstoppable tide

Westward. Uncompromising and insidious, it seemed no one was immune. All ages and ethnic groups succumbed. Past vaccinations had no effect controlling the new disease. Under normal circumstances, new vaccines would have been developed and the health care providers could have quickly vaccinated people. But the resources were not there, and with people already weakened, doctors and hospitals were overwhelmed, the death toll mounted.

The net result? Society East of the Mississippi unraveled at frightening speed. And when the shit hit the fan, some people could only smell opportunity.

Those itching to pick a fight with any kind of authority now had their chance. The mobs who rioted against the White House in 2021 and a dozen other fringe groups now resurfaced and attacked state and federal buildings. Conspiracy theories ran rampant—everyone found someone else to blame. With nothing to lose, the mindless groups ran riot. The police, and what was left of the National Guard and Army, had too many fires to fight on too many fronts to control them.

For most Americans, the rule of law and order began to irretrievably, hopelessly, break down. And no one seemed likely to restore it any time soon.

The neighboring states West of the Mississippi, who had managed to avoid the natural disasters, soon had their own problems. While at first willing to help, they were quickly swamped as hundreds of thousands attempted to flee to safety from the East.

However, with fifteen of the major Lower Mississippi crossings damaged by floods, it was easy for governors, who saw their states in danger of becoming refugee camps for millions of homeless Americans, to close the remaining ten bridges and stop the Westward tide of starving Americans.

Governors Jackson of Louisiana, Killingham of Arkansas, Branson of Missouri, and Davidson of Illinois all declared states of emergency and effectively closed all entry points to people trying to cross the Mississippi. While not directly affected by the storms and hurricanes, they were also suffering from chronic shortages of fuel, gas, and food. They couldn't feed their own citizens, let alone the exodus from the East.

Governor Jackson of Louisiana speaking on behalf of the all the states bordering the Mississippi told the media:

"We are all overwhelmed by the enormity of the disaster that has befallen our fellow Americans East of the Mississippi. Nevertheless, for the safety and wellbeing of our communities on the West coast of the river we have no alternative but to stop any more refugees entering our States.

We hope, and pray this is only a temporary measure until our mighty nations' resources can be put to work bringing back to the East everything a civilized society needs to survive.

We can assure our citizens in the East we will not abandon you in your time of need. Our thoughts and prayers are with you during these unprecedented troubles. We will now start actively planning how we can help the millions in distress rebuild their lives.

God Bless America.

In reality they did nothing to help their fellow Americans in their 'time of need'. Instead, they poured countless billions into building a security cordon 2000 miles long from New Orleans to

Duluth. Compared to the much-discussed wall between Mexico and the United States, (which never happened), this 'wall' went up in a matter of months. America wasn't just divided by a river, now it was severed in two by barbed wire.

Over the next few weeks and months, the specter of Armageddon came closer and closer.

Skittish as newborn colts, the financial markets had gone into meltdown and never recovered. With intermittent energy supplies, the whole electronic trading and banking infrastructure broke down. It became easy prey for hackers to infiltrate from around the World. Billions of dollars were wiped from Fortune 500 companies, and equal amounts of money siphoned away into the ether before the whole system collapsed.

No electricity meant no air conditioning or heat, no light, no public transport, no cellphones. Telecommunications was one of the first utilities to be hit as cell phone towers were irreparably damaged. Soon the major communications providers were unable to offer any service. It didn't matter: how do you charge your cellphone with no electricity?

By Christmas, an estimated fifteen million people were on the move. For the few who had planned ahead and had self-sufficient cabins in woods or mountains, they hunkered down and put prepper plans into action.

The first two years saw millions die of starvation, murder, disease, and cold. The government managed to mount a half-hearted relief effort in the spring of the first year following the Collapse. They soon realized, however, their resources had to be focused where they could produce the best results for the most number of people: in the West. What was happening in the East was too big a problem to solve. They were on their own.

Many believed the basics needed to survive would be outside the cities and suburbia. By the millions, a plague of starving, desperate people invaded the countryside. They foraged, pillaged, and stole as best they could. But for the majority, whose closest connection with the country had been a barbecue by the lake, they were doomed to failure. Soon, it too, became a wasteland of a different kind. They had swapped the empty shelves at Walmart for the supposed bounty of the countryside. Tragically, they found little to help them in the freezing outdoor temperatures. They starved, surrounded by the beauty and Nature's hidden resources, not knowing how to take advantage of either. Winter in the countryside is not for the faint hearted or ill prepared. It inevitably proved fatal to most.

Those with health problems soon began to suffer and perish: from seniors in nursing homes dying in the Florida heat to those needing regular medications. There was no help for them. At that time, some fifteen percent of Americans had diabetes, twenty-one percent heart problems, and thirty percent were receiving cancer treatments. Within months, supplies of medications dried up and hospitals closed. The resulting death toll was horrendous: some forty-five million Americans succumbed to painful, lingering deaths.

And with this death and carnage came diseases of every type, as sanitation services ceased working and dead bodies lay unburied in streets and hospitals. An illness that six months before might have been cured by a trip to the local pharmacy now became a death sentence. Diseases practically unheard of in America for decades became widespread in such a toxic, unhealthy environment: Cholera, Zika virus, Measles, Yellow Fever,

Malaria, and Polio rampaged through a weakened, undernourished, and unvaccinated population.

The speed at which over half of America's population descended into chaos astounded the government and countries around the globe. Those in a position to help—Europe, the Middle East, and Japan—looked sympathetically at the catastrophe unfolding in America. While willing to send aid, they could identify no coherent plan for how it could be used effectively on such a pan-continental scale. Absent any sound guidance from Washington (whose President had either insulted, ignored, or bullied them), these country's humanitarian feelings soon ran thin. They promised a lot but delivered very little.

The underlying problem was, as always, financial. The government at every level was bankrupt. Past years of spending vast sums on COVID, the war in Ukraine and profligate handouts had resulted in a multi-trillion-dollar deficit whose interest payments were in the millions daily and were tied to the value of the dollar. As its value plummeted, countries around the World called in their debts. America couldn't pay them and soon defaulted as the dollar dropped to almost worthless levels.

And for those who viewed America as an enemy? They were either privately gloating or publicly sympathizing, simultaneously weighing up how they could take advantage of the "greatest power on Earth," now sinking and disintegrating into a third-world country.

"America First" for most of the World became "America Last." Meanwhile, for its beleaguered population, the meaningless phrase provoked memories of government incompetence, arrogance, and promises of a better future destined never to be fulfilled.

It soon became apparent there was no quick way to rescue America or its economy when half the country had reverted to the days of the pioneers.

CHAPTER 5

It was those living in rural areas that found it easier to survive. Many still had basic skills, knowledge, and resources to keep food on the table. They had skills that would prove essential for an agrarian economy. For that is what half of America had become: a country learning to live in the 19th century.

Across rural America, many villages had to not just pull through the famine but also protect themselves from the hordes of city dwellers who sought refuge in the country. During the first months after the Collapse, they began the formidable task of rebuilding sustainable communities using long-forgotten techniques. These often meant back-breaking work, fueled with hearts full of determination and hope.

Ironically, the people who could not afford food and store-bought produce had become experts at growing and saving their own. Now they found it relatively easy to become self-sufficient. If they worked with neighbors to coordinate and pool resources, they could survive.

They realized early on—the two priorities for survival were: security and the preservation of resources.

So it was with French Creek. Originally a community of around 110 souls, after the Collapse their numbers dropped as the old and infirm died. Gradually, it increased to over 180 as the Council imposed a rigorous and brutal selection process from the hundreds of homeless and begging who wandered into the village in search of help. Only those with proven, valuable skills were allowed into the Community. Doctors, nurses, farmers, carpenters, biologists, mechanics, and veterinarians were granted access, as well as the youthful and strong who could help create the next generation.

French Creek quickly made a crucial decision: if their lives were to be saved and the Community to survive: Food production must be given top priority.

Which often led to awkward questions: Who should grow what and where? How much should people keep of what they grew and how much to share? What if a crop failed? Where were the best places to grow certain vegetables and not others? Who should be responsible for all of this?

Many people already had a good selection of vegetable seeds. Rather than let each villager grow what they liked, the expert gardeners pooled all these resources then decided what should be planted and where. Communal gardens were created to ensure enough was grown for everyone to eat. Every household had to start growing their own too, but in ways that ensured the cultivation of a broad selection of produce.

Those with livestock were told to keep their animals in areas where the pasture was good enough to feed them but didn't take all the fertile land away for food production. Fruit was more of a problem, especially apples, pears, and plums. Few people had such trees. Growing and caring for them to improve their yield proved a lengthy process. Eventually, after three or four seasons, an increasing number of healthy, productive trees were providing wholesome and tasty fruit.

The health workers were concerned about diseases like scurvy reappearing. Still, those who had canned their own produce or had good existing stocks of supermarket-bought cans saw the first years through without any real problems. They also discovered from an old foraging book that boiled Spruce tree needles provided an excellent source of vitamin C. Mother Nature's pantry was there for everyone to feed from if you knew the combination.

However, the lack of medicine was a real problem. Some twenty percent of the Community had diabetes, heart disease, or asthma. It became clear that little could be done to help them as their regular trips to the pharmacy ceased. Within weeks, most died. Others reliant on opioids learned to live without them. Thanks to marijuana growing in the far reaches of the hollows, this natural medicine became an acceptable alternative. The plant was now carefully and deliberately cultivated to help alleviate a variety of illnesses.

One of the long-forgotten skills, foraging for medicinal plants, took on huge importance. A group was formed to scour copies of Mother Earth News, Countryside journals and nature books to identify and find plants, flowers, shrubs, and trees that could take the place of the manufactured drugs upon which everyone depended.

This initially met with limited success. But each year, as herbicides and pesticide use ceased, many of these plants, dormant for years, started growing again. Likewise, the bee population recovered, offering much better pollination, and providing a regular supply of honey. Every home was made to keep a beehive.

Even with these initiatives and huge improvements in the land around French Creek, it could produce only so much food.

This subject regularly came up at every Council meeting. People were anxious over the future size of French Creek and its ability to feed the inhabitants.

Land in adjacent hollows could be worked however, the distance and lack of security made it of questionable value. Within twenty miles of French Creek, there were at least four other communities. While relations were good, they kept themselves to themselves. Nevertheless, there was always the danger that a year's work of growing a crop in a distant, unguarded field could be taken by those who preferred stealing to the effort of growing their own.

Despite these problems and countless setbacks in the five years following the Collapse, life had improved to a degree many thought impossible. People were eating well. Food, while not plentiful, was sufficient for the increasing population. It was a constant struggle to ensure the safety, health, and security of the community. Overall, however, most of the villagers in French Creek believed they had turned the corner and life was looking better.

Inevitably, not everyone was happy with the way things were being run. Soon, dissent would make itself known and begin to fray the fragile bonds that had held the community together for the last five years.

CHAPTER 6

Back in the makeshift prison, the newcomers who had been allowed to stay neared the end of their two-week quarantine. It wasn't too strictly enforced; a few people were allowed in though they had to wear masks to avoid any possible infections brought in from the outside. Though most of the infectious illnesses that had decimated the population five years ago had long since run their course.

"When can I get out of here?" Jane Davidson demanded again, as she had several times over the last few days.

"I'm thinking it will be tomorrow," replied Nurse Helen. "We have to find a place for you to stay where you won't cause any trouble."

"Trouble? I'm not going to be any trouble. I'm grateful to be here."

"We're talking about the type of trouble any new woman can cause in the community. You're going to be an object of interest to the men here. You'll have to tread very carefully. If the Council thinks you're being provocative...well let's put it this way: they have expelled women in the past who upset things" explained Helen patiently.

Jane flared up. "Jesus! My husband was murdered just two weeks ago. Do you think I'm on the lookout for a replacement?"

"You may not be but some of the men here might." Helen could think of several who would find this tall, slim, blonde, now cleaned up and looking much better, a tempting proposition.

"We're finalizing arrangements for you to stay with one of the elderly couples. Your job will be to look after them."

Jane flopped back down on the hard bed in her cell. She saw the plan: Keep her occupied and out of the way. No problem; she was happy to bide her time until she could execute her plan.

CHAPTER 7

In any community there's always a group who are not happy. In this case, it was the younger people in French Creek who felt things could be run differently. They wanted a little more freedom. They wanted to explore beyond the stifling confines of a small village. They believed that they could only discover a more interesting life by leaving and heading West.

As they grew from teens to young adults, they felt more needed to be done to improve their prospects. They were, after all, the ones who felt the full force of change from a technologically-led society to one that, within weeks, had retrogressed 150 years.

No cell phones, social media, computers, or televisions were now a fact. As electricity supplies failed, so their world collapsed around them. Many found their lives devoid of substance or purpose without a phone in their hand. Life had now shrunk to what they could see and who they could talk to in person. It was an electronic cold turkey they endured for several weeks until they realized their screen fix wasn't coming back. Entertainment and friendship had to be found in the people and environment around them.

Life was no longer delivered via a keyboard and screen. It now required effort, time, and patience to acquire information from books, old magazines, and people. They had to be proactive and persistent in learning new skills. YouTube wasn't there to help them anymore. Now they had to gain instruction by watching people, asking questions, reading, taking chances. Hell! Even reading books on paper was a novelty to many! All a time-consuming, frustrating process for those used to an era of instant gratification and answers to any question courtesy of Google. The mindset change left them angry and frustrated.

Immediately after the Collapse, everyone had no choice but to adjust to this new way of life. It was no longer a "me" society—the emphasis was now on "us." A willingness to take orders and do things for the benefit of the community became the new mantra. And it worked. By combining skills and knowledge combined with sheer hard work, French Creek had survived an apocalypse.

Now, five years on, the older teens were feeling a little rebellious. Just because an elder said it was the rule, didn't mean it was. Nothing new here; for generations, this had been the case. Their grandparents demonstrated against the Vietnam War, their parents for 'Me Too', and some even protested for gun control. It was a rite of passage now re-emerging as life became more settled, and people began to look beyond the next harvest for what their future might offer.

Dave Matthews and his best friend Alex were the informal leaders of such a group. For months, they had been discussing whether more effort should be made by them to look outside French Creek. Beyond the county, and even Kentucky to see if civilization was moving back to pre-Collapse times. If not, look to the West.

They'd had a series of casual meetings over homebrewed beer and dope to find out how many of them supported such a drastic move. No one wanted to do anything hasty, so currently the discussions were more talk than action.

Dave was twenty; his parents were teachers before the Collapse and had continued to educate the kids of French Creek. He was well aware of how life had been during his techno-focused teenage years and how much it had changed.

He knew how societies could pick themselves up from disaster and move ahead, often to better times than before. Look at Europe after the Second World War; it had been in ruins. But within a few years, Germany was an economic success story. Why couldn't the U.S. do the same? What was taking so long? Like everyone, he'd seen the occasional military plane fly over. Why weren't troops visiting the area? Where were the rescue efforts?

As Dave sat down on the decaying oak log next to the campfire, he looked at the group of potential "leavers." Steve Johannsen was a little younger than he, here because his elder brother Alex was one of the group's founding members. Alex was a strapping young man, an expert with animals, especially horses. Next to him sat Landy, son of Roger, the Council chairman and a valuable source of inside information on what the elders were thinking and planning.

The remaining members, Dick Stanford and Paul Davidson were probably the most determined to leave. Both came from broken homes and saw firsthand how divorces in a small community caused resentment. They wanted out.

Dave lit a joint and turned to Landy.

"What's your old man and his Council cronies up to?" he asked, getting straight to the point.

"Not surprisingly, they seem pretty interested in the new arrivals. They think the blonde woman is hiding something but can't figure out what it is."

"She's pretty cute to look at," commented Alex. "I wonder who she's going to hook up with once she's free from quarantine. Happy to show her around." He smirked at his own joke.

"She's a bit old for you," said Dave. He turned to Landy, bringing the conversation back to the topic at hand. "They think she's got something to hide? I was told she put on quite an act about losing her husband, but no one has any info on where she came from."

"I agree," said Steve. "First stranger we've had here in months and then six of them turn up."

Alex didn't add to his brother's comment. He poked the fire, which raised a cloud of sparks that evaporated in the cool evening air.

"I wonder if she's a spy or scout or something?" Dick suggested. He was always the conspiracy theorist and often the most negative. "Why leave somewhere that was well-supplied and go rogue with a bunch of other losers? That's a lot to keep fed and watered on the road. They all looked in reasonable health."

"Why the hell would anyone want to spy on us?" asked Landy, incredulously. "What have we got they could want?"

"We've got food and supplies. That's worth something to people like them," Dave suggested.

The conversation rambled on and circled around for a few more minutes. Dave brought it back to the Council's meetings. "What else have they been discussing, Landy?"

"Sorry to disappoint you guys, I'm not in the room when they have their weekly meetings," Landy admitted. "As I said, they are keeping a careful eye on blondie. She'll be put on oldie care duty any day. That's about it."

There were a few moments of silence as the group pondered what to say next. Talking about leaving French Creek was one thing; quitting was quite another. They couldn't just up and leave. They'd need supplies and a plan of where to go and what to do when they arrived there. It was a daunting prospect and one they couldn't start planning without getting their parents' and the Council's permission.

In truth, they weren't sure what the reaction would be when they asked. Certainly not enthusiastic. Probably downright hostile. Then what? Leave anyway, burn their bridges? Would they be welcome back if they failed to find what they were looking for, whatever that was? Pretty doubtful they all agreed.

What if the great unknown out there was worse than living here? Was French Creek all that bad? They had food, security, and, as far as they could tell, a relatively risk-free future. Was the gamble of leaving likely to pay off the way they hoped? Their lack of knowledge about life beyond French Creek was frustrating. Maybe the newbies could be tapped for information.

Alex broke the silence. "Time for some wishful thinking. What do we want that we don't have now?" He looked at each of them in turn. "Dick?"

"I'm not sure," Dick said. "I'd love to be back online. Have a working cell phone, and be able to play video games."

"Landy?"

"The same," Landy said. "Plus, a working truck so I could get away from here, go to a ball game, do some normal stuff."

"Just to be able to get away, see some new faces, new girls, get a job that doesn't break your back." Alex looked dejected as he mumbled his wish list. "Make some money, get drunk. All that dumb stuff."

Steve was more direct. "All of that shit. Just to be able to do all the stupid things we did before. Out of sight of parents and those dicks on the Council."

Paul added little to the others' dreams, quietly nodding his head in agreement." Just some freedom," he said simply.

Dave silently digested the comments. They mirrored his own—except he would have added going to college and finding a girlfriend to the list.

Even before the Collapse, he was tired of everyone knowing everyone else's business. The endless family responsibilities, his contemporaries' total lack of ambition. The goldfish bowl of a never-go-anywhere community. He just saw his life drifting away like smoke in the breeze, becoming invisible and forgotten.

He wasn't sure how, but he had to know, had to see for himself that the alternative out there offered nothing better. Just to satisfy his curiosity.

He stood up and kicked out the fire. Clouds of sparks flew into the air, briefly illuminating the group's young faces. At that moment, he wondered if they were as serious as he was about getting out. What would they do if the chance really did present itself? How far would they push to discover the unknown?

An ultimatum was needed. "OK, I reckon it's man up time. Now's the time to see what our parents say to our idea," Dave said. "If they think it's OK, then we can plan to leave with their help. If not, then we'll have to be a little more devious. Let's get together for another smoke in a few days so we can discuss their reactions. Are we all up for doing this?"

They all mumbled their agreement to Dave's suggestion, some with more enthusiasm than others. Nothing ventured, nothing gained was the attitude.

With that, they passed around the joint for one last drag each, finished their bottles of homemade hooch, doused the fire, and strolled back to their homes. No one looked forward to the conversations they were about to have with their parents.

Dave had little doubt any of them would receive their parent's blessing to leave French Creek. He knew in the past, others had tried and failed. One or two had gone anyway. Adults had also left following acrimonious divorces, unwillingness to follow the strict regime set up by Council, or just the desire for a change. None had returned.

In reality, this disparate band of leavers-in-the-making had no idea of the devastation that the Eastern half of the country had suffered. The resources needed—financial, manpower, and material—to bring the region back to the twenty-first century. It was simply beyond a bankrupt country's capabilities. They didn't know just how bad it was out there. How could they? Their dreams didn't factor in such realities. They wanted out.

CHAPTER 8

Within weeks of the catastrophic 'storm of storms' and the subsequent disasters across the East, the government bowed to the inevitable and decided to relocate to Sacramento, California.

The President, his Cabinet and senior aides felt they had no choice but to leave to fight another day. They and thousands of government employees moved quickly to the West as the unrest, violence, and disintegrating society made their jobs impossible. At least that's what they told themselves in an effort to justify their flight from the chaos.

Likewise, most State Government institutions, with no Federal help, soon became completely ineffective at controlling their desperate populations. The rich and powerful managed to escape before airports crumbled to a halt and planes stood idle on the ground for lack of fuel. They looked impassively down on the chaos they had left behind as they scurried to safety 30,000 ft in the air. It had all happened so quickly many had seen their fortunes dwindle in the stock market and banking crash. Though they had salted away enough to affect a hurried retreat to a safer life.

They left behind helpless aid agencies such as FEMA and DHS. Depleted of resources after years of cutbacks, they faced overwhelming demands on an unprecedented scale. Soon they too, had no choice but to abandon their posts leaving the population to implode into disarray.

Also left behind was much of the Nation's cultural and historical treasures.

Valiant efforts had been made to move the contents of the major art galleries, museums and depositories of their irreplaceable valuables. Shipping containers full of priceless arts and relics were hastily moved in containers onto ships and spirited away to the West. Much was left behind locked in vaults in the hope it could be rescued at some later date. Many were looted and sold to eager European and Far East collectors who bought some of the world's masterpieces and historical icons at fire sale prices. The money was used to obtain guns, food and supplies.

Financial institutions, realizing stacks of dollar bills were now almost worthless, left them locked in their vaults. It wasn't worth the time and effort to transport them Though billions in other currencies were shipped Westwards as these were still worth something of the foreign exchange markets. However, the value of these shipments paled into insignificance compared to the challenge of moving gold from the two main depositories in Fort Knox in Kentucky and the Federal Reserve Bank in New York.

While Fort Knox holds a lot of gold—about 147 million ounces or 4500 tons—the largest gold stockpile in the US is in the Federal Reserve Bank Depository in Manhattan, containing a whopping 6,700 tons of gold. Before the Collapse these two hoards had been worth a combined $300 billion. With the dollar now worthless on the foreign exchange markets, its value to the USA was now countless times that.

No one knows for sure how, or indeed if, it was all extracted and moved. Some say the gold in the New York vaults was too much to transport and the 90ton steel door protecting the vaults 80 feet below the bedlam of Manhattan was sealed with concrete for posterity. Others claim it was loaded into dozens of semis and quickly put on naval destroyers and shipped Westwards. The gold at Fort Knox was allegedly spirited away in convoys of trucks across to Mississippi and safety. The gold's whereabouts would be the subject of conspiracy stories for years to come.

Arguably of more importance was the stockpile of potentially lethal toxins and diseases stored at the Center for Disease Control in Atlanta. From Sacramento the Government claimed that any such plague carrying stocks of these diseases had been safely removed. Not everyone was convinced by the assurances. The cloud of secrecy surrounding this deadly stockpile and its whereabouts is still unknown.

Safe in Sacramento, the government started to try and assess the damage. Rescue committees were formed to strategize, help and organize resources. But with so much infrastructure out of action it was impossible to plan a cohesive rescue mission on the scale needed. The telecommunication companies were typical of many utilities who said they were not prepared to put men and materials into places where law and order had broken down. The same went for food suppliers, retailers, and distribution companies. If the government could make it safe for them, they said, they would offer help. The government couldn't deliver.

Weeks turned to months, by Year Two, the situation had only marginally improved. The flow of American refugees Eastwards had been contained in all directions. Normalcy returned to states West of the Mississippi. The government decided to send a small number of FBI agents back East to report on the situation to help formulate a rescue mission.

The reports coming back painted vastly different pictures. Larger cities, such as Chicago, Philadelphia, Atlanta, and Washington D.C., had seen their populations decimated by deaths and an exodus of people to the West. What was left was run by gangs who controlled the food and resources. They were heavily armed with everything from handguns to RPGs and military vehicles. To take back control of them would result in heavy casualties on both sides, said the agents on the ground.

In contrast, coastal cities, such as New York, Boston, Tampa, Baltimore, and Charleston, had received some aid and assistance from Europe and South America within weeks of the Collapse. The dollar was worthless, but enterprising foreign governments and corporations were willing to trade any valuable commodity for aid. Expensive cars, weapons, jewelry, even property was traded for food, medicine, and fuel. Some semblance of normality returned to these sectors; the rule of law partially reinstated. These were governed along similar lines to what had been in place 200 years ago—localized government attuned to the needs of the populace with minimal federal interference.

The FBI agents reported that if people had food and basic resources, violence and rioting decreased. Life went back to some version of normal. Over time, supplies might even come in to restart the power grids. Who knew? They were considered the lucky ones.

Overall, the Federal agents reported that the population in these cities seemed content with how things were improving. They would likely regard the arrival of government troops as unwarranted and meddlesome. It was by no means perfect. But, compared to two years ago, it was a vast improvement. In short, what could an underfunded incursion by a distant federal government do for them?

In the countryside, said the Agents, the scenario was mixed. Many small villages had begun to pick themselves up and organize basic amenities through community action, cooperative farming, and shared security. Many combined forces to share knowledge, experience, and limited local resources to gradually rebuild their lives.

In other isolated areas, progress was slower. Poverty and desperation made for a miserable existence. The agents doubted many of these communities, most in the Appalachians, would survive another winter.

Based on all this information, 'Washington' (now Sacramento) had to decide where it would be best to start the work of re-instituting the role of the federal government East of the Mississippi.

All the displaced governors and state legislatures demanded theirs be the first in line for any reconstruction. But the money wasn't there for a broad scale project, so a test state was chosen—Kentucky. The process would then be rolled out gradually across the other states, depending on the outcome of the Kentucky operation. No date was set for its implementation, that would have to wait until government funding was available. This could take up to ten years, the President warned.

CHAPTER 9

Jane scrutinized herself in the mirror. It was her last day in quarantine. She looked clean and well-rested. The two week stay had replenished here physically and mentally. Her blonde hair had regained its luster. Her filthy clothes had been replaced by those donated by other women. She felt fit and motivated. Confinement away from the rest of the community had given her time to plan her next move. Whatever it was, she'd have to tread carefully. To some in French Creek, she was the grieving widow, trying to make a fresh start. Others had warned Jane her presence would be greeted with suspicion by the other women—she had to make it clear finding a man was not on her agenda.

What the entire village didn't know was ending up in French Creek had been no accident. Her planning hadn't foreseen the well-organized security and subsequent shootings of three of her group. She was lucky that the two sisters had been asked to stay-they were crucial to her future success. The expulsion of three of them had gone according to plan—it removed any suspicions that their arrival was anything but coincidental.

Her first job was to meet up with everyone else being released today. To observers, it would be quite natural for them to get together. They were "friends," after all. Even so, Jane knew their movements would be carefully watched, so care and subterfuge would be required.

She needed to return to her cache of materials—satellite radio, guns, and ammunition—hidden a couple of miles down the road.

That trip would be best left until she had a better idea of the community's routines. There seemed to be no curfew or restrictions on going into the surrounding woods for food, but she didn't want to push her luck until she knew more.

The cell door swung open. Roger, Chairman of the Council, stood there expectantly. His gray hair, tied back in a ponytail, made him look like an aging hippy, a far cry from the image he must have sported as an Army officer. Jane surmised, beneath the laid-back exterior, he was someone who could spot a fraud a mile off. His eyes never moved from hers as he talked to her. He listened with an intensity that was unnerving. Tread carefully, Jane thought.

"Time for you to start settling in now we know you haven't any lethal diseases! Thought we'd have a quick chat so I can outline some of the basic rules we follow here. They keep things running safely, smoothly, and happily."

"Sure," Jane said. "I'm all ears. Fire away."

They walked over to a handmade oak table, where the nurse set out water and a bowl of fruit. They sat at opposite ends, Roger not wanting to encroach on her personal space for this chat. He locked eyes with her to make sure she was listening and understanding.

"We don't have a written rule book obviously," he started casually. "We expect people to behave like adults, use their common sense when making decisions. Buy into the belief that we are here to help each other. Look after each other, and respect each other's opinions. If we have any major disagreements, I am the judge and jury. Though it seldom comes to that."

He poured some water, took a drink, and continued as Jane sat in silence. He offered her some, she declined.

"We would not have survived if everyone hadn't pulled together. It's been hard work—there's been setbacks—but as I sit here today, we are in the best position we've been in since the Collapse. And I'm not going to let anything, or anyone, jeopardize that." He paused to look at Jane. It wasn't an accusation in his voice—more of a challenge.

"Are you with me so far?" he asked.

Not wavering from his stare, Jane answered, "One-hundred percent,"

"Good," he said. "Let's walk and talk some more. Then I suggest you get settled in with the Grayson's. They have a spare room where you can stay and look after them. We think he has early onset Alzheimer's. Mrs. Grayson just needs some help and company. As a nurse, it should be easy for you. Obviously, you'll be on call 24/7, and also take your turn in the health clinic on the days it's open. I'll show you to their house."

He got up and led the way out of the church along the only paved road that ran the length of French Creek, parallel to the river.

It was a perfect Kentucky fall day, clear blue sky, the last of the leaves clinging to the trees, waiting to be dislodged by the next strong wind. It was warm enough to not require a coat. Jane relished the fresh air and the opportunity to stretch her legs after two weeks of confinement.

It was the first time Jane saw the village in daylight. It was remarkably neat and tidy. Each house had piles of logs stacked up outside. Most had runs and coops for chickens, ducks, and other domestic animals. A grow-your-own culture meant every house had gardens devoted to raising vegetables. Many had fruit trees as well with fruit ready to be picked.

Roger kept up a commentary that was a mixture of pride and lecture.

"Everyone must be as self-sufficient as possible. But we must also produce enough surplus to contribute to the Central Store for those who can't, whether because of age, illness, or injury. We take it very seriously; the community works together on this. It's been essential for our survival". He stopped walking for a moment. Feeling the need to expand on the point he just made, added, "I remember my father saying to me once. Your food always tastes better if you grow it yourself. The things you make give you greater satisfaction than those you bought. Basically, the more of yourself you put into something, the greater the satisfaction you get out of it. That's how it is here."

Jane nodded in agreement. Then asked, 'What happens if people become ill or injured? How have you coped with that?"

"That's one area where we will always be at risk. Traditional drugs and medications ran out years ago. We're back to basics using herbal remedies where possible. That was a real learning curve, I tell you what. Luckily, one of our early immigrants was a herbalist who knew what we needed. Finding the plants and herbs was a huge problem. At the Barter Fairs, we swapped or collected more to create an effective collection of natural medicines. We've made great strides. But safe to say, you don't want to break a bone or get something infected. We have limited ways to handle pain and illness."

"What about diet? Everyone I met seems healthy."

"In general, they are. With no fast foods, candies, and sweet drinks obesity has disappeared. We did worry about scurvy in the early days until the fruit trees produced. But we coped, and now I guess you could say we are back to...what was it called?"

"The Paleo Diet?" Jane offered.

"That's it. We know what to eat and drink for good health. We are still working towards learning how to grow and produce enough of it. It's a never-ending challenge. Overall though, we're a pretty healthy bunch."

"You seem satisfied with what you've achieved. Is there anything you miss?" Jane asked, weary of hearing about Roger's mini-Utopia.

"Me, personally? Not much," he shrugged. "I've long since gotten over the need to watch TV, go on the internet, follow social media. They're not essential. The way social media was being used and abused just before the Collapse played its part in the way the whole system unraveled, I'm sure. It was a toxic environment, in my opinion. Pandering to the worst in human nature. I'm glad it's gone."

He continued. "On the negative side, having no air conditioning or hot water on tap can be miserable. Power tools would save a lot of hard work. Popping down to the supermarket to top up on beer and the week's food is a long-forgotten dream." He sighed. "I've gotten used to it though. I think most of us have. There's not much I want from the twenty-first century right now."

He stopped for a moment to admire the village, the peace and quiet creating the feel of a country idyll. With a surge of enthusiasm, he added to his list.

"What I really don't miss? Interfering government. Never-ending taxes. Every year, some new law took our freedom away from us bit by bit, so slowly most people don't even notice. We've none of that here. It's refreshing—liberating."

Probing, Jane asked. "You have rules here, isn't that the same thing?"

Defiantly, Roger replied, "the difference here Jane is everyone has a say in how the community's run. It's an open book, no bought and paid for politicians. We're all in this together, not one person looking after some corporate interest with a big wallet. That's the benefit of keeping the government small and local I guess."

"Does everyone else feel the same?"

"You'd have to ask them," Roger said. "Most people seem pretty content. Happy to have survived the Collapse and the shitty years after it until we could get some comfort and safety. No one's forcing them to stay. They can leave anytime—but we don't want them back if they do."

"Why's that?"

Roger stopped walking and turned to face her directly, closing the gap between them. He was just inches from her face.

"Because I—we—don't need people coming back here with stories about what's happening out there. Nothing good as far as

I can tell at the moment. If there is, I'd rather this community not hear about it, not just yet. It'll get people all riled up and unsettled. We can't afford a huge exodus. It will ruin everything we've worked for."

Not waiting for a reply, Roger strode off and stopped outside a small, well-tended white, single-story house. The front porch had the obligatory two rocking chairs and some well-tended flowers. It was a typical cozy Kentucky house.

"Welcome to the Grayson's. Let me introduce you."

Minutes later, Jane was comfortably ensconced on a worn but ancient sofa. A fussing Elsie Grayson served homemade apple tea with cookies, delighted to have some new company to regale with stories from her decades in French Creek. Roger departed without saying a further word.

"What a lovely house you have, Mrs. Grayson," Jane said, looking for a start to the conversation.

"We've been here fifty years and have loved every minute of it. Such happy times, haven't we dear?" she said, turning to her husband who sat silently in the chair by the fire. He stared vacantly into the flames.

Jane sighed. This was going to be a tedious few weeks. But at least her charges were not likely to be too concerned about what she did and where she went.

CHAPTER 10

Jay McDonald was a thin, dour-looking man with permanently greasy hands and clothes who kept himself to himself. His wife's death soon after the Collapse had left him taciturn, withdrawn and bitter. His remote location at the furthest end of French Creek, where the river was barely a trickle coming out from the woods, reinforced his reputation as the community's hermit. He would have preferred a more permanent antisocial existence, but his uncanny ability to fix anything mechanical brought the villagers to his door on a regular basis.

In his solitude he did enjoy the rare visits of the few remaining deer, hogs, and coyotes. Once so plentiful, now hunted to near extinction they emerged from the woods in the evening or early in the morning. He never mentioned the sightings; he didn't want noisy hunters camping outside his house. He certainly didn't like the company-his mind was on other things.

He sat on his back porch thinking of happier days with his wife when they had money, cars, and a big house near Atlanta. That was before his brother-in-law siphoned off their life savings in some investment scam that left them only enough to afford a small house, workshop, and few acres in the boondocks of central Kentucky.

Worse still, his wife believed the brother-in-law, Stewart, had some part in her sister's sudden disappearance months before the Collapse. She had gone to her grave believing she had been murdered. No proof was ever found; no criminal investigation was possible after the Collapse. Jay, though, was inclined to agree with his wife. A decade later, the resentment was still there, and he was ready for justice to be served.

He believed this scheming relative had used his money to buy a well-equipped bug out cabin in the southern Appalachians, where no doubt he spent the last five years living in comfort and style. As Jay brooded on his unhappy past, his desire for revenge fermented inside him like a cancer, growing every day. Well, Stewart, payback was on its way. He was leaving French Creek—and soon.

To accomplish this ambitious goal he had a plan that was approaching finalization.

While the rest of the community believed him to be a simple curmudgeonly mechanic, what they didn't know is that Jay was getting close, so close, to finishing the construction of a very basic ultralight aircraft.

It required all his skill and subterfuge to make, scrounge, and secretly re-build the 400cc motorbike engine that would power his method of escape. He painstakingly made the wings out of recycled wood, canvas, and tarp, all of it based on a design from an old issue of Aviation Monthly. Jay had spent more evenings than he could count doing his best to adapt the specs to allow for the lack of materials and tools at his disposal. The result wasn't pretty, but Jay was convinced it would work—well enough to get him out of French Creek and to the door of his crooked brother-in-law's cabin.

While he was mechanically sure the ultralight was sound and workable, he had no way of taking any test flights to check the controls and its flying ability. He had flown ultralights as a hobby before the Collapse; he didn't doubt his abilities to fly the contraption. But first, he had proved it was mechanically sound and flight-worthy.

Jay forced himself to be patient. He would have to wait until the spring to leave French Creek. In the meantime, he tinkered and refined the ultralight at night and played the dutiful mechanic during the day.

CHAPTER 11

Every month the council held a meeting This one was to review how well-prepared the community was for the upcoming winter. Plus, any other issues the members felt important to discuss.

The council consisted of ten senior members of the community, all with specific expertise or knowledge. French Creek tried to be a democratically-run community. Every year, elections were held for places on the council; however, they rarely saw any new faces elected. Most villagers accepted that being healthy and secure was a pretty good indication that things were running well, so there was no need for change.

The council meeting began promptly at five PM in the church hall, as dusk fell and outside work stopped for the day. It was a warm fall evening, and the council arrived in an upbeat mood. There had been a good harvest, and the gardens were producing healthy amounts of fruits and vegetables. The atmosphere was positive and optimistic.

One of the community's wood-powered generators had been fired up for the occasion and produced enough power to light the sixty-watt bulbs hanging over the large wooden table and its ten chairs.

Sandwiches with beef, ham, and chicken on homemade bread plus flagons of deceptively strong home brewed beer were arrayed on a table by the wall. Not a big spread, but recognition enough that the meeting was an important event and likely to go on for several hours.

Roger took his seat at the head of the table and looked at the nine other members. All good men and women, he thought. Dedicated to keeping French Creek thriving and prepared for the future. Most had been on the council since its formation four years ago. There was little dissent or argument over most matters. Most times, it was common sense and practicality that drove the conclusions and decisions.

No one under thirty was on the council; villagers seemed to agree that older heads made the best choices for all of them. However, most were aware that some of the younger community members were beginning to question where French Creek was heading and their role in its future. It was a problem that had to be addressed—it wasn't going away anytime soon.

Roger knew that dealing with this could create divisions within the council. Older members with no children were likely happy with the status quo. Others with teenagers knew that a future of manual labor, limited horizons, and lack of opportunity was neither appealing nor practical to their children. Like a summer storm, the clouds were beginning to appear on the horizon. Before they knew it, it would be rattling their doors, comfort zone, and future.

"Okay, ladies and gentlemen," Roger announced. "Shall we get started? There's a lot to get through." Roger's voice boomed over the chatter and brought everyone to attention.

"First up," he continued. "Let's have our annual review on the supply and demand side of things. Jason?"

Jason, a former accountant, now math teacher, looked like a mad professor: with a scruffy jacket over an ill-fitting shirt and long dank, gray hair hanging limply over his collar. An unkempt beard completed the illusion of brains with no concern for appearance.

He got straight to the point with the blunt announcement, "We're reaching the limit of how many people we can support here. We're staying healthier, and more babies are being born than anticipated. The lack of reliable contraception is contributing to this increase," he explained in a matter-of-fact voice.

"What's the current population now?" asked Craig "Fix it" Phillips, the village's top maintenance worker. He was one of the oldest inhabitants at sixty-seven years of age. His experience of pre-computer-controlled machinery had been a godsend in the community's early days. Some credited him with a significant role in helping it survive at all. He and Jay were essential members of the community.

"189, with ten women in various stages of pregnancy," Jason said. "Our current food reserves look okay for the winter. But if it's long or severe, they could be heavily depleted by spring. All we need is a poor harvest next year, and we could be in trouble. Ideally, we need to keep the population at no more than two hundred until we can convert more land for food production."

In the past, a group of farmers and growers produced a report explaining how food production could be increased. The main problems were: The limited number of farm workers restricted production levels. In addition, the lack of chemical fertilizers and herbicides meant yield per acre was limited to pre-Industrial Revolution levels. Furthermore, their two tractors could only function when scouting groups found-or bought- more diesel. With careful rationing, it would last another two years. Some progress had been made in converting one of the other tractors to steam power, but the technology was still unreliable. The engineering team, with the help of old issues of Popular Mechanics, were hopeful a more reliable and efficient engine could be made by spring.

In the meantime, the ancient art of blacksmithing had been revived. Some reluctant horses and cows were now trained to pull plows and other implements. It was a painfully slow way of farming. They found that the old measurement of an acre being equal to what a horse-drawn plow could till in a day was all too accurate and punishingly hard work. In essence: more land would need more labor or extra working machinery.

Jason continued. "What we cannot risk is demand outstripping our limited resources. Progress is being made on all fronts in the food production chain, but it's slow. We cannot let the balance get out of sync. If we do, we could end up in the same place we were five years ago."

The room fell silent for a moment. Daphne Cortez, one of the experienced gardeners in the group, asked how many extra acres would be needed to safeguard food supplies.

Roger asked Joe Burke, a farmer, to answer the question.

"Difficult to say," Joe admitted. "Probably another twenty acres to grow corn and wheat, plus ten more for cereals for both animal and human consumption. Then we have to find the manpower to cultivate it. And, I should add, we need to increase our supply of dairy and beef cows as well. If we do, we'll get more fertilizer. The other problem we've discussed before; security as the extra land we need will likely be in the next hollow. Out of sight and difficult to guard."

"Good point, Joe," Roger said. "Maybe you could put together an action plan to start in the spring. Identify the best land and come back with what you need to make it work."

Joe agreed he would. The meeting moved on through the normal agenda of topics—security, water supply, maintenance of common areas and buildings. Then discussions of any major infringements of the community's rules, and what penalties, if any, should be applied.

In truth, there were rarely any significant problems. People were too busy working to get into any major arguments or trouble. What was there to argue about anyway? People had little worth stealing. Neighbors by and large got on with each other. No electricity meant no loud music and no noisy cars or machinery. People co-existed without resorting to anything close to physical altercations.

While nearly all adults had guns, the ammunition was centrally stored in a large safe box with limited access to avoid any accidents or theft. Hunters could request a supply before going out into the woods. In times of emergency, everyone could be given a supply of ammunition quickly and easily. This way, the limited arsenal could be rationed and not wasted.

After a refreshment break, the council reconvened to discuss the next point on the agenda: possible "leavers" in the village.

He stood up, hands planted on the table, and stared down at his fellow council members.

"I wanted to raise this potential threat to our community before it gets out of hand. There was information given to me that some of the younger members of the community have been discussing leaving French Creek."

He paused to let the news hit the council. Some were less shocked than others, Roger noticed, indicating to him they'd also heard the rumors. So why hadn't they come to him before the meeting? Never mind—the subject was now out in the open.

"Who are they?" the group asked.

"Before we get to that," Roger said. "Let's try and keep calm. It's not the first time we've had this problem. What's worrying this time is that the ones I know of are all teenagers or a little older. I'm ashamed to say that one of them is my son, Landy. Others include Dick Strepfield, Stephen Landow, Dave Matthews, Jo Philips, probably more. I found out because Landy asked me straight out last night if he could leave. He mentioned some of the others were keen to as well."

"What did you say to him?" Daphne asked.

"I asked him why. He said he wanted to see what was going on out there, experience life beyond French Creek and a load of other bullshit. I told he was out of his damn mind, and no way would I let him go."

"I guess that's the reason the others want to go too?" Daphne asked. "Do we know what their parents said?"

"Some don't have much of a home life. Broken families, lousy step parents, that kind of thing. They have good reasons for wanting a change. Of course, what they don't know is whether what's out there is any better than here."

With that, the meeting descended into several noisy discussions between various Council members. Roger decided to let them rant for a while, eavesdropping on the conversations. Surprisingly, some seemed sympathetic to the youngsters' demands. Others took Roger's view that they were too young to make such decisions, let alone venture outside the safety of French Creek. In such a small community, everyone knew the boys involved and were shocked by their rebellion.

After a few minutes, Roger bought the meeting back to order and then posed the simple questions to which there were no straightforward answers.

"What are we going to do about these young leavers? They are at an age when we can't physically stop them. How can we convince them that staying here for another year or two is the best thing to do? That it's the safest option? And that it's not good for the community to have such trouble fermenting among us?"

There was little consensus on how to tackle this situation. No one had an answer. After another half hour of fruitless discussion, Roger took the age-old route to an intractable problem. He suggested he would put some ideas together for the next meeting.

Roger decided to leave any discussions about the new group for another day. So far they had done nothing to arouse suspicions. Let sleeping dogs lie, for the moment.

With that, the meeting adjourned and the members, temporarily forgetting the problems facing them, started enthusiastically attacking the food and drink. Roger left quickly, his mind working overtime to figure out ways to keep this community intact. He could understand why some of the younger villagers wanted to rebel against what they might see as the oppressive regime at French Creek. How to convince them that what lay outside wasn't any better? Or even potentially dangerous?

Roger walked to the front door of his small house, lit one of the lamps, refreshed the wood burner, and settled down with a glass of homemade wine to further mull things over. Before he had finished his drink, fatigue overtook him, and he fell asleep in his chair, no closer to finding the answers he so desperately sought.

CHAPTER 12

It was mid-November and time for the Fall Barter Fair, in nearby Glasgow. A vast gathering place for everyone in the surrounding villages and communities. The Fair was a chance to trade unwanted or surplus goods, from tools and furniture to farm and household products, food and animals, seeds and saplings. It was also a chance to catch up on the gossip, and exchange advice on anything people might find of use from farming to canning, health care to mechanics. Perhaps most of all it was a chance to let your hair down and have fun. It was one of the highlights of the year and everyone wanted to go.

Glasgow was about thirty-five miles away. A two-day journey on horseback with a camping stop overnight.

The council only allowed around thirty people to make the trip, chosen by lottery from those who wanted to go. After days of preparation, the community agreed upon what was needed and what was available to take for trade. Then individual families made similar choices for themselves and for the ones who weren't lucky enough to be going.

On the morning of the departure, the excited group was all saddled up and ready to go by dawn. They made for quite a wagon train as they lined up to leave. Wagons and carts full of produce and materials of every kind were all packed carefully for the journey.

It was a beautiful Fall morning, the sun still warm enough to allow people to travel without heavy overcoats. The mood amongst the travelers was upbeat and full of expectations. They'd be away for nearly a week.

The Fair wasn't just a place to sell, swap items and gossip. There were dances, barbecues, and all kinds of entertainment, talks, and lectures. Every need was catered, good and bad. For some men, there was the attraction of some intimate enjoyment with the prostitutes who made their presence known discreetly in tents set up some distance from the Fair. Others indulged in quick, casual liaisons. In essence, the Fair was a chance for people to let their hair down and forget about the hard work and drudgery that would soon face them as Winter approached.

The road to Glasgow was still in reasonable condition. Where it had previously flooded made it impassable in some places. These caused diversions into surrounding fields and made for slow going. Downed trees were frequent hazards that had to be overcome. Any abandoned vehicles had long since been pushed to one side. In places, dozens of them had been shoved into fields to rot away. Once their owner's pride and joy, now worthless piles of scrap metal.

As the convoy lumbered slowly away from French Creek past the security outposts, they numbered some five carts and fifteen horse riders. Progress was slow, but the countryside passed by at a pleasant speed. Aside from the sound of horses' hooves and the groans of the old wooden carts, it was silent. No cars, planes, or engines of any kind. This was the America the pioneers had found and worked so hard to cultivate. Unlike the untouched woods, forests, valleys and hills they had discovered, the group from French Creek saw nothing but abandoned houses and cars. Once well-kept farm buildings and shops now in dilapidated disrepair. In just five years, Mother Nature had long reclaimed the land so casually used then abused by its last human inhabitants. It was eerie, fascinating, and sobering.

Few people lived out here on their own. Being some distance from your neighbor was once considered a luxury. After the Collapse, it became a dangerous liability as the countryside was swamped by hungry, desperate people. Those with any sense moved quickly to communities like French Creek that offered security and a chance to rebuild alongside other survivors.

Every now and then, when the group stopped to let the horses rest and people stretch their legs, the curious and adventurous among them wandered off to search empty houses and shops. Hoping something of use might have been overlooked by previous scavengers. Most came back empty-handed. Occasionally, a potentially useful farm implement, machinery part, or household item was found much to everyone's excitement. More to keep, swap, or sell at the Fair.

Dusk approached when without warning several shots sliced through the convoy. It was such a total surprise, no one at first reacted. Then Pat, serving as convoy guard, screamed at everyone to take cover behind the wagons and a stone wall that ran parallel to the road.

No one was seriously hurt. Only Debbie sustained an injury to her leg. Helen, the nurse, had come on the trip in case of a medical emergency. Now her expertise was needed, she crawled along behind the wall to Debbie to see how she could help.

Pat shouted for everyone to keep their heads down as more shots peppered the wall and splintered the woodwork on the carts. The horses panicked and were in danger of bolting, taking their wagons careening down the road. Some of the group ran to the horses and tried to calm them down.

"Anyone see where they are?" Pat screamed over the noise of gunshots and scared horses.

A male voice bellowed," Across the road over in that barn. I think the church as well."

Pat peeked through a gap in the stone wall and saw two rifles, one poking out from the first story of the barn and another on the ground floor. He couldn't tell how many there were in the church.

Roger crawled to Pat, keeping the wall between him and the shooters.

"How do you want to play this? Any idea how many there are of them?" he asked Pat.

"I can't tell at the moment. At least four I think. How many of us have guns? I know Dave and Stuart bought theirs."

"Not sure, maybe ten all told," Roger answered. "Though we've a limited amount of ammunition."

"I think we have to try and get behind them," Pat suggested. "If there are only four or five of them, they won't want a long gun fight. Probably just want some horses and supplies. Which way do you want to go?"

"Let's see if we can flank them," Roger said. "If I remember correctly, this wall runs a good distance alongside the road. I think it's about a quarter of a mile. Some of our guys could use it as cover then cross under the creek bridge further up. Might be able to get behind them using the creek and woods as cover?"

"It's worth a try," Pat said. "I'll pull together some of our best shots and explain the plan. Everyone else needs to keep their heads down, shoot only when necessary".

Roger worked his way to where people had found shelter. Occasional shots still came from the attackers but safe behind the old stone wall they were ineffective.

Four of the better armed men in the group started the move to flank the shooters under cover of the stone wall and creek. The rest kept a steady stream of fire to distract the attackers. To further confuse them, two more grabbed a couple of the horses and made a dash down the road in the opposite direction, heading back the way they came. Hopefully fooling the gunmen into thinking they were retreating for help. Unlikely, as they were nearly a day's ride away. The attackers didn't know that, it was just a further distraction.

Roger heard a shriek and groan of agony followed by someone moaning in pain. He turned to see Landy clutching his head as blood cascaded from a gaping wound above his right ear.

"Christ, fuck, I've been hit," he screamed. He tried, unsuccessfully, to stem the flow of blood with his hands.

Roger crawled over and looked at the wound. It didn't look good. Then again, head wounds always bled like a slaughtered pig so it was difficult to know how serious it was. He shouted for Helen to make her way over.

"Try to calm him down and patch him up," he shouted to Helen. He turned to his son, "You'll be fine Landy, hang on in there. I'll be back soon to see how you're getting on." Roger crawled off to the wall and let loose a volley of shots towards the barn, more in anger they had injured his son than in the hope he'd hit anyone.

Helen was some distance away still tending to Debbie's injury, "Gimme five, and I'll get there."

In truth, she couldn't do much more than dress the wound and douse it with a herbal antibiotic. A few stitches could be administered later if necessary.

"Got the bastard," someone exclaimed. Roger looked up and saw one of the attackers jerking on the ground in front of the barn, blood pouring from a bullet wound to his neck.

The attackers actually numbered only eight people. Four were armed, plus two mothers and two children hiding out of sight and danger. They had been expelled from a community near Dale Hollow Lake for theft and were trying to make their way West to Memphis and across the Mississippi. They were scared, hungry and desperate. The decision to attack was spontaneous and ill thought out. All they wanted was food and some horses to speed up their journey. They hadn't expected such a spirited reply to their initial attack.

"What do we do now?" shouted one of the women to the man at the front of the barn. "Jake, there are too many of them, and it's getting dark. They could attack us later, and we'd probably be killed before we see them. Can't we try and talk to them? Persuade them to give us food and leave us alone?"

"Too late for that. We've severely pissed them off, and we just lost Ryan. They shot him right in front of me. We've got to make a run for it back into the hills." Jake shouted back at the cowering woman with a young child clutched close to her. The other woman in the barn with a baby wrapped in her arms started to sob uncontrollably when she heard her husband, Ryan, was dead.

Before they could say more, the other group members spotted the flanking move from their viewpoint high up in the abandoned church.

"They're trying to get behind us," a boy shouted down Jake. No older than fifteen armed with an ancient revolver, he had yet to fire a shot. He was too terrified to do anything useful. "I can see four of them. What do you want me to do?"

Jake called back to the women in the barn, "Oh shit, we're fucked. I'm practically out of ammo too. Lacy, why don't you go out and try talking to them? They won't shoot an unarmed woman. See if we can get out of this crapshoot alive."

"Oh, that's just fucking great," Lacy screamed. "You come up with this bullshit idea and when it goes belly up, I have to pick up the pieces. You're a complete ass, Jake."

With that, Lacy tore off part of her dirty white shawl and found a tobacco stick to tie it around. Telling Jake to look after the child, she moved to the front of the barn, waving her makeshift white flag nervously before walking out into the open. For a second she stood rooted to the ground expecting to be shot.

She glanced at her cousin Ryan as he lay bleeding out on the ground. What a waste she thought. Losing a life because you wanted food. Gaining confidence, she wasn't going to be shot,

Lacy walked slowly towards the road, frantically waving her surrender flag in the air.

"Don't shoot. Can we please talk?" Lacy shouted. "This has all been a terrible mistake. I want to stop this now. Please, we have kids in there." She motioned with her head back towards the barn.

Roger looked at Pat, who nodded and told everyone to hold fire.

"Okay, what do you want?" Roger stood up cautiously, gun in hand pointed at the woman standing just yards from him. She was in a terrible state. Filthy, skinny, her clothes torn and worn almost past the point of offering any warmth. Despite her pitiful condition, she held herself defiantly.

"Just to stop this before anyone else gets hurt or killed," she said. "We're starving. We just want to get to Memphis. My shithead of a husband thought attacking you would be an easy way to get food and horses. Like most of his plans, it didn't work. It was his loudmouth got us thrown out of the Celina community. We're out of options. I know we don't deserve it, but please help us."

"There's a better way to get help than shooting us," Roger replied, not yet convinced the woman was sincere. "What's your name?"

“Lacy, Lacy Thomlett. Originally from Burkesville."

"Thomlett, as in Bruce and Mary Thomlett who ran the ACE store?" Roger asked.

"They were my mom and dad," she said. "Both dead now. Caught smallpox after the Collapse."

"I remember them," Roger said. "Used to go there from time to time. Nice folks." Roger felt a little more comfortable about this woman's intentions. "Tell the rest of your group to come out. Lay down their arms and get down here."

Lacy repeated the instructions to the rest, and they cautiously approached the road. They made for a pathetic sight. The two kids looked half-starved. The adults looked like vagrants. Roger could smell them from twenty feet away.

He turned to Pat, "Get a message to the others to come back. Start rounding up the horses and getting the carts back in shape. We may as well make camp here. Get some fires going and food ready. I'll talk some more to these folks. We can then decide what to do with them".

Roger signaled for the group to come closer. "You attacked us," Roger said. "You talk first."

After a pause to gather his wits, Jake answered in a despairing tone, "The last people we tried to stop and talk to just started shooting." He pulled at his greasy hair and took a long slug of water from his canteen. Then continued. "Me and my family here are desperate. We didn't know what else to do when we saw you coming along. If we'd known you knew Lacy's mom and pop, we woulda done things differently. But we're hungry and tired. All we want to do is get to Memphis. We've heard people there can help us get back West?"

"Oh yeah," Pat said. "Who told you that?" He couldn't keep the skepticism out of his voice.

"Some people who turned up at Celina in the Spring. That's why we were thrown out of the village. These newcomers started stirring it up with all this talk about how good it was back West. How they could help us get across. As soon as we said we wanted to go, the Celina people kicked us out with no supplies. We don't know what happened to the other people. They gave us an address in Memphis saying a man there would help get us across."

Hearing this Roger felt a stab of suspicion. Could French Creek's recent intruders and the group Jake was talking about be one and the same? He decided to probe a little more.

"Can you remember the name of any of the people in this group that were spreading these rumors?"

Jake looked at Lacy for help remembering. Before he could say anything, Lacy answered.

"We didn't have much to do with them, but one of the guys was called Austin. I think the women may have been Jane. Why's it so important?"

"Just interested." Roger did his best to look unconcerned while his mind raced. Could they be the same people? Seems probable. Did that mean they have a hidden agenda? Or was their appearance at French Creek just a coincidence? If there was another reason than wanting safety and food, what was it?

"That's an interesting story you told there, Jake," Roger said. "I'm inclined to believe you for the moment." He stood up, asked one of his group to give them all some food and any clean clothes they could spare. He walked to the other side of the camp and grabbed a flagon of homemade beer on the way.

Concern over what he had just heard pushed his hunger aside. He needed to learn more about Jane and her group when he returned to French Creek. Then figure out want to do with them.

He sat alone as the evening closed around him. With it peace and quiet descended. No cars or planes or any other man-made sounds disturbed the tranquility. The distant yipping of a coyote looking for a mate was the only sound to be heard. Despite the worries fluttering up inside him, Roger found it difficult not to love and welcome the undisturbed calm of this rural existence.

It was a simple life of hard work, without the help of modern technology and endless resources. French Creek proved it could be done, and surely in thousands of other places around the country as well? How well were they doing? How were they being governed? Did they have the same problems as French Creek? Were any close to living a pre-Collapse lifestyle? Would the Federal Government ever come to help them?

Roger often pondered these questions and discussed them with friends over dinner or at Council meetings. Everyone had their opinions and ideas on how they'd respond when the time came to face the new outside world. So far, no one has had to decide on these life-changing decisions.

As Roger sat in solitary silence, doubts bubbled up again about the new group at French Creek. Jane did have a kind of arrogance, confidence—chutzpah. Was she hiding something when he first questioned her? He sensed that all was not as it seemed. Something was lurking below that tough veneer he couldn't see through. He'd need to confront her sooner rather than later to try and extract the truth.

While the camp settled down for the night, Roger stood up and walked back to the fire, checked that Pat had organized some sentries on the perimeter, and made sure their new guests were safe. Pat had given them some food and water then locked them back in the barn until a decision could be made about them in the morning.

"Thanks for your help today," Roger said. "How are the wounded?"

"Doing okay," Pat said. "They'll live, Landy will have a headache from hell for a few days. I'm just doing one last check around the camp before I get some shut eye. My watch starts in a few hours."

Roger wished him goodnight, collected his bedroll, and laid it on the cool ground. Within minutes, he was asleep.

CHAPTER 13

It was late afternoon when they reached the Barter Fair in Glasgow. As always, it was organized chaos. It took a while, but everyone managed to find a place to set up their stalls and start displaying their wares. There were hundreds of other people doing the same. Each year, the Fair grew larger and larger as people found it safer to travel and had more surplus goods to bring.

Every conceivable type of structure was erected—yurts, teepees, tents— anything that was portable and weatherproof. Larger tents and marquees were set up to house the entertainment. Music and singing clashed with the mournful sound of the cows, the bleating of sheep, and a dozen other animal sounds, all creating a cacophony that battered and excited the senses. The smell of cooking from a thousand campfires was mouth-watering.

By the evening, hundreds of parties were in full swing. Noisy, raucous, and bawdy, it was more medieval than twenty-first century. Music came from musicians playing every type of instrument, creating an ear-numbing, jarring noise. There were no police or security. If someone became too drunk or out of hand, cooler heads (and heavy hands) calmed things down.

On the edge of the Fair the hookers were already doing a brisk trade. Men of all ages took advantage of a service that was unavailable back in their communities. No one was judging. It was just a fact of life, the normal equation of supply and demand being played out as it was elsewhere at the Fair.

By the next morning, the crowds were even bigger. Over three thousand people from as far away as Bowling Green, Paducah, Louisville, even Nashville had converged on Glasgow.

If it wasn't fun or supplies people were seeking, it was information. Many were keen to find folks living on the Mississippi River who could tell them what was happening on the other side. Once the country's greatest transport artery, the Mississippi had now become America's own Berlin Wall. Even after five years it was a perennial quest, a fatal fascination to find out more about something that was unattainable to most. They wanted to know how much better it was in the West, knowing full well they would never get to sample its delights.

Roger and Pat walked by dozens of stalls, amazed at what people had on offer. Machinery, tools made or well-worn from years of use were everywhere. More tempting was the huge range of food, vegetables, meat and home brews to sample and buy. There were no prices on anything. Products were bartered, their value based solely on what the seller and buyer considered fair.

As they walked past another large tent with a temporary bar, Roger overheard someone talking about refugees trying to flee to the West. He stopped and waited for his chance to join the conversation. A brief lull between the two men allowed Roger to introduce himself.

"Couldn't help but overhear you guys talking about refugees trying to cross the Mississippi. What's the latest on that, if you don't mind me asking?" The men looked suspicious. Such questions answered in the wrong way could lead to trouble.

Roger sensed that a drink would help open up the discussion. Pat went to the bar and came back with four tankards of disconcertingly strong beer. As the conversation opened up, Roger ascertained one of the men lived in Paducah and worked as a dockhand. The other was a blacksmith from Harrodsburg.

The dockhand went by the name of Jock. He was short and stocky, with a completely bald head. His hands were calloused and dirty. He seemed amiable and willing to talk—especially when presented with another beer.

He was honest and to the point, "Still fucking chaotic at times," he said. "We never know from one day to the next if the rest of the country is open for business or not. The refugee camps are slowly emptying as people go back East or have their visas issued to go across and start again in the West."

"They're issuing visas now?" Pat asked.

"Had to," Jock explained. "Too many people, not enough jobs, housing, or food, even over there. Lot better than this side so I'm told, but still pretty shitty if you don't know the right people. Just like it was with Mexico ten years ago. Lots of coyotes charge a fortune to get people over there illegally, if they even survive the trip. The states along the Mississippi have pretty good security after five years. It's not easy to get through. But just like in the past, people are so desperate, they'll pay anything, try anything."

Roger thought this over for a moment. "Do you know anyone who's looking to smuggle people across?"

Jock looked uncomfortable for a moment, staring intently into his beer as he thought of an evasive answer.

"I might. Why are you looking to go West? You don't have to look very hard to find these coyotes-or their recruiters. They're traveling all over the place. They persuade folks that they can get them across to a better life, but then when they get to the river, they charge them a fortune. I hear some go across and pay back the money by working like slaves. It's a fucking shame. People shouldn't believe a word these recruiters tell them."

"I agree," Roger said. "It's terrible." Before he could pry any more information from Jock, a band started to play, drowning out the rest of their conversation.

"Thanks for the information. Be safe," Roger shouted, bringing the discussion to a close. He and Pat finished their drinks and made their way into the sunshine.

"Why were you so interested in how to get to the West? Thinking of doing a runner?" Pat said half-jokingly as they strolled back towards their campsite.

"No, not at all. Just trying to get a handle on how things are changing at the border. We're bound to be asked when we get back. I just wonder how far those recruiters have spread out to find potential leavers? They could stir up a lot of trouble with people who are looking for something better."

Pat didn't answer. He stopped at a stall packed with ammunition to see if he could get any for his gun collection. Roger moved on alone, deep in thought about what Jock had told him. He wondered if he should warn Jake and Lacy before they made the trip to Memphis? He also wanted to learn more about the visitors to their Celina camp that had persuaded them to start this perilous journey. Could there be a connection between them and the group who had just attacked French Creek?

Elsewhere, the rest of the French Creek visitors were taking advantage of the delights Barter Fair had to offer, good and bad. Many sought out doctors and dentists for checkups or to see if some medications could be obtained that were unavailable at home. There was no doubt such goods were increasingly making their way in from the West. Health products were becoming more readily available—for a price. No one asked how they had been sourced, and there was always the danger they could be fakes. For many, it was a risk worth taking.

The Council had given Nurse Helen some valuables to exchange for medicines and first aid products. They hoped she'd find something useful, specifically modern pharmaceuticals to use alongside their range of natural remedies.

Over-the-counter drugs, guns, and ammunition—it wasn't illegal to bring stuff like this across, though much of it required permits as they were still considered controlled in the West. Roger wondered who was behind these imports—the government, organized crime, or just budding entrepreneurs? He noticed most were only interested in bartering for gold, silver, or valuables they could convert to cash when they returned to the West.

The three days went by in a blur of fun, shopping and doing business. By the last evening people were exhausted, hungover, and sad. The Barter Fair had that effect on you. A three day high followed by a dose of reality-months of hard work in the cold Kentucky Winter lay ahead.

Soon the roads and tracks were full as everyone packed up and headed home. People said their goodbyes. Overflowing wagons and pack horses spread out across the countryside. Within a few hours the Barter Fair had been dismantled and was deserted for another six months

They said farewells to Jake, Lacy family and friends. Roger gave them a horse and small cart to make their way to Memphis. He repeated the dangers he heard from Jock in the bar about the unscrupulous coyotes. He even offered them a home back in French Creek, but they seemed determined to take the risk.

"Thanks for the offer," Lacy said. "But we've had enough of the East. We just want something better for us and the kids." She looked much healthier after a few days of rest and decent food. "We really ain't got much to lose, so we'll give it a go. We appreciate your help though."

After three days of blessed relief from the hard work back at home, and despite a few hangovers, the group left refreshed from their Barter Fair trip. They'd picked up supplies, gossip, news, plus, one other thing they didn't realize—the flu.

CHAPTER 14

"Hey guys, what's going on?" Jenny, one of the newcomers, strolled up to a group of teenagers sitting around an old barrel they had converted into a table. It was the end of the day with few villagers around as many were away at the Barter Fair.

Jenny had kept a low profile since being released with Jane and Bryanna. She'd been given a job helping out canning, drying, and smoking food. Her past experience of selling homemade goods was sufficient for her to be allowed to stay for this purpose.

Jane, conscious that she might be observed, suggested Jenny ask around and see if there were any villagers who might not be happy with their current situation. It didn't take long for her to hear about a group of teenagers who wanted to quit French Creek. She spotted them as she walked back to her house and decided now might be a good time for a chat.

Jenny was in her mid-thirties, tall, willowy, with short blonde hair. A perpetual smile on her face and an open demeanor made it easy for her to strike up a conversation with strangers. She took full advantage of it.

She looked down at the group of teens and guessed these were the ones she'd heard were not too happy with their lot. She decided to find out more.

Flashing a beaming smile, she asked, "Mind if I join you? Anyone with a beer to spare? I'm so thirsty I could drink horse piss. Spent all day over a hot oven, canned God knows how many tomatoes."

Dick invited her to sit down and dug a beer out of his backpack. They weren't used to adults joining them for a drink. "Might be a bit warm, but you're welcome. Should taste better than horse piss."

"Thanks," she said. "Appreciate it." She took a long slug and pronounced it much, much better than horse piss. Then took another lengthy slurp, nearly emptying the bottle. The boys were impressed.

It didn't take long for the group to start asking questions about what she'd been doing before they came and attacked French Creek.

"Whoa, steady on," Jenny said defensively. "That was Jane's husband's fool idea. I wanted no part of it. Unfortunately, he had the guns and made it clear we were either with him or on our own, so we tagged along. It all went pear-shaped because of his stupidity. We're all really sorry for what happened."

"Yeah, you should be," Alex said. "You shot my cousin. He was a good guy."

"What we did was stupid and ended badly for lots of people," Jenny said. "But I can't change that. All I can say is I wish it had never happened. Sorry again guys, really."

Searching for a change of subject, Jenny asked them about French Creek and what they all did for fun. It was obvious most were bored and frustrated with their lives. Within minutes, the questions were coming back at her thick and fast about what it was like "out there."

"What are the other communities like?"

"What did you see while you were out there?"

"Was it dangerous?"

"What places did you visit? Any big cities?"

"Is French Creek better or worse?"

"Why do you want to stay here?"

"Do you know what's happening in the West?"

Jenny spent nearly half an hour and three beers trying to answer their questions. Their thirst for knowledge was insatiable. She was one of the first outsiders they had ever met or talked with, and they wanted to know everything. Everything.

The more she told them, the more animated and excited they became. It soon became obvious that some desperately wanted to explore the outside world. She may have exaggerated a little as to how good it was out there and in the West. By time they found out, it would be too late.

Their ignorance and naivety gave them a rose-tinted view of life's potential outside of French Creek. Jenny did nothing to convince them otherwise. Even when she explained how she was almost raped and killed on more than one occasion, it didn't seem to concern them. However, there were no girls in the group, she noted.

"Guys, guys, hold on a minute here. Have you given any thought to what you'd do out there if you left? You can head West to the Mississippi and try to get across. I've heard it costs a fortune and can be dangerous. It can be done of course lots of people do it, every day. It's not easy, you need help"

Dick intrigued, asked Jenny, "Do you know how they go about it?"

Jenny decided the conversation had gone far enough for now. She certainly didn't want to get into any more detail with these wannabe leavers. Or arouse any suspicions. She learned enough to report back to Jane.

"I don't know the details," she said. "But some other members of our group do know a bit more than me. Let me have a word. Maybe we can meet again in a few days. But don't get your hopes up. There's no easy way to get to the West, I warn you."

Having primed the fuse, Jenny got up, tossed her empty beer bottle at Dick to catch, and walked back towards the village, leaving the youngsters buzzing with excitement. Let them stew on it for a few days, she thought. She'd go talk to Jane about what to do next.

CHAPTER 15

The rumblings of discontent among the community's younger members continued to fester. The chat with Jenny had only fanned the flames. Like migrant birds in spring, they were restless to get moving.

Not surprisingly, Dick, Dave, and the rest of the campfire group received no encouragement from their parents when they suggested a trip to discover the wider world. With Landy away at the Barter Fair, they had done little more than brood on their parent's unwillingness to even entertain the idea. They were awaiting his return before deciding their next move.

Jane had listened to Jenny's report on her meeting with the boys. She needed to find out more about their intentions. Wary of getting into trouble with their parents and the Council, she had to tread carefully. One afternoon, Jane casually bumped into Dave as he walked home. She took the opportunity to bring up the conversation he and the group had with Jenny. Dave responded evasively. He claimed they had been 'shooting the breeze and weren't serious'. Jane countered that if they wanted to know more, she had some information they might find useful. Just come back to her if they are interested. Having sowed the seed, she left the conversation hanging. Dave and his friends could follow up if they wanted.

Jane knew she had to be cautious. Reveal too much too early and she could blow it, not just for herself and the group, but for the potential new recruits as well. Experience told her these things couldn't be hurried. To her, there was a lot at stake. She could wait a few weeks for the right moment.

In the meantime, she dutifully looked after her elderly companions and kept her ears open for any information that would help with her plans. Jane had to admit that French Creek was the most well-organized, harmonious, and comfortable of all the communities she had infiltrated. She admired how they had managed to take modern technology and combine it with old fashioned graft, and wisdom to make life bearable.

As she walked along the creek, she saw Herb. She knew he was one of the teachers. Today he was trying to fish in the pond. It had been stocked with bass, trout, and catfish. Jane hadn't yet met him properly. With nothing better to do, she introduced herself.

"Hi," she said, walking up quietly behind him. "Any luck so far?"

"Not a bite. How's it going with you?" Herb asked without looking up from his fishing line.

Jane tried to get the conversation going. "I'm OK. Just getting some fresh air before going back to work. It's certainly beautiful here. Do you look after the pond?"

"No, Billie did that. I guess we need to find someone else to take care of it now, since you guys killed him." Herb's comments carried only a hint of anger. "In truth, he was an asshole. Looking after this pond was about all he was capable of. Fact he got himself killed just about sums up how useless he was."

"Well, that put him in his place didn't it? Mind if I sit down?" Jane asked, easing herself onto the bench next to him. She looked at Herb, trying not to appear too interested but there was no doubt—cleaned up, he could be a nice-looking guy. Time to deploy some feminine wiles.

"Yes, that was really bad news about Billie. I'm sorry that happened". Jane moved onto safer ground, "How long have you lived here?"

"I was living in Somerset when the shit hit the fan," he explained. "It quickly went to hell so I canoed down the Cumberland. Got as far as the Dam, then walked the rest of the way. My cousin lives here so I thought I'd try and find her. They took me in because I was a teacher. Can't complain—it turned out pretty well."

Jane looked more closely at Herb. She guessed he was in his early thirties. Like most men, he had a beard (shaving was a luxury) and the most piercing blue eyes she had ever seen. An attractive package if he scrubbed himself up. He seemed a philosophical, easy-going type, thought Jane. He had the patience, not just to deal with a classroom of kids, but to sit here fruitlessly fishing for hours at a time.

"So, you weren't keen on Billie?"

"He was OK," Herb said. "He just didn't really contribute. He was one of the originals living here, so we couldn't kick him out. Sorry to see him go, but no great loss if I'm honest."

Jane probed a little further, "I like honest people. Pleasant change from everyone keeping too many secrets."

Herb flicked the lure across the pond with ease. It plopped into the water and didn't move. The fish weren't biting today. "Do you think we're a secretive bunch here?"

Jane knew she had to be careful how she answered this. Everything she said could be reported straight to Roger and the Council.

"No, not really." Jane said. "Cautious might be a better word, I guess. Certainly around me and the rest of my group."

"You can't really blame us. We've had people turn up over the last few years and cause problems. It takes a while for newcomers to be accepted, trusted. You'll just have to be patient. Forgive me for being blunt, you did, after all, come in here with guns blazing. Not a great way to make friends."

"True. Our arrival didn't go to plan. But it wasn't my idea to do it in a way that would cause trouble. Blame that on our impatient captain—my husband." Jane kicked herself for the slip of her tongue. He wasn't her husband at all but a phony arrangement she had concocted to garner some sympathy from her captors after the shoot-out. It worked and gained her admission into the community. The end justifies the means.

Herb didn't notice her hurried correction and carried on, aimlessly casting the fishing line back into the pond. For a moment, nothing was said. Jane allowed Herb to break the silence.

"Do you like reading?" he asked.

Taken aback by the oddness of the question, Jane paused before answering. "Long ago, when I had the time. Yes, I did enjoy it."

"Who was your favorite author?"

"Not sure I had a favorite author. I loved true crime, mystery, and thrillers. Historical fiction, as well."

"So not a Nicholas Sparks, romance novel kind of gal?" he laughed. "Suppose I shouldn't be surprised."

"What do you mean by that?" Jane replied, feigning insult.

"You seem too practical and down to earth for all that mushy stuff. Prefer action rather than talk."

Jane realized Herb was quietly flirting. To her surprise, she not only liked it—she was happy to play along.

.

"What about you? What do you read? Zane Gray-are you a wannabe cowboy?"

Herb laughed. "Not a fan of him, otherwise anything, especially in the last few years. Not a great deal of choice. Within the community there is a reasonable selection, and we all swap books," he said. "But so many people trashed them when they got iPads and Kindles. Now they wish they hadn't. If I had to choose, I would say history. The American Revolution, Civil War, some European history, as well. We never learn from our mistakes, or rarely. Every great civilization comes to an end. Sometimes suddenly, sometimes gradually—but it always happens. They become too big, too rich, too complacent. Look what happened to us."

Warming to the subject, Herb carried on. "America was just too arrogant to see the signs. The Collapse was destined to happen.

We were bankrupt. Not just financially, but morally, politically—in every way. If it wasn't a series of natural disasters, it would have been something else. Just our shitty luck it happened on our watch."

Herb paused. "Sorry for the rant." His voice went to a whisper. "It just pisses me off. The people we put in charge turned out to be so corrupt and selfish they turned tail and ran when the shit hit the fan. Personally, good riddance to them. We are managing quite well without them. Long may it continue."

"But it wasn't anyone's individual fault," Jane replied. "Just a perfect storm of unforeseen disasters."

Herb looked up from the fishing lure that had become the center of his attention. He turned and stared straight at her.

"Of course no one could see what was coming," he said. "When it did, it was our inability to deal with all the disasters, natural or man-made, that annoys me. After COVID, we should have spent time and money building up our disaster preparedness. These disasters were going to happen again sometime. Not all the Cassandras were wrong. Climate change, rising sea levels, depletion of natural resources—they were all contributing to this eventuality. Billions being spent on the military and not on FEMA or other emergency services. Where's the sense in that? The shortsighted belief that problems can be dealt with only once they've happened and not headed off is just plain wrong. And when the shit did hit the fan? What did our government do? Run for it, leaving millions of Americans like you and me to pick up the pieces and millions more to die. So yes, I am pissed about where we've ended up and the zero help we've received. To be honest, if the government turned up today to offer help, I'd tell them to go fuck themselves. Others here might even string them up. Doesn't it piss you off?"

Jane admired his spirited argument and mentally rehearsed her reply before answering. She couldn't be too honest; it might reveal too much about her reason for being in French Creek.

Before she could respond, the sound of horses' hooves, creaking wagons, and chattering people could be heard down the road. The group had returned home in high spirits from the Barter Fair.

"Maybe we could continue this conversation later?" she said, frustrated that an enjoyable afternoon had been curtailed.

"You want to come round for a beer later?" Herb asked.

"I can be at your place after my shift."

"See you then," Herb replied. He packed up his fishing gear and headed up the road to meet the returning travelers. Jane walked back to her elderly charges, for the first time in months with a smile on her face.

As he rode in, Roger saw Herb and Jane going their separate ways. He made a mental note to chat with Herb, to see if their conversation had revealed any useful information about her. In the meantime, he raised a hand and shouted for Herb to gather a few folk together to help unload. There was plenty of work and gossip to share, plus a couple of people who still needed medical attention.

CHAPTER 16

The first person to show symptoms of the flu was Bryan, a giant of a man who sported a huge bushy beard and scruffy hair tied back in a ponytail. His normal ruddy complexion wasn't quite so healthy when he came to the clinic run by Dr. Joe Brown. He immediately recognized Bryan's symptoms and sent him to the same quarantine room that recently housed Jane and her friends.

They had nothing to give him except yarrow and elderberry infusions. "He's a big guy; he'll probably be OK," Doc Brown said to Nurse Helen. "It's the older folk we have to worry about. Put on some masks, wash your hands, and keep well away from him." He then ordered the staff to raid the medicine store for more herbs likely to be of help. "I'll go tell Roger what's happening. We'll have to quarantine everyone who went to the Barter Fair."

"Flu? Jesus," Roger said, pacing around his kitchen, mug of mint tea in his hand. "That's all we need going into Winter. If we quarantine everyone from the trip, that's thirty people out. Where the hell are we going to put them?"

"And you, Roger," Doc Brown said. "You'll have to quarantine too. We don't have a place big enough for everyone."

"Then everyone will have to stay at home?" Roger asked. "How long?"

"Two weeks before we can hope we've seen the back of it. That's if everyone stays inside."

"Let's do it," Roger said. "The list of people who went are on the Community Notice Board. You and the other nurses go round and tell everyone they can't leave their houses for two weeks. We'll convene the Council tonight to plan how we handle food, workloads, and lockdown."

Doc Brown bustled out of the house, leaving Roger to plan how to overcome the community's latest problem. There had been no flu outbreak since the Collapse. The nearest epidemic had been a nasty bout of measles two years ago. Luckily as most people had been vaccinated, the disease was short-lived and only claimed five lives. This could be way worse. Those thirty travelers had already gone home and been welcomed by husbands, wives, and children. A hundred people could have been in contact with these potential carriers—over half the community.

If the flu took hold, it could be a calamity for French Creek. It would decimate families that had worked so hard and been through so much to see their lives torn apart because of a trip to the Barter Fair. A steep drop in population would create a host of problems—not enough people for security, a workforce too small to keep the community fed. It had to be contained at all costs.

Roger was about to leave and inform the Council members when he checked himself. He couldn't leave the house either. He scribbled a note to each of the members, and when one of the villagers walked past his window, he asked them to take the letters, leave them in the members' mailboxes, and shout that there was an urgent note they needed to read immediately. Avoid any contact at all costs.

Later that day, the Council gathered.

The scene was strange, to say the least. All were wearing makeshift face masks and sat outside Roger's house on the porch. They kept a safe distance apart. None had gone to the Barter Fair except Roger, however some of their relatives had. Roger ran the meeting from inside his house with a window cracked open for him to address the scattered assembly.

"Thank you for coming," he said. "How are you all feeling? Are any members of your family showing signs of the flu yet?"

Two members reported family members showing symptoms. They were already on a regimen of herbal remedies provided by Doc Brown.

As they talked, it soon became apparent that the biggest problem wouldn't be caring for the sick, but keeping people from breaking quarantine rules. Those with kids and teenagers could already foresee problems.

"They're not going to stay cooped up with their parents for two weeks, I can tell you that," said Daphne. "And I won't be sane either if I have to see them all day every day for two weeks. Does it have to be that long?"

Doc Brown answered the complaint with his best bedside manner, "If a lot of people get the flu, that's how long it will take to run its course. If it looks to be dying out sooner, we can review the situation. But let's be crystal clear—if we don't stick to this quarantine and the virus takes hold, it could wipe out dozens of people in a matter of weeks. The community would struggle to survive."

"So, we either die by flu or commit murder when our kids have driven us insane?" Daphne replied.

"Yep, pretty much," the doctor chuckled. "It's what's called a Hobson's choice."

"That much is clear," Roger said, steering the conversation back to practicalities. "What isn't is how we're going to keep this place running with two-thirds of the people quarantined."

"I suggest we just wait and see what happens over the next week or so," the doctor said. "Maybe we caught the virus in time and contained it. Not everyone who does get it will die. We need to protect the very young, the old, and the infirm. Let's not act in haste and repent at leisure."

"Good advice Doc," Roger said. "I can't really see an alternative at this time. I'll put together a roster so that people doing the essential work do it at different times."

"I'll organize some people to enforce the quarantine," Doc Brown said. "I hope people will be sensible. Anyway if that's all, I have some patients to see." He packed up his papers and walked off the porch into the dark, cool evening air.

The other Council members stayed outside on Roger's porch, chatting. They asked for a report on the trip to the Barter Fair. In all the excitement, many had not yet heard about what had happened. He filled them in on all the goings on, notably, the altercation with Jake's group and the conversation with Jock from Paducah.

"There's an actual trade in people who want to get back across the Mississippi?" Daphne asked, a look of horror on her face. "And people are prepared to risk their lives for this?"

"Seems so." Roger answered, wondered what Jake and his family might be enduring at this very moment in Memphis.

"Those people are fucking depraved, trading in peoples' lives. Like the slave trade." Eddie spat. "Sorry about the language, Daphne."

"No," Daphne said. "My sentiments entirely. Those people are parasites trading on peoples' hopes and dreams. They deserve to be strung up."

"Interestingly, they are now sending out recruiters to persuade people to take the risk," Roger said. "There's so much to be made that it's proving very lucrative for everyone involved. To them, it doesn't matter whether the people make it across or not—they still profit. We have to assume that these recruiters might come here. In fact, I wonder if they haven't already?"

Realizing what Roger meant by this comment, a collective silence descended on the group, halting all conversation. Then they began to pepper Roger with questions.

"I didn't want to say anything until I was sure about my theory," Roger said. "But now that I've raised the matter, here's where I'm at."

He took a long swig from his beer and composed his thoughts. If he was wrong, it would cause a lot of resentment, recriminations, even reckless actions. But if he was right, the sooner the better for the community.

He stood at the open window and felt like he was preaching to a congregation. For five years, he had been their leader, pleading, cajoling, and bullying them at times to do what he thought best for everyone. He was sure some thought him high-handed, even arrogant at times. But to him, it was the only way at times to get things done. Most people, he believed, prefer to be led, have decisions made for them, responsibility taken off their shoulders. Few can see the bigger picture, the knock-on effects a whole village could suffer if certain actions, sometimes unpalatable, weren't taken. He had always been prepared to stand up and take the consequences.

Maybe this was one of those times.

He relayed the information he'd gleaned so far, combined with his own gut feeling. Neither represented proof. He knew certain Council members would want a lot more of both before taking any action. But sometimes a person has to take that leap of faith, trust their instinct, and ask for forgiveness later if it all goes wrong. He wasn't one to beg for permission and wait.

It didn't take long, just a few minutes. When Roger finished, his small audience reacted with collective concern.

"You admit you haven't much proof that this woman is a recruiter," Daphne said. "Just the stories from the Barter Fair, hearsay from around the village, mainly your son, and a gut feeling that she isn't all she claims to be."

Roger had to agree with Daphne, "Yes, I know it would hardly convince a jury. But we may not have time to gather all the proof before she does something irreversible. I just can't sit here with this nagging feeling that she is a fake. And if she convinces a group of the youngsters—our children—to take their chances and go West, the consequences could be heartbreaking, even deadly."

Roger found himself for once at a loss for words. He couldn't put together a watertight argument that his feelings were one hundred percent right. But he couldn't dismiss them either. The evidence was there—but not enough of it.

"If she is a recruiter, why didn't she just walk in here asking for help? Jo asked. "Rather than shoot her way in? She could easily have got herself killed."

"That's true," Roger said. "Maybe it was an elaborate cover. Maybe it wasn't her husband we shot…maybe she was using him for her own purposes. I don't have all the answers yet."

"That's a lot of maybes," Jo said.

"You're going to have to trust me on this," Roger pleaded. "Please keep this to yourselves. Keep your eyes and ears open; see who she talks to, what she's saying. If she's going to recruit someone, she will have to start pushing the idea soon. We need to get ahead of it if we can."

Roger paused, leaning on the window sill. "First things first, go back home and keep a close eye on this virus. Let the Doc know if anyone starts showing symptoms and keep to the quarantine arrangements. I suggest we meet again at the end of the week."

The Council stood up, gathered their belongings and drifted off, careful not to get too close to each other. Jason, another teacher, lingered behind and knocked on the window to get Roger's attention.

"It may be nothing," he said. "I was talking to Herb yesterday. Said he was meeting Jane for a beer, I think tonight, though with the quarantine, that may not be happening. Seems they're getting quite friendly. I can ask him to try and find out more if you like."

"That's useful to know," Roger said. "If you see Herb, ask if he can come and see me—through the window, of course. I guess school will be closed for the next couple of weeks?"

"Sure will. I can drop a note in his mailbox."

Roger thanked Jason and moved back into his house, a dull headache making itself felt behind his eyes. A hot herbal tea and an early night would be a good idea he thought to himself.

CHAPTER 17

Jay McDonald was perversely delighted with the news that the flu was in the village. It meant less visitors coming to see him with their broken pieces of machinery. He was keen to try out his homemade ultralight, and less activity around the village made a test flight a possibility at last. How to take advantage of this lockdown?

Late one afternoon, as he sat on his porch enjoying a typical Kentucky downpour, complete with thunder and lightning of an apocalyptic intensity, he had the germ of an idea.

Why not use this weather and the lack of people out and about, as a cover? Not to fly in—too dangerous—but to move the ultralight to a neighboring valley, where a small country lane could act as his airstrip. Then, he could test-fly it there. The construction was light enough and the wings were in four pieces—all easily transportable on a small trailer. He could use one of the tractors in his workshop to pull everything a couple of miles through the woods.

The more he thought about it, the more Jay believed it might work. It wasn't without risks; he could be discovered, the machine might suffer some damage on the cart, and of course, it might not fly. Hell, he could crash and injure himself and no one would find him. But life was about taking chances. When again might the village be quarantined, with all the prying eyes confined to their homes?

He made a checklist of all the things he had to take: the tools he'd need, the fuel he'd been saving and scrounging for months. (In his defense, he'd been one of the first to devise how to extract alcohol from wood and create a poor man's gasoline. Jay had been perfecting it for years, it was nearly ready for a trial run in the Spring).)

The two hundred miles to Atlanta where he intended to fly and confront his crooked ex brother-in-law should only need about four gallons of fuel, he estimated. That was 160 pounds in weight, with room for a little extra baggage. This modest amount made it all the easier to prepare for his trek to the next valley.

It took a couple of hours to collect all he needed and a further hour to load it up and hitch the trailer to the ancient John Deere. He'd barely use any fuel for the short journey—not enough for anyone to notice when they came to collect it.

By early evening, he was ready. The sky was abnormally dark because of the storm. It was unlikely anyone would see him as he trundled out of his barn. Within a few minutes, he disappeared along an old cart track and into the woods behind his house.

He wasn't completely sure where he was going. He rarely went hunting, so the woods were not familiar to him. Looking at the map, he knew if he took a North East path, he'd come to a hollow near the village of Columbia.

As evening closed in, Jay crept along the not-so-clear track, stopping every now and then to move fallen trees out of the way. It became increasingly difficult to make steady progress as the weather turned the ground into a deep, thick, muddy quagmire. But the John Deere chugged along, impervious to the conditions.

Jay held tight to the thin steering wheel, drenched, but with a look of stoic determination on his face.

After an hour, Jay arrived at the edge of the hollow. With the aid of the tractor headlamps, he managed to identify the road meandering through the valley. He needed to find somewhere to safely store the ultralight until he could return another day.

It took another few minutes of crawling down the road until he spotted an old wooden barn, complete with a faded quilt design above the main door. It was in poor repair but with enough roof left on it that Jay hoped would protect his precious cargo.

Now dark, Jay reversed the trailer into the barn and started to unload the ultralight and all the tools and equipment. Finished, he used some old hay bales to weigh down the tarp he'd bought to cover his prized possession. Jay stood back and felt a sense of pride, achievement, and excitement. Finally, after five years, he was close to leaving French Creek and getting revenge on his brother-in-law.

Though he was freezing and soaked to the skin, he didn't care. His plan was coming to fruition. He couldn't be happier. He hadn't given much thought as to what he would do when he got to Atlanta. How he'd find his brother-in-law, what he'd do when he did. He'd worry about that later. Jay's all-consuming desire for revenge blinded him to the practicalities of the journey ahead. All he wanted was to get on his ultralight and head East. He had nothing to lose. His wife was dead, his life in French Creek was going nowhere. He needed a challenge, and he was relishing this one.

The alternative? A never-ending succession of complaining people whining about their life, the hard work, the boredom, their broken machines. He'd had enough. Now he could see his way out; he couldn't wait to leave. He knew there was still a lot to do. Test fly the ultralight, build up a modest store of provisions, get some ammunition from the Community armory. None of it fazed him, he was on a mission.

With these problems bouncing around in his mind, he took one more look at his precious machine. Then climbed onto the tractor and started his journey back home, barely noticing the crackling lightning and pounding thunder of the storm.

CHAPTER 18

Jane broke quarantine to see Herb. As neither of them had attended the Barter Fair, nor had her elderly patients, she figured the chances either of them carried the flu were remote.

She waited until the couple retired to bed, then quietly left the house to cross the village where Herb lived by the school. It was almost dark as she walked along the deserted road. Candles filtered a soft glow from the windows of the few homes along the way, but they didn't do anything to light Jane's path. The storm snuffed out the last of the evening light. In the gloom she stumbled a few times and arrived at Herb's soaked to the skin. She climbed onto the porch to find him sitting there with a bottle of beer in his hand.

"I wondered if you'd still come, what with this quarantine business and the storm," he said. "Can I offer you some of my fine homemade beer?" He waved the bottle back and forth like a windshield wiper.

"That would be most welcome," she replied. "Maybe a towel, too? If you have one."

"Sit yourself down and I'll be back with both in no time."

Jane sank down into an old armchair. Despite its well-worn appearance, it was surprisingly comfortable.

It was a typical Kentucky homestead front porch. Old sitting room furniture that had migrated to the outside once its useful life inside had finished. Fishing tackle, various tools, piles of neatly chopped wood ready for the fire. Under the eaves, a huge 350-gallon rain barrel rested on stilts with pipes leading into the house. There was even an old rug on the floor, an attempt to add some degree of comfort. The table between where she sat and Herb's seat was piled high with books on history and related subjects.

Herb reappeared with a towel, bottles, and glasses.

"Sorry," he said. "The towel may be a bit threadbare. I haven't been to Walmart this week! Joke. Hopefully it'll dry you off a little. If not, I have an old sweatshirt you could use."

"This'll do fine," Jane said. She rubbed the towel through her hair and around her neck. "I've survived worse. Thanks for the beer."

"You're welcome," he said. "I'm glad you came over. It's not often I have company. Did anyone see you? You won't want to incur the wrath of the quarantine police."

Laughing, she said, "I think I escaped their prying eyes. The weather's made everyone turn in early."

Jane slumped back into the chair and gazed out towards the distant hills intermittently lit up by the storms. The lightning seemed to stab them with a crackling ferocity. It was a breathtaking light show. For a moment, neither felt the need to say anything.

Finally, breaking the silence, Herb asked: "So what's your story? How'd you survive when the shit hit the fan? You don't sound from around here."

"No, I'm an Ohio girl born in Columbus," she explained. "I was in Atlanta when it all went south. Was making good money as a nurse, had my own apartment, nice car, blah blah, blah… you know what happened next."

Herb nodded. She continued.

"I hung around Atlanta for a few days, then realized it wasn't going to get any better, so I jumped in the car and headed north towards Chattanooga. By the time I got there, it was even worse than Atlanta. The place had gone to hell in a hand basket. I put my nursing skills to use helping out a FEMA center, then at the rescue camps, which bought me some security. But after a couple of years, they ran out of everything and the rioting started, so I hooked up with a group of aid workers and we headed West."

"That sounded fun. Then?"

"Then what?" Jane turned to Herb. In the candlelight, she could barely make out his face. She couldn't see if his question was a casual inquiry or something more.

"Then you ended up here. With a husband…?"

"We all make mistakes."

"Yours was getting married?"

"Not getting married—marrying Hal."

Herb said nothing, tempting her to continue. He didn't have to wait long.

"Hal was a big mistake. A hot head with a big mouth that just kept getting all of us into trouble. Whatever place we stayed at, he always thought he knew how to run it better. Folks don't take too kindly to unwanted advice. I could always get us in because I'm a nurse; he managed to get us kicked out because he was a jerk."

She paused, remembering her cover story. "I married him for protection. Being a single woman out there wasn't fun. Answer your question?"

She wanted to keep as close to the truth as possible in case the same questions were asked by others in the village.

"There's one more question that I know has been bugging a few folks here," Herb said. "If all you wanted was somewhere to stay, why creep in here in the middle of the night and start shooting? Seems a dumb way to do it."

"Hal's idea again. He didn't realize there were so many of you or that you'd be so well-armed and prepared. He thought killing a couple of you would be enough. You'd all just hold your hands up and let us in. I told him it was stupid, but we were tired, hungry, and desperate. I got pissed off arguing and went along with it. We all did. He got his just desserts, as it turned out."

There was no pity or sadness in her voice. She, it appeared, was over it, over him. No time for recriminations or grieving. Life was genuinely too short nowadays to spend wondering what might have been. She had a job to do and time wasn't on her side. Events here at French Creek had somewhat derailed her plans.

In truth, she found the pace of life, the relative security and comfort a pleasant change from the hand-to-mouth, live-or-die scenarios she'd experienced over the last three years.

Maybe this would be her last job. She could keep her bosses happy, somehow make a home here. It was difficult to see how to square the circle. However, for the moment, this evening, it was something she'd prefer to put aside. Herb was an appealing and entertaining character. If she could move him on from the questions about her past, she could have a pleasant evening.

She waved her empty bottle in the air. "Is the bar open for another?"

"Be right back," Herb nodded. "Do you play chess, by chance?" he asked as he walked back into the house.

"I do. But not in a long while."

"Wanna play?"

"I'll give it a try," Jane said, not too enthusiastically.

Remembering all the piece's moves and trying to put some kind of game plan together quickly ensured that conversation was diverted onto less troublesome topics. More beers helped, too. By the end of the evening, the two giggled like a couple of teenagers as their chess-playing abilities descended into a mass suicide of all their pieces.

"That was one shit move, Jane," slurred Herb as she allowed her Queen to be taken by one of his pawns. Before she could answer, he grabbed her Queen from the board and held it to his lips.

"Ever seen the Thomas Crown Affair, with Faye Dunaway and Steve McQueen? The one where they seduce each other over a game of chess?" Herb asked, a wide smile on his face.

"No I haven't. That was before my time. Who won?"

"Neither of them. Halfway through, McQueen stands up and grabs Dunaway and says, 'Let's play something else.' And they do. Great scene. One of my favorites."

Jane laughed. "Never would have guessed chess could have that effect on people. Is that why you wanted to play? Are you trying to capture my heart as well as my Queen?"

Herb smiled then quickly backtracked, "That's quite a poetic thought, but not what I had in mind. Just wanted to get the brain cells moving. It can get pretty mind-numbing around here after a while."

"I hear you." Jane stood up, deciding it was time to leave. She pushed herself up from the sunken chair and stepped off the porch, thankfully it had stopped raining.

"Honestly Herb," she said. "That was one of the nicest evenings I've had in a long while. Maybe we could do it again sometime?"

"That would be fun," Herb agreed. "You're good company but a lousy chess player."

"Next time we'll play my game," she said. "Poker. Be prepared to get your ass whooped."

"I'll look forward to that," he smiled. "You take care walking back."

Jane waved acknowledgment of his advice then walked unsteadily back to her house. Herb went inside, decided a nightcap of mint tea would be better than another beer. He sat at his kitchen table and scribbled a few notes on this evening's conversation so he could report back to Roger tomorrow.

He hadn't learned much. Nowadays, anyone can turn up with any story. It was nearly impossible to check up on them. No Google or Facebook to hunt down past indiscretions, old friends, memories.

Maybe there was enough to discover if Jane's friends contradicted or confirmed what she had told him. Perhaps she was being honest. Who knew? Who cares, mused Herb, as he drained his tea and went to bed. She seemed like a fun lady. More than that, she seemed interested in him.

Let Roger worry about her tomorrow.

CHAPTER 19

Roger raised his head from a very damp pillow. His bed sheets were soaked. He felt like shit. The aching in his neck and head had now spread to his whole body. His throat was so constricted he could hardly breathe, let alone drink.

The flu had hit him with a vengeance.

He had to get a message to Doc to try and get some medicine. He knew the herbal stuff had only a slight chance of helping, but anything that could keep the fever down would be welcome. It was a virus, and his body had to fight it—he just had to stay alive long enough to give it a chance.

After a couple of hours, Roger crawled out of bed and to the window. He pulled it open and sat there, praying someone would come along who could take his message. Mercifully, one of the farm workers came within shouting distance, and Roger explained the problem.

Later, Doc knocked on the door and peered round into the gloom. "Not feeling too good I hear?"

"That's a fucking understatement," Roger croaked. "Is there anything you can do to help?"

"Not much. Your body just has to do the hard work. Even if I had Tylenol, it would only cover the symptoms, not cure them. Just keep yourself hydrated, gargle salt water for your throat.

Believe it or not, a fever means your body is already beginning to fight back. I can get my wife to come over later with some hot soup if you'd like. You've gotta eat." He tapped the door frame as he left. "You're a strong guy. You'll see this through."

"I'm in for a few shitty days I guess," agreed Roger. "I appreciate you coming over. Soup sounds great. Now let me suffer in silence."

"Try not to have too much fun," Doc said. "I'll drop in later if I can. You're patient number twenty-five with the flu. I hope to God we have it contained now."

"This day just keeps getting better and better," Roger groaned. "Go help and heal the wounded, Doc. I'll see you soon."

Doc turned to leave, then stopped. "By the way, where's Landy?"

"He's been staying with friends. I told him to not come back for a few days."

Doc nodded. "Someone will be around later to see how you're doing. Behave yourself."

Roger lay back and fell asleep. Later, a knock at the door woke him from his sweaty, restless nap. He shook himself awake, unsure what time it was.

"Jane here," the voice said. "I've been helping Doc. He asked me to come over and see how you're getting on. I'm probably the only one round here with a vaguely up-to-date flu vaccination. Albeit, four years old."

She walked over to Roger's bed and sat down. "Feeling any better?" She reached across and stuck a thermometer in his mouth. It was quiet as she refilled the water jug and put it back on the nightstand.

She checked the thermometer. "102 degrees. Well, you're not fit for purpose, are you? Been drinking and gargling like the Doc said?"

Roger struggled to talk through the sore throat. He managed a reply. "Yes, nurse. Any other helpful suggestions?"

"Just practicing my rusty bedside manner. Anything else I can get you? Dinner will be over soon. Ultimate comfort food, chicken soup. Should do you a world of good. I've also got some homemade throat syrup. Honey and moonshine. Should dull the senses."

Roger took a long swig of the liquid. His throat eased a little. "It's good of you to pitch in. You've only been here a short while. I'm sure Doc really appreciates it. Are you settled in okay? We haven't spoken in a while."

Jane wasn't sure where the conversation was heading. "Yes, all okay." She decided to keep it vague. "My two patients are behaving themselves, I've met a few of the other villagers... No complaints really. This flu business makes me feel a little more useful."

"Well, I appreciate your help."

"You're welcome. Anyway, I don't want to tire you out. You need to rest up and get loads of sleep. Someone will drop in later with a liquid dinner."

"Thanks again." Roger flopped back onto his pillow, exhausted even from such a brief conversation. He wondered if his concerns about her were realistic or if he was just overly suspicious of any newcomer. Before he could think about it anymore, he drifted back to sleep.

For three days, Roger was confined to bed, only capable of dragging himself to the bathroom before collapsing back into bed from the exertion. Aside from the Doc, Jane was his most regular visitor. She brought herbal remedies to help him sleep, and meals—she even changed his sheets when they became embarrassingly in need of a wash. She was charming, helpful, and attentive. It was disconcerting to Roger, who still harbored doubts about her real reason for being at French Creek. But he couldn't help but be swayed by her caring and thoughtful behavior throughout his illness.

By the fourth day, Roger was able to move about the house, cook himself some basic meals. He invited Jane to stay for lunch; it was the least he could do after all the consideration she'd shown. She was beginning to look a little worse for wear, admitting that being a full-time caregiver was exhausting.

She declined his first offer of lunch but agreed on second asking and turned up obviously having made an effort to tidy herself up for the occasion.

"You look better," Roger said. "Not quite so stressed?"

"Yes, things are calming down a bit," she said. "I think we're through the worst of it. As Doc probably told you, we've lost ten people so far. A few are still on the danger list. Could be closer to twenty by the time it's done."

Roger tried to hide his shock; twenty was a good percentage of the community's population. He didn't yet know who the individuals were. Whoever had passed, it would mean grief for all the families. He would have to deal with that in the coming days and weeks. Then figure out with the Council the long-term effects on the community. It was a setback, a bad one. But not, as it stood, a terminal one.

Trying to set the bad news aside, he brought out a simple meal of bread (donated by Doc's wife), cold chicken, and some fresh vegetables from his cold store.

"Wow, quite the host!" exclaimed Jane, looking at the spread. "This looks great. Thanks so much. To what do I owe this honor?"

"You've been a wonderful help over the last few days. Doc says he couldn't have coped without you. It's the least I can do to thank you for looking after me and all the others, as well."

"Funnily enough, I enjoyed it in a stressed-out kind of way. Good to get back to nursing..." She paused a moment too long.

Jane's slight hesitation in finishing the sentence didn't go unnoticed. Roger decided to find out a little more about her. "What else have you done besides nursing since the Collapse?"

"Survive. Deal with the shit you face when moving to new places, meeting new people. Spend more time looking out for yourself than others. Not what I was trained to do. Not what I enjoy. It's a waste of my talents, such as they are."

She hoped the explanation would prevent Roger from probing further into her background. She was confident she could offer adequate explanations, though the more she said, the more questions it might raise.

For the moment, Roger seemed satisfied and busied himself with serving the food.

The food was simple but delicious. It was the first decent meal Roger had eaten in over a week. Washing it down with some beer finished off the meal in fine style.

Jane was suitably impressed at Roger's efforts. "Thanks so much. It's most kind of you when you must still be pretty washed out. Have to say, I just loved the home-grown veggies. Do you manage to have a year-round supply?"

"We do," Roger said. "As long as we get a decent break with the weather. Like all farmers and gardeners, we're at the mercy of the elements. But we've learned so much in the last five years. What grows and what doesn't, where it thrives and where it doesn't. The meat supply is well under control and easy to store. The vegetables are more difficult, we all have underground cold stores which is the only way to save them. We also keep some in a central store in case people find theirs ruined. We're still fine tuning the process, but it gets easier each year. We don't have a huge choice—no fancy fruit or exotic meats and vegetables—you can exist quite well without mangos or pineapples, veal, so on and so forth. And no chemicals! Though that does make controlling the weeds and pests a never-ending problem. We just have to use nature's own pesticides where we can."

"It must have been hard work," Jane said. "A lot of trial and error."

"It was. Being thrown back a hundred and fifty years almost overnight was an unbelievable challenge. Though we've managed to keep a few bits of modern technology going. Some limited electricity from a small array of solar panels and generators. It's still pretty tough."

Roger was clearly proud of what French Creek had achieved, and with good cause. Jane could understand and appreciate where he was coming from, even if she hadn't given much thought to the trials and tribulations communities like theirs must have gone through.

"It all comes at a price," he continued. "Hard work, seemingly relentless at times, to get even the simplest task completed. Everything takes days where it once took a few hours. Ever tried milking twenty cows by hand? Every day? Or chopping enough wood to see you through the Winter? Cooking and canning a hundred jars of fruit and veg, then if they go bad, you starve? There's little room for error here, which is why we have to run the place almost along military lines."

"So I've noticed!" Jane agreed. She pushed her chair back from the table and stretched her legs. "Don't some people find that a bit restricting? Personal choice and all that?" She moved over and sat down on the old comfortable sofa, feeling more relaxed after her meal and a couple beers.

"Needs must," Roger shrugged. "I'd like to say it's a wannabe democracy, but it's really more of a benevolent dictatorship. It has to be—there's no room for much dissent on major issues. If everyone starts doing what they want, we'll end up dead. Simple as that."

"And everyone's okay with that?"

"Of course not," Roger said. "Especially the younger ones who can't remember what it was like five years ago and seem to think it's way better 'out there.'" Roger pointed outside in no particular direction. "To be honest, from what I've seen and heard, I have my doubts. This mystical Shangri La that people think exists beyond the Mississippi is just that in my opinion: mystical. America was conquered on the idea that the grass was always greener elsewhere. Somewhere else there must be a better life, more opportunity, more freedom. Maybe it was once true, but not now. What's out West is just a replica of the clusterfuck we had before the Collapse, and I want none of it. I don't believe most people here do either."

Roger's comments opened up a subject Jane had been trying to avoid. Still, she couldn't resist prodding it along to see where it would go. "But shouldn't they get the chance to find out? Maybe they will find a better life elsewhere? You can't limit people's freedom just because you think they won't like it. Let them find out for themselves. Isn't that possible?" Jane knew she was pushing Roger's buttons, still, she was interested to see his reaction. Roger's arrogance, coupled with his absolute belief that what he did was for everyone's benefit was narrow-minded, even selfish. She plowed on.

"Where's the danger in letting people experience what's out there? See it firsthand. What's the problem with that?"

"I'll tell you what the problem with that is," Roger replied. Taking the bait. The heat of the argument made him forget his post-flu exhaustion. "It'll end in tears for everyone. Those who leave will find out that just getting to and over the Mississippi is fraught with danger. Finding the money, or whatever currency is needed to pay all the coyotes who promise safe passage then screw them or worse? Probably leaving them destitute-or even press-ganged into slavery. If, and it's a big if, they make it, what will they find? An overcrowded, disorganized society still trying to get its act together years after the Collapse? No jobs, no welfare, no family to fall back on. And what about the people left here? When a bunch of youngsters, who should be preparing to take the community forward, leave it in search of greener pastures? Tell me, what's attractive about that? Everyone's a loser."

He paused, taking a breath. "No. For the time being, we have to remain as we are. Maybe sometime in the future some semblance of government may reappear and impose all those old rules and regulations, and people will feel safer moving around. I hear on the Eastern seaboard some places are running like in the 1700's—state control, but no central government. Perhaps that might work. Hell, maybe we'll see Walmart re-open, or the hospital, who knows? Welcome back, civilization! God help us!"

He paused mid-flow for a moment, then continued. "Until that happens, we have to look after ourselves. Because if we don't, no one else will. If that means keeping this community together in ways some might not like, well… That's just the way it has to be, in my humble opinion."

Jane listened, beginning to see why Roger was the community's driving force, the glue that had held them together. How his passion and total belief in what he was doing was right and keeping it that way might save them in the future. But at what cost?

She knew from her experience that much of what he was saying was right. While she hadn't been across the Mississippi herself, she knew plenty of people who had. If they could reconnect with relatives or rich benefactors who could get them back on their feet, the risks, once they got there, were small. For those without those safety nets, it was all too easy to become ensnared in the never-ending demands for money from the coyotes who helped them cross to the West at huge expense. Failure to pay meant working it off. Too often, that was nearly impossible. They became the modern enslaved. Years ago, when she lived in Florida, she read the book Angel City she knew such conditions now existed, this time on the other side of the Mississippi.

But that wasn't her problem. If people were desperate or foolish enough to want to try for a better life, who was Roger to stop them? She had helped some take that gamble. A few succeeded. She didn't care to think too much about what happened to those who hadn't been successful.

"I can't argue that you haven't succeeded in keeping French Creek safe and secure. But as things get easier and people aren't living hand to mouth, they may get the "grass is greener" itch. And it'll be a tough one to scratch, especially for the kids."

"You're right," Roger conceded. "I have to fight my battles as they come. For now, my battle is sorting out how we cope with losing ten or twenty people. Then surviving Winter, which is always tough. Come Spring, I'll worry about those wanting to sample the greener grass."

Deciding to bring the conversation to a halt, "Rather you than me," Jane said, rising from the settee and taking the dirty dishes to the small kitchen. She started to wash up using the gravity-fed water from the rain barrel. "Clever set up," she said. "Does it ever run dry?"

"Not often, thankfully. The alternative is to heave water up from the pond, and then you have to sterilize it. At least rainwater is pure."

They chatted amiably as she washed the dishes and Roger dried and put them away. It struck her as a somewhat surreal scene of faux domesticity. It didn't make her uneasy; disconcertingly, she found it almost comforting. A feeling she hadn't experienced in a long, long time.

Drying her hands, she turned to leave. "Thanks again. It was a lovely lunch, but I must be getting back. Doc is a hard taskmaster, and I have a few more patients to visit. Take it easy now, and get your strength back."

"Thank you, nurse," Roger said. "I promise I won't do anything too strenuous." He made a mock bow.

CHAPTER 20

It was Thanksgiving in every sense of the word. For the last five years, the date had become as symbolic and important as it had to the original Pilgrims. They had survived another year, a flu epidemic, an attack by outsiders, plus all the normal trials and tribulations an agrarian Community had to battle.

The village hall was laid out with tables and chairs, with more outside. Bunting and flags were festooned from the trees. The buzz and laughter of a hundred people created a party atmosphere. Nearly everyone was there.

Every family had contributed to the feast of homemade and home-grown food, washed down with gallons of hooch, moonshine, and other (almost) drinkable concoctions.

While everyone was there to enjoy themselves, it was a slightly more somber and subdued affair than usual.

While they had avoided a complete disaster with the flu epidemic, they had still lost 15 souls. The last burial was only a week ago. For many families it was still too early to be out celebrating, so they stayed at home.

In practical terms, the effect of losing so many people had yet to be felt by the community. While the majority who died were elderly, there were several important people, including nurse Helen who had done such a brave job during the attack on the way to Glasgow. Her medical knowledge and skills would be difficult to replace. She was an immensely popular person, always willing to help the sick anytime of the day or night. Doc Brown in particular, was devastated by the loss.

The Council met a few days earlier to discuss the possible labor shortage caused by the flu. They were working on alternative plans to make up for the shortfall of knowledge and help the dead had taken with them to their graves. For the moment, those at the celebration put on brave faces determined to enjoy themselves. The weather was still pleasant enough for people to sit outside and enjoy the last warm days of the year.

Jay sat at a long table piled with food, making a rare outing to mix with the rest of the villagers. Since his excursion during the storm, he managed to sneak away a couple more times to his ultralight to make further preparations. To date, he'd assembled it, got the motor running, and taxied it up and down the narrow lane outside the barn. So far, so good. He was frustrated and impatient to get it flying. Though cautious enough to know he had to complete building it safely before he could prepare himself for the final getaway.

He was so distracted with his mental planning that he barely noticed Roger sit down next to him.

"Hi Jay," Roger said. "How's it going?"

"Fine. You? Over the flu?"

"Yes, just about back to full strength. Wanted to have a quick word."

"Oh? What about?" Jay said guardedly. "Something wrong?"

"Not really," Roger replied. "A couple people said they'd been up to your place to get some help but couldn't find you. One said they'd seen you coming back from the woods. I didn't think hunting was your thing?" Roger shifted in his seat, he didn't like confronting people in public. "You know the rules, Jay. You can't go wandering off by yourself. We only leave the village if we have someone with us."

"I was just looking for trees to cut for winter fuel, that's all." Jay paused. "I'll be sure to take someone with me next time."

"No problem," Roger said. "It's just for everyone's safety. You have a good Thanksgiving."

"You too." Jay breathed an inward sigh of relief.

Roger got up and mingled with the happy crowd, taking advantage of the plentiful supply of food and drink and the chance to congregate after the quarantine alarm.

Jane sat with Jenny and Bryanna. It was one of the few occasions they could get together without someone suspecting they might be up to something nefarious.

"Have you had a chance to talk to that group of youngsters I told you about?" Jenny asked, shielding her lips with a large glass of tea held close to her mouth.

"Not yet," Jane said. "The Grayson's have been sick. Haven't had a chance."

"For Christ's sake, Jane," Jenny said. "Time's moving on. It'll be Winter soon, and there will be no chance to get people to Memphis once that starts. Can't you find the time? We've got commitments, we've made promises...you know what'll happen if we don't find people soon."

"Yes, yes I know," Jane said, irritation in her voice. "I'm just being careful. This place... I'm beginning to think it wasn't such a good choice for us to come here."

"Why?" Bryanna butted in." Are you going soft? Getting cold feet?"

"No. I'm just being realistic. Except for those bunch of headstrong teens, I haven't come across anyone who's really pissed off with this place. It's not proving to be particularly fertile ground in my opinion. What about you? Have you found any potentials?" Jane tried to put the responsibility back on the two sisters.

"Well no," Bryanna admitted. "No one but those teenagers. But if we can hook those, that'll be enough to keep the boss happy, right?"

"The trouble with trying to shift teenagers is that they have parents, and they ain't often too happy to see their kids go," Jenny reasoned. "Is it worth concentrating on them? I reckon there's four or five that are pretty serious. The others are just talk. Or should we try and find others?"

"It'll be an uphill battle," Jane prevaricated. "Let me think about it."

"Don't take too long thinking," Jenny said. "The clock's ticking." Before Jane could muster a withering reply Herb wandered up, amiable and slightly drunk. "Hi ladies," he said. "I'm not interrupting anything, am I?" He plonked himself down on the bench next to Jane before waiting for a reply.

Grateful for the interruption, Jane replied. "No, nothing exciting going on here," she said. "Please join us. How are you doing?" She asked as though they barely knew each other.

In fact, Herb and Jane had seen each other several more times since their first evening of chess and had been getting quite close. Another reason Jane felt ambivalent about the group's proposed plan for the French Creek villagers. She had to try and keep her doubts from Jenny and Bryanna until she could resolve her dilemma. Stalling for time was all well and good, but Jenny was right—their bosses wouldn't accept any delay. Excuses did not sit well with them. Results, clients, and money, that's all they were interested in.

"Well, we'll leave you two to it," Jenny said tactfully as she and Bryanna got up from the table, adding. "Let's chat again soon. I'll bring the guys along next time."

"Sure." Jane knew the sisters were growing anxious about their plan's delay and any backlash from the boss. Bringing the rest of the group into the meeting meant more pressure to get things moving. A lot was at stake.

For a moment, Jane was lost in thought, trying to figure out how to keep everyone happy while reconciling her concerns that the task before her was becoming less feasible. Indeed, whether she wanted to do the job at all.

"Penny for your thoughts?" Herb leaned across the table and took hold of her hand to get her attention. Instinctively, she withdrew it and grabbed her drink.

Seeing the surprise on his face, she apologized.

"Sorry Herb. I didn't mean to react like that. I have a lot going on. I'm not in the best mood. Let's start again. Happy Thanksgiving!" They clinked glasses.

Herb's mildly inebriated state meant he was too relaxed to take real offense. "No problem. The same to you. Is there anything I can help you with? You look… worried."

"I appreciate your concern," Jane said. "But this is one I have to sort out myself. Trust me—you don't want to get involved. If I need any help, I'll ask." Changing the subject, she suggested they get their drinks refilled.

Herb got up unsteadily from the table and went for more drinks.

"Let's go for a walk," Jane said. "I need to get away from these crowds." She grabbed Herb by the arm and walked towards the woods.

Landy and his buddies watched the festivities from the sidelines, chugging their beers, tactfully they had left their dope behind. The age limit for drinking had been banished with the Collapse, though getting drunk was still frowned upon. Still, they enjoyed seeing their elders get tipsy.

Talk eventually returned to the subject of leaving French Creek.

Landy regaled all of them with his adventures at the Barter Fair, getting shot on the way, the people he'd met who had come back from the West. Their experiences in a place where televisions, computers, phones, and jobs with paychecks were to be had with apparent ease captivated them all.

No one doubted the truth of his stories, and no one questioned how accurate the sources of his information might be. It was just what they wanted to hear—and believe. Dick repeated the conversation they had with Jenny, but no one was quite sure how to proceed from there.

"All I know is, there are scouts out there looking to recruit people for the West," Landy said. "I overheard Dad and Pat talking to the guys that shot at us. They think Jane and them might be one of them. Your recent conversation with Jenny makes me think they could be right." He'd been mulling these thoughts for some time and now gave the group the benefit of his recently acquired knowledge.

Landy paced around, waving his beer in the air while he thought out loud, trying to puff himself up and act like a leader. The others seemed to expect some more words of wisdom to come forth, so he obliged.

"Look," he said. "If we are gonna leave, we're gonna need help. There's a lot of shit out there, no doubt about it. We can't just wander off. We don't know the way, we have no supplies, we don't know where to go and who to ask when we get there—wherever "there" is. Most importantly, we don't have any money. We need help."

He paused to let his words sink in with the others.

"I'm not just going to walk out. I want to leave, but it's got to be planned. Properly planned. We've got to find people who know what to do. Maybe Jane or Jenny can… Or maybe they're full of shit. Who knows? The only way to find out is to ask."

He looked around at the group. Most nodded in agreement, though a couple seemed unconvinced—Steve being one of them.

"You got a better idea, Steve?" Landy challenged.

Steve looked at Landy, then the rest of the group. He was becoming less enthralled with this idea as time went on. Landy's recounting of the attacks on the way to Glasgow and what he'd heard from the others had left him concerned this whole thing would be too risky and dangerous.

"I'm not so sure about this," he started hesitantly. "My dad went to the Fair and spoke to people who'd sent family to Memphis. They never heard from them again. All kinds of wacko stories about being ripped off, even killed. I'm having second thoughts, I gotta be honest."

Landy looked at Steve with barely concealed contempt." So you're chickening out? Well, fuck you and fuck the rest of you. If you think I'm going to sit around here and die of boredom or the next disease to hit us, you're wrong. I'm going to talk to Jenny and see how I can get out of here as soon as I can. If any of you want to join me, come on."

With that, he grabbed his beer, turned his back on the group, and strode back to the celebrations.

Meanwhile, Herb and Jane walked arm in arm through the woods along the edge of the community. The drink, the celebrations, the solitude—all began to release their pent-up emotions. With surprising speed and few words, they were on the ground, embracing, fumbling with clothes, frustration blowing away any inhibitions.

Herb stopped and sat up, panting with exertion, his shirt tossed to one side." Wait."

"Wait, what?" Jane asked. She peeled off her shirt." Is there a problem?"

"No," Herb said. "Won't it be a bit hard and dirty to do it here?"

Jane laid back with a suggestive smile on her face. "I sincerely hope so." She pulled Herb down on top of her to dispel any further concerns.

As the afternoon turned to evening and the air began to cool, Jane rolled onto her stomach, her head resting on Herb's chest.

"I guess we better get going," she said. "People will talk. They already have enough to say about me without giving them more ammunition."

Herb looked down at Jane, his face inches from hers. "True. You and the other ladies are the subject of some gossip." He smiled and winked at her. "Around here, people are suspicious about strangers. Many think you have a hidden agenda. I get where they're coming from. And since I've got to know you, I'm not totally convinced they're wrong."

Jane rolled onto her back, hands locked behind her head. She looked up at the trees, the sky turning blue to pink. Was it time to come clean? Not just with Herb and the community, but with herself too?

For two years, she practiced deceit and dishonesty, living a lie wherever she went, re-inventing herself to suit the circumstances. How much longer could she continue like this? At some point, she had to admit she was cornered and being used by people more powerful than her. These people had trained her to manipulate and mislead gullible folk searching for a better life, new opportunities. Promising back to the way life was before the Collapse. Was now the time to confront these people, extricate herself from this complicated double life she was leading and be honest about her intentions? She could only imagine the grim consequences if she did. Was that worse than the alternative? For now, should she unburden her soul and be honest with a man she believed she could trust-and accept the consequences?

She sat up, facing Herb, and held both his hands in hers.

With a resigned voice, breaking with emotion, Jane finally opened up, "Okay, you asked for it," she started. "You asked me to be honest. Make yourself comfortable, because this could take a while."

CHAPTER 21

The day after the Thanksgiving celebrations, Roger had dinner with Landy. He sensed something was wrong; his usually garrulous son was silent and sullen, barely able to hold a conversation or look his father in the eye.

Roger tried gently to open him up, and discuss whatever was troubling him, but he received only monosyllabic replies. The more he pushed, the less Landy acknowledged his questions.

Frustrated, Roger said. "Alright son. Suit yourself. If you don't want to talk, that's fine. I'm always here if you need me. You know that, right?"

"I know," Landy grunted as he got up from the table and made his way to his bedroom, slamming the door behind him. God save me from teenagers, Roger thought. He wished Landy's mother was around to deal with all this angst. He missed her dreadfully, even five years after her death from an asthma attack. One that could have easily been controlled with a new inhaler had it been available. She'd have known how to get their son to talk, mused Roger. The house was definitely lacking her personal touch. It was neat, tidy, and well-organized, reflecting Roger's personality. But it lacked warmth, that welcoming atmosphere only she had brought to the home.

In the five years since her death, Roger never looked at another woman, though there were several candidates in the community. His whole life in that time had been consumed with making

French Creek a safe and healthy place to live. He hadn't sought the role of Council Chair, but his experience in the military and then in the National Guard had made him an obvious choice. The community was now strong, well-run, and despite flu epidemics and other problems, things were far more manageable than ever before. People had food in their stomachs and a reasonable standard of living. Perhaps it was time to step down as Chairman. Maybe it was time to look after himself a little more. There were others out there who could do his job.

His interactions with Jane made him aware of how much he enjoyed and missed female company. Was there any chemistry between them? Probably too early to tell. He certainly didn't want to get involved before it was clear what she and the rest of her group's intentions were. He needed to catch up with Herb and see if there were any updates. Once he knew more, Roger could make some decisions. Depending on what he found out, plan how to move forward, with or without Jane.

With that in mind, Roger sat down with a glass of elderberry wine and his latest book, The Alice Network, a story of female spies in Paris during World War Two. He loved war books, especially those with strong female characters. Maybe that's why he was drawn to Jane. She had survived tough times since the Collapse and seemed to have come through it without too many scars. Since arriving at French Creek, she'd proved capable, willing to take responsibility and get on with whatever job was given to her. The more he thought about it, the more he realized she was just his kind of woman.

CHAPTER 22

After Jane's revelatory conversation with Herb, his mind was full of conflicting emotions. On the one hand he promised to keep her secret until she felt she could tell Roger and the rest of the Council. On the other hand, the information was so explosive he felt duty-bound to tell someone about it as soon as possible.

If she was to be believed, and he had no reason to doubt her, her group could cause considerable disruption in French Creek. He couldn't let that happen. Delaying the truth—Jane pleaded for him to wait until she confronted Jenny and Bryanna—could be tragic. He tossed and turned all night, wrestling with the dilemma his loyalty to Jane versus his obligation to protect the community.

Unable to sleep, he rose at dawn and went, coffee in hand, to sit on his porch and try to make sense of the impossible position he now found himself in. He was still churning over the options when Roger appeared, walking directly towards Herb's house.

"Morning Herb," Roger waved. "How's it going? I hope you don't mind me coming over. I wanted to follow up on that conversation we had about Jane recently. Good time to talk?"

Herb looked at Roger shaking his head with disbelief. "Your timing is either shitty or perfect," he said. "I would've had nothing to say about it up until yesterday. Now that's just changed in a big way—a clusterfuck kind of way. I really don't know what to do."

Roger sat down, astonished at Herb's outburst, concerned about his state of mind. This was not the levelheaded teacher he had known for years. What the hell had happened to turn him into a nervous wreck?

"Christ Herb," Roger said, looking worried, "It can't be that bad. What's causing you so much grief? I've never seen you this upset before. Tell me. Let me help you."

Roger's soothing words calmed Herb down to a less hysterical level, but he was still caught between his loyalty to Roger and Jane. Whatever he did, someone was going to get hurt.

"Roger, I'm between a rock and a hard place. If I tell you what Jane told me yesterday, I'll blow her trust in me. If I don't, I'll lie to you and face some awful consequences later. Shit. I don't know what to do."

Roger chose his words carefully. "I can't tell you what to do. You have to decide that. Who will suffer the most if you tell me what she said— Jane, or the whole community? These people are your friends, relatives, students. You can't ignore the history you have with them, the hardships you've suffered together, the future you have here in French Creek. That's a lot to sacrifice Herb. Maybe there is a way we can make this work for everyone?"

Herb turned to look up the road. A couple of his students waved to him as they walked by. He gazed back to the hills, the land that was French Creek, his home, his sanctuary. It was a lot to lose.

He sighed. Inwardly he knew Roger was right; he had to tell him—tell him everything.

The story took nearly an hour to tell. Roger interrupted on numerous occasions asking questions, probing, drawing out awkward answers. As Herb recounted Jane's confession, it became clear her story was a mixture of tragedy, love, and hope.

Most of what she told Roger over lunch and during other conversations was true. She had been a nurse in Atlanta, worked for FEMA, and then left when the shit really hit the fan. This is when the story diverged from the one she had told everyone else in French Creek.

Jane did have a husband, but it wasn't the man killed by Pat. She had a child too, and all three had tried to make it across the Mississippi.

They had gotten as far as Memphis, with promises of passage across the river. At the last moment, she had been separated from her family due to the price of "immigration" to the West increasing at the last minute. They could only afford passage for two. Jane insisted her injured husband go with their son to the West for treatment and safety. His experience as an Atlanta cop would be useful over there, but worthless in the East. Jane promised to make the extra money quickly and join them as soon as she could.

Despite her promises, her plans soon fell apart. The coyotes who made fortunes from this illegal trafficking saw Jane as someone who could move freely around and get access to any community with her nursing experience. They made a deal with her: recruit fifty people who wanted to move to the West. Once she'd done that, she could cross free and be reunited with her family.

In the meantime, they would be kept 'safe', working on a farm close to West Memphis, until her debt was paid. If she reneged on the deal, she'd never see her family again.

The smugglers teamed her with others who found themselves in similar positions and told them to head East to find people who wanted a new life in the West. They gave the group one year. As the twelve-month deadline approached, Jane was close to meeting her target of fifty people. Six to go, and she could cross with them to the Mississippi and see her family again.

Hal's death rid the group of a member who had shown zero tolerance for failure. With him gone, it fell to Jane to lead the group. The rest of the group had been either potential leavers (including the ones refused entry by Roger), or in the case of Jenny and Bryanna, anxious for their own reasons to get back West.

Now there was a wrench in the works: Jane had grown to love the people of French Creek. Herb admitted to Roger his burgeoning relationship with her and was surprised to see hurt and surprise on Roger's face. Not realizing why, he continued on with Jane's story.

She didn't want to help anyone leave the community. She didn't want to harm anyone—especially the kids, which included Roger's son. However, her own family was in danger, and she was anxious to be reunited with them. This quandary was a circle she couldn't square. The group was pressing her to act fast and get leavers on the road to Memphis. Time was running out—they had only a matter of weeks left before their deadline was up.

The ensuing silence between them allowed both to digest what had been said. In Roger's case, to start corralling his thoughts on what should happen next. When he'd finished, Herb fell back in his chair, mentally and physically exhausted.

After a painfully long pause in the conversation, Roger said, "Here are my initial thoughts. You do and say nothing to anyone, especially to Jane. I need to digest all of this and figure out the best way forward, for us and her. There are so many factors at play here… Give me time to think it over. I won't say anything to anyone, even the Council. Though we can't keep this quiet for long."

Roger stood up and put his hands on Herb's shoulders. "You did the right thing telling me. I don't know if there will be a happy ending, but I'll do my best. Go get some sleep."

With that, Roger left, leaving a confused, relieved, and exhausted Herb in his wake. He needed to think seriously about whether there would be a way to save Jane and keep the community intact. With only a few days in which to do it.

Following his conversation with Herb, Roger locked himself away at home to think. The numerous inter-connecting factors presented a real conundrum, but he was hopeful a solution could be found.

He ran through each element of the problem:

First, Jane's dilemma: Of course, she needed help to rescue her family. But at the cost of trafficking people to keep the smugglers happy? Or she could stay here and lose her family—if they were still alive.

Second: Several members of French Creek, including his son, wanted to move West. If they were persuaded to make a run for it with Jane, then Roger would lose all control.

Third: Others in Jane's group had their own families to reconnect with in the West. He felt obliged to help them as well.

Fourth: If he lost control or did nothing, everyone might opt to take matters into their own hands, causing chaos in the community.

It seemed to be a question of choosing the lesser of all evils.

Around lunchtime, there was a knock at the door. Roger was tempted to ignore it, but whoever was on the other side hammered with increasing urgency.

Roger got up and wrenched the door open, glaring at the noisy culprit, demanding to know what was so damn important?

Pat stood with a look of nervous excitement on his sweating face. "Sorry," he said. "But I think you'll want to hear this."

"I've got a lot on my plate at the moment," Roger said. "Can't it wait?"

"'Nope." Pat was out of breath. "One of the hunting parties found something really interesting near Columbia. You'll never guess."

"Cut to the chase," Roger demanded. "I've got some really important stuff to sort out here."

"As important as finding an ultralight?

CHAPTER 23

Following her tryst with Herb and the unburdening of her worries and fears, Jane, too, felt exhausted. Now she was concerned at the unknown ramifications her confession might create. That was out of her control.

To Herb's credit, he neither judged nor tried to tell her what she should do next. On the contrary, he seemed so confounded by her story he offered little in the way of advice at all. On the plus side, it was a huge relief to finally tell someone the truth.

Now that her subterfuge was shared with someone outside her group, she had to wonder: how long would Herb keep it a secret? She'd asked him to tell no one, of course. Nonetheless, she could tell he was desperate to help. He suggested she talk to Roger next.

"Let me first figure out how to get myself out of this mess with the others." She begged him. "I need to tell my group what I've done and see their reaction. I have a feeling it won't be pleasant. Just give me a few days. Please?" Herb couldn't refuse and agreed to keep her secret to himself. As Jane left, she gave him a lingering kiss—a thank you or a please, wondered Herb? Either way, he felt desperately sorry for her as she trudged back to the village.

As Jane returned to her house, she felt a sense of relief: her secret was finally out. Now, she'd have to battle Jenny, Bryanna, Roger, and all who wouldn't hesitate to point fingers at her. Delighted to proclaim how right they'd been all along to mistrust her.

It was late in the evening. The Graysons were long gone to their beds, leaving Jane alone to compose herself and plan her conversation with the group

She initially didn't hear the gentle tap on the window. It took her a moment to realize she had a visitor. Jane hesitated. Surely Herb hadn't spilled the beans already, and Roger was here to demand an explanation?

She peeked through the door, and to her relief, saw Jenny, a smirking grin on her face.

"So, you got some news to tell me?" Jenny said as Jane opened the door. "I saw you wandering off with Herb. You weren't looking for local wildlife, were you I bet? I see that little glint in your eye, sister."

Jenny licked her lips with mock lasciviousness. "Come on, admit it. You two were at it, weren't you? Naughty, naughty, you being married and all. I can't blame you though. He's pretty cute."

Jane stood speechless, embarrassed, and relieved at the same time. Quickly regaining her composure, she smiled and winked. "You got me there. Sometimes you just gotta let those urges take over. It was pretty good too."

Jane didn't want to go into detail with Jenny. Inviting her in would lead to another conversation about the progress, or lack of it, in recruiting leavers for Memphis.

"While I really appreciate your interest in my sex life, it's been a long day," Jane said. "I'll tell you more next time we meet. I need to get to bed. Can we take a rain check on this chat?"

If Jenny minded being cut short mid-gossip, she didn't show it. She turned to go, adding a throwaway comment over her shoulder. "Hope you're not going soft on us girl. There's too much at stake."

As Jenny receded into the darkness, she offered some unwanted advice. "Talk soon. Sleep well. Don't do anything I wouldn't!"

"You too," Jane replied. As she closed the door, she breathed a sigh of relief. She had dodged a bullet, though only for a short while.

A major confrontation was in the air. Jenny, her group, Roger—it was like a noose tightening around her neck. There wasn't a resolution that wouldn't entail pissing a lot of people off she realized. Usually, never one to dodge a fight, this time Jane felt overwhelmed, the odds stacked against her whichever way she turned.

There had to be a solution. So far, it had escaped her. She went to her small attic bedroom, opened the window to let the cool Fall air drift in, hoping inspiration would come to her. It didn't. Exhausted, she lay down, and within moments, was dead to the world.

She woke early and went downstairs to prepare breakfast, tidy the kitchen, and start a fire. The days now started with that crisp feel, sometimes close to freezing. Her morning routine kept Jane from dwelling too much on her mounting problems. Once Mr. Grayson had been fed and settled in front of the fire and Mrs. Grayson was busy with other household chores, Jane sat down with a cup of coffee, searching for solutions to her predicament. Later that morning the germ of an idea formed in her mind.

She would talk to Herb first, bounce her thoughts off him. If he felt she was on the right path, the next step would be the real battle. Jane knew her idea was risky, but it was her best shot. She hoped Herb would agree.

CHAPTER 24

"An ultralight? Are you fucking kidding me?" Roger couldn't believe what he was hearing from Pat.

"Wouldn't BS you about something like this, boss," Pat replied with a smile. "Do you want to come take a look at it? It's about a forty-five-minute tractor ride from here."

"Let's get there as quick as we can. Is anyone guarding it?"

"Couple of the hunters who found it are still there. Austin came back to tell me. This is going to blow you away."

They went to the main barn and cranked up an ancient John Deere and attached a trailer, the same Jay used to tow the ultralight there in the first place. They went as fast as the tractor would allow, Pat hanging on at the back as Roger dodged branches and downed trees. An hour later, they arrived at the barn.

"How'd you guys find it?" Roger asked, staring in wonderment at the contraption in front of him.

"We were hunting a wild hog and saw tracks in front of the barn," Austin said. "We decided to have a quick look inside, saw loads of human footprints, and figured something must be going on. We poked around and found this thing under a tarp and hay."

"I wonder who built it," Pat asked. "Do you think it actually flies?"

Roger shrugged. He'd never seen anything like it.

"What do you want to do with it?" Pat asked. "Someone spent a lot of time building this. I hate to steal all their hard work."

Roger pondered for a moment. "Fair point. But if we don't take it, it may just end up rotting here if the owner doesn't come back. We may find a use for it. As for who made it, I may have an idea about that."

Pat looked at Roger. "Who?"

Roger chose to ignore Pat's question and turned instead to the rest of the group. He instructed them to load the ultralight onto the trailer and get it back to French Creek as soon as possible.

It was close to dusk when Roger and his crew chugged back into the village, towing the ultralight behind them. They couldn't wait to tell everyone what they'd found.

Jay was sitting on his porch drinking homemade wine as the tractor passed his house at a snail's pace. When he saw his prized ultralight, his wine suddenly tasted sour.

Horrified, he stared blankly as his long-planned route to freedom was carted off into the village to be housed in someone else's barn. He quickly realized that was the least of his problems. The community would soon start to investigate who built it and why.

Depressed and angry, he went back inside, poured himself a full glass of moonshine, and decided the first thing to do was to get blind drunk. Tomorrow was another day, one he didn't care to think about right now.

A night and one head-splitting hangover later, Jay lay sprawled, still fully dressed on his bed. He pried his eyes open. There was hammering outside his window or maybe from inside his head. It wouldn't stop wherever it was coming from. He flopped out of bed to go to the bathroom. Through the alcohol-induced haze, he finally realized the noise was coming from downstairs, and the hammering was someone loudly—too loudly—trying to get his attention.

Grabbing the banisters, he lowered himself delicately downstairs and opened the door to see Roger and Pat.

"Can we come in? Thanks," Pat asked rhetorically as he and Roger pushed none-too-gently past him.

"Please, help yourself. Just talk quietly. I got a bit of a headache." Jay could hear himself whining.

"Should think you have," Roger said, sniffing an empty bottle of moonshine. "This stuff smells lethal."

Collecting his thoughts, Jay went into the kitchen and came back with a glass of water. He sat down on the sofa and watched his two visitors through half-closed eyes.

"So what do you want?"

"You probably saw the new toy we brought back to the village yesterday," Roger said. "Quite a find. Wondered if you knew anything about it?"

"What—ultralights? Sure. I had one years ago."

"Do you know anything about that particular ultralight?" Roger asked, with a little more steel in his voice. He wasn't in the mood to play games.

Jay hesitated. What would denying it achieve? They'd find out eventually, as some parts had come from other redundant machinery in the village. A bit of detective work would soon reveal Jay's hand in its making. Still, it was months of work gone to waste, and he didn't feel like cooperating. In the end, through his alcohol-fogged mind, Jay decided to own up. What could they do to him? What penalties would they impose? He figured nothing too draconian, and in a way, he didn't care. He mumbled his admission of ownership.

"I built it. Guilty as charged." He paused. When the others said nothing, he continued. "So what's my punishment? Banishment, half rations, six months in the cell? Go on, tell me. I can take it." His tone was resigned and sarcastic.

"No punishment," Roger said. "None at all. In fact, we want you to finish it. Get it up and running—but with one change."

Jay's mind, despite the hangover, became crystal clear. Nothing like a big surprise to ease the pain.

"What do you want me to do?"

"Adapt it to carry two people, not just one. Can you do that?"

To say Jay was relieved hearing Roger's request was putting it mildly. He launched into a series of garbled questions at Roger. "It may need a bigger motor. Have to increase the wingspan, maybe. But I suppose it could be done. Why, though? What's the plan? So, I'm not in for a hard time from you and the Council?"

"Not if you do what we want," Roger said. "As to why, we'll tell you and everyone else in due course. We'll get the ultralight back to your shop. You've got a month."

CHAPTER 25

Jane was caught flat-footed when Herb and Roger unexpectedly came to her house. Neither looked to be in a good mood. Without any preamble, they suggested a walk.

As they left the village, what small talk there had petered out. Jane waited in trepidation for the real purpose of the meeting to start. She had no idea which way this conversation might be headed.

"Jane." Roger stopped and turned to face her. He looked serious but not annoyed. Jane held her breath, waiting to hear his next words.

Roger didn't mince his words. "Herb told me about the conversation you had a few days ago. Don't be annoyed with him; I had already guessed a lot of it—he merely filled in the blanks. Let me be clear, I don't appreciate being lied to, or fed a load of BS as to why you turned up there. That said, I can see you're in an impossible position. While some is of your own making, a lot of it was down to bad luck and circumstances."

He paused and suggested they sit down on some fallen tree limbs before continuing.

"Your arrival coincided with some problems in French Creek—a group of youngsters hatching a plan to leave. You, Jenny and Bryanna exacerbated that problem by feeding them a lot of garbage about how they might get over to the West. Then giving them vague suggestions how you could help."

Jane stood up. "That's not what I said at all….."

Roger held up his hand and stopped her mid-sentence. He suggested she sit down and let him finish before making any more excuses.

"You'll have your turn in a minute. Hear me out."

Herb chipped in, "Please, Jane. Do as he says. This might be a solution that suits you and us."

Jane retook her seat, a flicker of optimism rising inside her.

"As I see it, you need to get back to the Mississippi with a few more people in tow," Roger said. "You want to get back to your family in the West. We have, as you are well aware some people keen to leave. However, I'm not prepared to let them go by themselves. You might be able to help to a degree based on your knowledge. I think there's a lot more to it than any of us realize. So, we'd like to be involved in this process. I hope, with some careful planning, a little finesse, and a lot of luck, everyone might get what they want from this sticky situation."

Jane felt her jaw drop. Gathering her wits, she blurted out the first thing that came to mind. "Roger, that would be a fucking miracle if you could pull it off. Tell me what I have to do. Anything at all."

"We've a lot more details to sort out," Roger answered. "I'm going to meet with a few more people to discuss this. Let's get together again in a couple of days. In the meantime, keep this to yourselves, both of you-OK?"

Both Herb and Jane nodded in agreement.

"In that case, I'll leave you and get back to work." With that, Roger abruptly stood up and walked back to the village. Leaving the two of them in stunned silence

Once he was out of sight, Herb and Jane looked at each other. The relief they both felt soon turned to something else. Before they realized it, they were embracing, kissing, and undressing.

"Was that a celebratory or a sympathy fuck?" Herb asked with a smile, as they disentangled themselves twenty minutes later.

"I'm not sure, bit of both probably. Who cares? It was amazing." Jane beamed a wide grin as she dressed. "C'mon, you. We have work to do."

"Jesus, so much for my post-coital cigarette," Herb laughed. "You're just using and abusing me."

"You should be so lucky." Jane winked at Herb then turned to head back to the village, a sense of relief sweeping through her.

CHAPTER 26

Roger had been stretched physically and mentally over the last few days trying to get all his ducks lined up in a logical row. With help from Herb and Pat, he believed he might have created a workable plan. Unlike in the military, he couldn't order and force people to follow his instructions, so some delicate negotiations might be needed.

Time was against them; Jane had a deadline to meet, otherwise, there was a good chance her husband and child might be hurt. To keep these coyotes happy, Roger planned to offer his son and any other leavers as payment—and bait. Meanwhile, Jay and his ultralight offered a previously unavailable method of transport to reach the other side of the Mississippi

Deception, bravado, and a large helping of luck were needed, along with careful planning and coordination. The number of moving parts that could fall off at any time was fearsomely high. Despite that Roger and his team thought it was possible. God willing.

In the week after his chat with Jane, they had all met several times to thrash out as many variables as they could, fine-tuning what they knew they could control and making backup plans for when the unexpected arose. Now, they just had to get everyone else on board—the Council, and the rest of the village. They would then have to deal with anyone who wanted to leave. Explain the dangers, cost and a dozen other factors. Especially awkward if they were part of the teenage group as they had become known.

Roger called for a specially convened village meeting to put everyone in the picture. Not surprisingly, it was crowded. It was a rare occasion when all the villagers were invited to a meeting. Most decisions were made by the Council. Not this time. Too many people were involved for this to go ahead without approval from the whole community.

Roger sat with Pat and Herb. Jane and Jay sat to one side facing the group of nearly hundred people. Jane felt uncomfortable; she knew as the meeting progressed much of the focus would be on her. So she sat up straight, staring into the middle distance, not daring to catch anyone's eye.

Jay, unused to being the center of attention, looked like he clearly wished he was somewhere else. He had smartened himself up for the occasion—for the first time in months, he was not dressed in greasy overalls.

Pat and Roger already seated at the top table were deep in discussion, heads close together. The hubbub of an excited group of people filled the room. People took their seats and looked around expectantly.

Roger took a deep breath, cleared his throat, and stood to address the villagers. Talking in public didn't worry him, but the message he was about to deliver was one of the most important and potentially inflammatory since he took over as chairman of the Council.

He paused, looked around, and started in a commanding, slow, steady voice.

"Thank you all for coming. The discussion we are about to have any the decisions we are going to make aren't going to be easy for many of us. I ask for your patience and understanding while I explain the problems—unprecedented problems—facing us. Then I'll outline how I and the other people you see in front of you have put together a plan to solve them. A proposal that we hope will keep this community viable and happy".

Roger paused to gather his thoughts. He wasn't using notes; he didn't want this to appear as a formal speech. Though he had to get the message across in such a way as to keep the alarm to a minimum.

"Over the last few months, since Jane and her group arrived, not in the most auspicious manner I think we'll all agree, those that stayed have proved valuable members of the community. It now seems some of them came here with a hidden agenda. An agenda forced on them by others criminals who have little regard for the lives of their fellow human beings. Those who merely see them as a way of getting rich, no matter the consequences. However, that agenda has changed. Why? Because while staying here, they came to know us, made friends, and settled into our way of life. They became part of the community. This forced them to realize that they no longer wished to be part of this evil undertaking and came to us for help. They had given promises under duress. They were put in an untenable, unenviable position. And now I am proposing to the community of French Creek we help them out of this almost impossible predicament."

Roger went on to explain the blackmail the group had been under to recruit 'leavers' who wanted to head West. The deadly threats to their families if they didn't deliver enough people who wanted to make the dangerous trip.

To the astonishment of many at the meeting, Roger revealed the demands from a group of youngsters who wanted to leave French Creek. These problems were not going away. They needed to be addressed, Roger argued.

"Taking all these factors into account, I would like to propose a plan that will help Jane and her friends get what they need. Give those who want to leave our help—and keep the French Creek spirit intact."

Before he could continue, Jane stood up. She faced the gathering and nervously asked if she could say something. If Roger was annoyed at the interruption, he didn't show it. He nodded for her to continue.

"I hadn't planned on saying anything, but I feel I owe you all an explanation." Apprehensive what the reaction her words might provoke, her tone was conciliatory. She continued in a voice not much beyond a whisper.

"Now you all know why we came here and what our intentions were. They weren't decent or honorable. It's what we felt we had to do at that time in order to survive and get our families back. Now times have changed, and I have too. I believe the others in my group have changed as well. The reasons are simple. You folk here at French Creek have proved so welcoming and accepting that for the first time in five years we found somewhere that feels like home."

She paused. All eyes were focused on her, waiting to hear what she had to say, her explanation as to why someone who had misled them from the start should now deserve their support and trust.

"Before, I didn't see a way out of my dilemma. I thought I would have to make a choice between never seeing my family again, or causing hurt and unhappiness here as we broke French Creek apart. Now I hope—really hope—that with your help, we can all end up getting what we want. It won't be easy or without risk. I urge you, from the bottom of my heart, to hear Roger out and accept his proposal. It's not perfect—nothing ever is—but I have to believe it's the best option. I know and have experienced what kind and understanding people you are. I am begging you to show that generosity of spirit just one more time. I know some of you will think we don't deserve it. Maybe you're right. But, I ask you, what would you have done in my position? We could have chosen a different path, we didn't. We were wrong. I ask for your forgiveness and understanding. Thank you."

Jane sat down, close to tears, and leaned against Herb for support. The room was silent. Everyone sensed this was, not for the first time, a life and death decision in the making. They wanted to hear exactly what Roger had planned before making their decision.

Roger rose from his seat and began to explain his proposal.

CHAPTER 27

The community, with some reservations, gave Roger's plan the green light.

Immediately, Roger, Herb, Pat, and Jane went to dig up the cache of weapons, materials, and radios stashed prior to the original attack on the village. Much was ruined from frost, rain, and vermin—but the solar-powered satellite phones were still intact and serviceable, with a little help from Jay. They were how Jane and her group communicated with the coyotes; it was via these that the first phase of the group's plan was put into action.

The most difficult part of the operation was discovering who wanted to leave French Creek and make the trip West.

The initial group of dissenting teenagers, when faced with the option to leave, had been reduced to just two—Roger's son, Landy, and his best friend, Dick. Pressure from parents and Jane supplying further details on what the whole process might entail dampened their enthusiasm. To everyone's surprise, some other residents, all single men, came forward wanting to make the journey West.

Roger couldn't hide his disappointment that his son still wanted to leave. In the end, he reasoned that it was better to be in control of Landy's trip than leave it to others. He felt a little happier knowing he'd be alongside him should trouble arise.

Others wanting to leave included: Austin, who'd arrived with Jane and had family out West he wanted to try and find. Dwayne, an arrival from two years earlier whose skills as a carpenter, would be sorely missed. He had found it difficult to settle in and had not yet found a wife. There was a good reason—Dwayne was gay. He feared the repercussions of revealing this within the small French Creek community, so he made the decision to leave. He didn't explain this—just said he thought it was time to move on.

Lastly, Bryan, a 40-year-old handyman had lost his wife to someone else within the community three years ago. Though now divorced, he couldn't accept the awkward and upsetting situation of seeing her every day with another man. When this opportunity came to leave, he decided to join the group. Bryanna and Jenny also opted to go as they had family in the West. With Jay and Jane, it made a total of nine, plus Roger and Pat.

Jay and Jane were flying ahead in the two-seater ultralight. She had a pretty good idea where her family were in the West. She needed to find a more precise location-and hopefully rescue them-before handing over the rest of the group.

The first satellite call Jane made to the coyotes did not start well. They were less than impressed at the time she had taken to re-establish contact. When they heard she was bringing a group of 'around' nine, they became less aggressive. After several calls, she found out where her husband and son were staying—near Marion, Arkansas. They had been moved due to her husband's poor health. With the aid of false papers, he had rejoined the local police force on the understanding that he would keep the coyotes informed of any potential raids or arrests that might cause problems.

Jay managed to convert his ultralight to carry two people without major difficulties. With him officially 'on the team', he could practice and fine-tune its flying capabilities and brush up on his navigation skills without any more subterfuge.

The deal they offered Jay, aside from help and materials to finish his ultralight, was the freedom to leave the community with their blessing when the expedition was over. As an added incentive, Jane reminded him that her husband had been a cop in the Atlanta police force and could give him some useful names to contact in his quest to find his brother-in-law. That was enough for Jay to come on board and play a crucial role in the plan.

It was late February before the group was ready to leave for Memphis. It was a clear, crisp morning when they assembled at the church and made their farewells to the rest of the village. Erring on the side of caution, plans were put in place for Roger's and Pat's replacements should they not return. Herb had been thoroughly briefed and was to stay behind as link man. He kept one of the satellite phones to communicate with the two groups in case of emergency. Jane and Herb said their tearful farewells, accepting that their relationship was destined to be short, though Herb begged her to come back if it all went awry. Prudently, she offered no promises; she was torn between the prospect of seeing her family and leaving the man of whom she had become so fond.

Four were on horseback, and the other five in a wagon with supplies. The impatient horses shot funnels of hot breath from their nostrils as they pawed the frozen ground, ready to get moving. Farewells complete, Roger turned his horse and prodded him forward into a trot. The rest of the group fell in behind. They cut an almost silent path through the slight dusting of snow on the road. Soon, they disappeared from view.

They anticipated the journey to Memphis would take the better part of seven days, Roger estimated. They wanted to avoid major cities, such as Bowling Green and Nashville. For most of the way, they saw few people. It was cold, not tempting many to come out and greet them. Roger decided to break the journey by visiting an old friend near Jackson. A fellow ex- soldier, Roger had not seen Jeff in over five years. As they approached the village of Oak Grove, Roger went ahead to see if he was still at the last address he had for him. A farmer, Roger thought it unlikely Jeff would have moved. To his delight, as he rode up the long drive to the old farmhouse, he was greeted by his friend toting a shotgun and demanding, "Now what the fuck do you want?"

"Jeff, always good to see you too," Roger laughed. "Such a warm welcome from a fellow officer"

Jeff lowered his gun and drew close to Roger's horse, peering intently at his surprise visitor.

"Roger? Captain Roger Makefield? Jesus, it is you." Jeff's face lit up as recognition dawned.

"Indeed it is, Lieutenant Johnson. Good to see you after all these years. I hope I'm not arriving at an inconvenient time? Looks like you've been fighting a few battles since I last saw you in Afghanistan."

Jeff looked nonplussed for a second, then reached up and touched his scar.

"Yea, one or two run-ins with some undesirables," Jeff explained, "Let's save that story for later. More importantly, what the hell are you doing here? Last I heard, you were making your way back to see some relatives in Kentucky? Guess that's where you've been since the shit hit the fan?"

"Yes, I made it back okay," Roger acknowledged. "We managed to survive the last five years pretty well, considering. Jeff, before we start reminiscing, would it be okay if my fellow travelers and I stopped over for a couple of days?"

Roger briefly explained who was with him and why they were going to Memphis. Jeff, happy for some company, told Roger to go and get the group. In the meantime, he'd get some hot drinks brewing and food prepared for dinner.

Jeff quickly and expertly prepared a meal of roast lamb, potatoes, and vegetables, delighted for the first time in months, to be cooking for someone other than himself.

After Jeff's stomach filling meal, they all sat in his large farmhouse kitchen, thawing off in front of an ancient wood-burning AGA stove, drinking hot milk spiced with some of his homemade moonshine.

Roger, feeling relaxed, warm, and more comfortable than he had in several days, reclined in a battered old leather armchair, his legs stretched out in front of a crackling and bone-warming fire. The others had gone to unpack and find places to sleep in the various bedrooms upstairs.

Eager to catch up with his military friend's news, Roger looked at Jeff quietly sipping some brandy he'd 'kept for special occasions'.

"What's your story since I last saw you?" Roger asked. "You've been living here all by yourself since the Collapse?"

Jeff leaned back in his chair, a look of pain on his face as he recalled what had happened to him when he returned home. He told few people of his ordeal—reliving the memories was difficult and upsetting. But Roger had been a good commander and always a sympathetic listener. With the brandy relaxing his body and loosening his tongue, Jeff opened up for the first time in a long while.

"How long have you got?" he asked. "It's a pretty miserable story, Roger. No real happy ending except that I'm still alive, and I sometimes wonder what the point of that is".

As Jeff recounted his story, he seemed to find the retelling at times painful but somehow therapeutic, releasing long-held demons of a deeply upsetting episode in his life.

"After we split from Fort Bragg, I made my way to Memphis with an idea to take a boat up the Mississippi to Tiptonville, then cut across to here. It was a nightmare, Roger. The refugees trying to get across were already causing panic and chaos, so I went up the I-40 towards Jackson. There, the looting, killing, and armed mobs made me divert East. I was going across the country when I met a group of people heading for a hideout in the Tennessee River at Saltillo. I tagged along for safety and found a bunch of ex-marines staking a claim to an island slap bang in the middle of the river called Goat Island, if I remember rightly."

Jeff kicked back a long slug of brandy. "Because I was ex-military, they invited me in, but I only stayed a few days to stock up. The vibes were bad, Captain, more like an internment camp than a reservation. So I skipped out and headed North, bypassing Nashville as I'd heard it was a dangerous mess.

He paused. "I eventually got here." The words caught in his throat as he explained what he found when he arrived.

"My wife and daughters had been held hostage as slaves by a bunch of evil bastards who made the farm their home. Two teenage girls were too much of a temptation to those animals. It was sickening, Roger, what they did to my family, my home. I can still see it, feel it. God knows what my wife had been through as well.

He took a breath, another sip of brandy. "I had to do something. My military training kicked in and I watched and waited for the right moment. They weren't expecting me or anyone else to bother them, so it was easy for me to pick off the first couple of them. Then they barricaded themselves in and threatened to kill my family if I didn't leave. I couldn't bear the thought and felt utterly helpless. I was determined to save them, no matter what. So early one morning, I became a one-man SWAT team, burst in, and killed the rest of them, but not before they shot my girls and wounded my wife."

Roger leaned forward and touched Jeff on the arm, "Jesus Jeff, that's awful. I am so sorry you had to go through this nightmare. Did your wife make it?"

Jeff replied in a whisper, "No. No, she didn't Roger. She tried, but without doctors and medicines, it was hopeless."

He stopped talking, lost in the terrible memories.

"I buried all three out in the field and set to work making myself self-sufficient. Thanks to Ruth we had a good supply of food and essentials. She'd always been a great preserver of fruits and vegetables. I survived the first Winter and then went back to being a farmer."

"Did you get any further unwanted visitors?" Roger asked. "We're still getting them in French Creek."

"Yes. From time to time. A few people straggled up to the farmhouse however, I was always well-armed and made it look like I had nothing worth stealing. Had to kill a few, but most went on without too much trouble. I'm a mile from the main road so the farm takes some finding, thankfully."

"How are things now?" asked Roger, interested in how other communities were managing.

"Not too bad most of the time. In the last couple of years, there's been a regular farmer's market in Jackson so I can get any basic food and supplies I need there, swap excess produce, ammo, that kinda thing. I'm surviving, if not thriving. Just like everyone around here. People close by are always coming over. I visit them; we keep busy and informed. Long way from what it was, but a lot better than five years ago."

Placing his brandy aside, he looked at Roger. "My turn now. What have you been up to, Captain? You're a long way from home and going to a shit hole of a place."

Initially unwilling to reveal everything about the trip, Roger ultimately decided that Jeff deserved to know the full story. He explained their plan, hoping Jeff might spot some failings in their thinking or make any helpful suggestions. When he finished, he sat back to gauge Jeff's reaction.

"Christ, Captain, that's an ambitious plan you've got going there," Jeff said thoughtfully. "The ultralight guy really adds an interesting dimension to it. If it wasn't for him, I'd say you were stretching it. But I gotta admire you—it looks just about feasible."

"That's good to hear," Roger said. "I always valued your input when we were in Afghanistan. It's even more useful now. It can't all go to plan...Does it ever? But we've got a few fallbacks in case the wheels drop off."

Leaning forward, Jeff whispered, "I can come with you if you want? I'd be glad to help in any way I can. Those smuggler coyotes are scum. If you can put a few away, you've got my blessing."

"Good to know," Roger said. "I think we've got it covered though having you available would be reassuring. I hope we'll not have to take you up on it. Your offer means a lot to me. I really appreciate it. Bit like old times, eh?"

"Indeed it is," agreed Jeff. "Indeed it is, sir."

With that, Roger got up, thanked Jeff for his hospitality, and went upstairs to bed. Jeff sat by himself, watching the fire gradually die down, the brandy ensuring he would get a sound night's sleep.

The following day, they rechecked their stocks, took some of the ammo Jeff offered free for the cause, and made sure everyone was doubly clear on what would happen as they neared Memphis.

Roger called Herb via satellite phone to check that Jane and Jay were preparing to leave in the ultralight. They would head for Millington, a town on the banks of the Mississippi, just a few miles north of Memphis. They estimated it should take about eight hours, keeping their speed to around sixty MPH to conserve fuel. Jane had the third satellite phone and would contact Herb and Roger to confirm safe arrival.

The group departed the farm at first light, aiming to complete the journey within three days. Jeff again offered to come along as extra firepower. He could easily get someone to keep an eye on the farm for a few days in his absence, he said. Both Roger and Pat were tempted. Having someone with knowledge of fighting, firearms, and tight situations would be a further safeguard. It could tilt any confrontation in their favor. In the end they demurred. Jeff had done more than enough. To know he had a safe house here if the shit really hit the fan was comfort and assistance enough.

Little did they both know how that arrangement would change within a few days.

As they approached Memphis two days later, the weather had taken a turn for the worse, with some heavy snow flurries and freezing cold temperatures. They discovered Jane and Jay had made an emergency landing near Dyersburg and hunkered down until the storm passed. Mercifully, the snow masked their landing on a deserted country road, and they stayed concealed in an old barn. They would take off as soon as the weather cleared.

Roger and Pat left the rest of the group in an abandoned farmhouse just south of Millington. Neither had been to a large city since the Collapse and didn't know what to expect. They hoped the looting, rioting, and violence had run their course, and some semblance of normality had returned. As they rode past Woodstock into North Memphis, the outskirts of the city shocked them with a depressing scene of burnt-out, abandoned, and derelict buildings on every street. In some gardens and parks skinny horses, goats and cows looked at them forlornly as they rode past. Few people were out and about. They stopped a man outside a church who turned out to be the local pastor and asked for directions to Harbor Town. He gave them the information, followed by a warning. "That's no place for those of a nervous disposition," he warned. "Lots of violence, gambling, drinking, and whoring. Watch your backs."

Roger and Pat thanked him for his advice. They continued until they reached Hernando de Soto Bridge. Then they turned to cross over it onto Greenbelt Park, which fronted the giant Mississippi. At this point, the river was nearly a half-mile wide. As they stood on the bridge, it gave them a view of the West side. Pat stopped and brought out his binoculars. He relayed what he could see.

"There's a pretty impressive checkpoint on the bridge. Armed guards, heavy duty artillery, a couple of tanks. Real welcoming."

He scanned down to the river's edge on the West side. "Jesus. Machine gun posts every hundred yards or so, what looks like a ten-foot-high brick wall, floodlights, the works. Reminds me of the Berlin Wall. I can see some docks further North. They look equally well-guarded. It will be interesting to see how these coyotes get people across. Can't believe it's fortified like this all the way along the West bank. Must've cost a fortune."

Pat lowered the binoculars and looked at Roger. "So where to next?"

"First port of call is to the Westward Emigration office. You can cross legally if you have the right paperwork. I want to find out how difficult it is to do that. I'd rather Landy and the rest of the group do it that way than being in the hands of the coyotes. I'm sure these people can't be trusted in any way. The pastor said the WEO was down on Island Drive, so let's head there."

The scene was like something from Deadwood—a modern wild West town met their gaze. Alongside the existing buildings, new ones had sprung up in haphazard style, offering everything from casinos, bars, hotels to boarding houses and warehouses. The main street ran parallel to the river and was busy even in mid-afternoon. Music blared from a dozen different places. As they rode warily down the street, they heard gunshots coming from one of the bars. Some motorbikes roared up and down the street, adding to the cacophony of noises. Roger and Pat hadn't heard such noises in years. They noticed with some surprise the amount of electricity that was being used. Clearly, people here had access to gas for generators and motors.

"That pastor was right. This place is a hell hole," Pat said, wide-eyed at the discordant sounds and sights that assailed them, spooking their horses and making them glance nervously around. Strangers on horses were a common sight. No one paid them too much notice. At the far end of the street, they found the Emigration Office. Roger told Pat to stay with the horses and their supplies while he went inside.

The large waiting room was packed with people waiting their turn to be seen by two disinterested clerks behind bulletproof glass. Roger went to a woman sitting behind a desk with a large sign reading INQUIRIES placed in front of her as though it offered some protection.

She ignored Roger until he got her attention. "Hello, ma'am," he asked loudly. "Can you help me?"

Barely looking up from her ancient Dell Computer, she demanded, "Purpose of visit?"

Roger, trying to stay calm and polite, replied. "I just have a quick question. What's the process for me and my son to get across to the West?"

"A long one," she sighed. "Unless you got a lot of money, relatives over there to sponsor you, guarantee you a job, you can forget it. Even if you have all that, it can take up to a year to get an exit visa. Read this." She tossed over a thick booklet. "Tells you all you need to know."

"Thanks. You've been most helpful," Roger said, trying to hide the sarcasm in his voice. He got up from her desk and headed out to meet Pat.

"How'd it go?" Pat asked as Roger mounted his horse.

"The lady there has obviously been to the same charm school most immigration officers attend. Suffice to say, doing this legally is a non-starter. It will take about a year and that's if you've got a bundle of money and influential friends. We're back to our original plan—trying to outwit the coyotes and get our group over there at the same time. We have to find our contact man among this den of thieves."

They mounted their horses and headed back down main street and North towards Millington, where the rest of the group had taken refuge. It was about a two-hour ride out of the city, and though the weather had cleared, it was still overcast and cold as they rode to the old farmhouse.

After a long miserable ride, they trotted up to the abandoned farmhouse. There was no sign of life, as Roger had forbidden any fires or candles from being lit for fear they could be seen by passers-by.

They put their horses in the old barn behind the farmhouse and entered through the kitchen door. They found the rest of the group huddled around an old kerosene burner, trying to keep warm and cook a meal for dinner.

"Where did you find the heater?" Pat asked, pleased he wasn't going to freeze tonight.

"This place hasn't been empty that long, it seems," said Dwayne. "Previous owners must've left in a hurry and didn't take this with them. Makes the room toasty warm." He stirred some kind of stew in a large pot. "We even managed to bag a couple of rabbits before it got dark. There is a God up there somewhere today."

"He might be smiling on you, but his generosity doesn't extend to emigration visas," Roger explained the findings from his visit. "Doing this legally isn't going to happen. Unless you know the right people over there, have a bag load of money, and can wait a year, you're fucked. If you want to know more, read this." Roger tossed over the booklet given to him by Miss Charming.

"Hardly surprising, but worth a try," Bryan said, trying not to look too disappointed at the bad news.

Roger sat next to Landy while he ate his meal. He asked one more time—did he really want to do this? Roger was petrified of what might happen to Landy if all did not go to plan. Though as someone who had run away to join the military at eighteen, Roger knew he couldn't prevent his son from wanting to see more of the world than Kentucky. They spent the rest of the evening enjoying a remarkably good meal and going over again the plans for the next few days.

"I know you're worried, Dad," Landy tried to reassure him. "So am I. But having got this far, I've just gotta go with it. After all, there's Uncle Peter in Little Rock for me to stay with. I won't be on my own for long."

Roger shrugged a grudging acceptance. "I understand. You can't blame me for wanting you to stay safe with me. I'm gonna miss you big time, son."

"I know…" Landy paused, on the edge of wanting to say more.

Before he could, the door crashed open three armed men barreled in, screaming for everyone to stay where they were. They fanned out around the room.

"Don't move a fucking muscle, any of you," shouted the leader, a huge bear of a man wielding a shotgun like it was a chopstick. "Don't even think about going for any firearms. You'll be dead before you can stand up. Who's in charge here?"

"I am," Roger said. "Captain Roger Makefield. What have we done to cause all this?" Roger hoped his army rank would impress his adversary. Fighting back right now would be pointless and dangerous. Besides, his gun was still in the holster on his saddle—nowhere close at hand. He gave Pat a look, willing him not to do anything stupid. He returned his attention to the man pointing a shotgun at his chest.

“Well, Captain Makefield, this is our property," the leader replied, unimpressed by Roger’s military credentials. "You're breaking and entering. What is your business here?"

"I must apologize," Roger was trying to keep the situation calm. "We had no intention of causing any problems. We are on our way to Memphis, and we thought this house was abandoned. We're only here for tonight, then we'll be on our way."

The leader glanced a meaningful look at his gun-toting sidekicks, then back to Roger.

"You can pay us some rent in the form of some food and supplies. Then we'll let you be on your way. Payment is due immediately." The man grinned, deadly serious.

"We haven't much to spare," Roger answered. "To leave now in weather like this will be deadly. We're happy to share what we have, but you must leave us enough to live on for the rest of the journey." Roger wanted to understand just how dangerous these people were or whether it was a bluff. Not that he intended to gamble their lives figuring it out. He'd play along for now and see if an opportunity to overpower them came later. Currently, it didn't look hopeful.

"Should have thought of that before busting into our place. Let's see what you got. I'll decide what you keep and we take." He raised his gun again and pointed it at the group. "All of you over by the wall, sit down with your hands behind your head. Don't try anything clever. Kenny here,"—he motioned to one of the other men—"is one of our best shots. He can take your eye out at a hundred yards. Kenny, check them for guns while Dave and I go look for their supplies."

Roger and his group were herded over to the wall. Before they sat, Kenny gave them a cursory pat down. None had revolvers or handguns on them. Roger did know Pat kept a hunting knife tucked in his right boot.

"Do you mind if I take my jacket off? Pat asked. "It's warm in here." Kenny grunted his assent. Pat took off his coat and threw it over his knees so it draped over his feet.

They could hear the other two rummaging around in the kitchen, searching their packs for anything worth stealing. Pat and Roger's supplies were still out in the barn.

After a few minutes, the two came back, looking disappointed. "You ain't got a lot worth having. We could take your horses… How many you got?" the leader asked.

"If you take our horses, we'll never get to Memphis," Pat said. "There is more food and brandy out in the barn—along with our guns." The glimmer of an idea formed in Pat's mind.

"Steve, let's you and me go take a look," Dave said. "Kenny—you stay here. Fire a shot if you need us. Shoot one of them if they try anything stupid. We'll be right back." The two disappeared out the back door. Pat estimated they had five minutes before they returned.

He caught Roger's eye. Kenny was briefly distracted, lighting a cigarette. Roger, Dwayne, and Bryan all nodded their heads. They understood the plan—diversion.

Roger was at one end of the group while Pat was at the other, stretched across the wall of the sitting room with the others spaced out in between. If Roger could attract Kenny's attention, he might not see any movement Pat made. Near Roger was a small table with a lit oil lamp on it.

"Any chance of a smoke?" Roger asked. "You know, for the condemned man and all that?" Roger smiled. "I haven't had a decent cigarette in years. What are those—Marlboro's? Used to be my regular smoke."

Kenny hesitated, then threw Roger a cigarette that landed close to his feet. As Roger scooted to reach it, he kicked at the table with the oil lamp on it, sending it crashing to the floor in a burst of flames.

"Stupid fucker," Kenny screamed, rushing towards the flames already spreading on the filthy carpet, vainly trying to stamp them out. Within seconds Pat was already on his feet, knife pulled from his boot, launching himself at Kenny. The two crashed to the floor. Kenny never stood a chance against Pat's physical strength and unarmed combat training. After a brief scuffle Pat sat astride Kenny's chest, knife at his throat.

"Two options here Kenny," Pat said. "You shut up and live, or you struggle, make a sound, and your blood will be all over this floor. What will it be?"

Terrified, Kenny stuttered, "I won't say a word, please. This wasn't my idea."

Pat cut him short. "Save the excuses for later. Turn over." Pat tied Kenny's hands behind his back with the man's own belt, stuffed a rag in his mouth, and dragged him out onto the front porch. Roger checked the magazine on Kenny's rifle—six rounds. Enough for what we need to do, Roger thought.

"Everyone, move out by the front door and keep an eye on this toe rag," Roger ordered. "Stay away from the barn, and don't come back in until you hear from us. If we're not back in five minutes, run for it."

The group followed Roger's orders without a moment's hesitation. Landy and Bryan retrieved their weapons before rushing outside to the front of the house.

Pat turned to Roger. "Quickly. They'll be back any second. I'll hide in the small pantry off the kitchen. You distract them and I'll take Dave. You take the other one."

With that, Pat, knife in hand, went into the tiny pantry and partially closed the door. Within a minute the noisy footsteps of two men stomped across the back porch. The kitchen door flew open.

"You miserable fuckers, you ain't got nothing worth having out there. Where have you hidden all your stuff—" Dave stopped mid-sentence as he confronted Roger, who pointed a rifle directly at his chest.

"Drop your weapons now," Roger said. "I told you we were traveling light. We can play this two ways. We can secure you comfortably and we'll leave in the morning; or you can try something stupid, and I'll shoot you both and leave you here to die. Your choice."

They reluctantly lowered their weapons onto the table in front of them. "Where's Kenny, asshole?" Steve asked.

"He's okay, but not in a position to help you," Roger answered. "So. Are you going to act sensibly and live? Or will you die an idiot?"

With a sly smile, Dave said. "There's one of you and two of us. You can't shoot both of us."

"True. So who wants to die first?"

Steve raised his hands above his head. "Dave, do what he says," he pleaded. "Ain't nothing here worth dying for."

Dave wasn't listening. He made a grab for his gun on the table. The noise of Roger's rifle going off in the confines of a small room was deafening. Dave's body was flung backwards across the kitchen, hitting the old stove with a solid, sickening thud. Blood sprayed all over his partner.

"Shit, fucking shit," Steve cried, staring at Dave's mangled body. "You killed him man, why'd you do that? The rest of the village will kill you for that." Before he could move, Pat was behind him, knife at his throat.

"Don't do anything stupid," Pat advised him. "It won't end up pretty. I'll happily slit your throat if you try anything. Understand me?"

Steve didn't argue, "Okay, okay, I got it. Please, I gotta wife and two kids. Don't kill me."

"Here's what we're going to do," Roger said. "You're going to join your other idiot friend tied up behind the couch and spend a really uncomfortable night on the floor. We'll leave in the morning. By the time you've released yourself, we'll be long gone.

"Understood Steve?" Roger said. "Do as we ask and you and Kenny will be allowed to live. Try anything smart and Pat here will be quite happy to separate your head from your neck. Do I make myself clear?"

Steve nodded. Pat led him into the sitting room, tied him up, and threw him to the floor. Roger gave the all-clear to the rest of the group, who dragged in a petrified Kenny and threw him next to Steve.

"No misbehaving down there," Roger said. "We'll be watching."

Pat gave Landy and Bryan the unpalatable job of peeling Dave off the stove and dragging him outside into the snow. Everyone watched in shocked silence as his limp, bloodied body was taken out. No one said anything.

"Listen up." Roger addressed the group. "We don't know if there will be anyone coming for these guys. We can't take the risk of waiting until dawn before we head out. Gather up your stuff. Take their guns and whatever food you can. Be ready to move out in fifteen minutes. Landy, take my gun and watch these two. If they so much as cough, shoot one of them. Now let's get moving, people. It's not safe to stay here any longer."

Within a short time, they were mounted up and heading South. The weather was foul. They were in for an uncomfortable ride into an unwelcoming city.

CHAPTER 28

Roger contacted Herb with an update and learned that Jay and Jane had made an emergency landing but were OK. Roger kept the conversation short as the satellite phone's battery life, even with a solar charger, was limited. He told Jane, via Herb, to contact her coyote in Memphis and arrange a time and place to meet. In the meantime, they were to stay put.

Late afternoon the group entered Memphis. Now they had to find somewhere to rest for the night, "There's plenty of places to stay, but none I'd recommend as safe, based on what we saw when we were here a couple of days ago," Roger warned, "Keep your eyes open for a half-decent place that offers shelter and security."

Roger then remembered the helpful pastor who directed them to the Emigration Office. "Pat, you remember that pastor? His church isn't too far from here, I think. Maybe he has an idea of a safe place to stay."

"Good thinking Boss," Pat said. "I think it's about a mile or so down here. Want me to go check it out?"

"Yes," Roger said. "If he's amenable to us staying, make sure it's secure. We need to be able to stable the horses and cart somewhere out of sight."

Pat trotted off and the rest of the group slowed to a walk. The events at the farmhouse had upset their plan; it was meant to be a safe house to wait at until they heard from Jane. Roger hadn't wanted to bring the whole group to Memphis, yet. Now he had to put some distance between them and Steve's irate friends. He didn't know how far the villagers would go to exact revenge.

Hopefully, they could find a place to stay while the rendezvous with the traffickers could be arranged. Then, the riskiest phase of the operation would unfold.

They waited half-hour for Pat to return, painfully aware they were exposed to anyone who thought they might be worth robbing, or worse. They checked out their surroundings, taking in the extent of damage and neglect the city had suffered over the past five years. When the Collapse started, Memphis was a prime destination for refugees trying to escape West. As the routes across were blocked one by one, thousands of dejected and desperate people found themselves marooned in the city with no place to go, no shelter, and short on supplies. Many took it out on the city itself. Graffiti was everywhere, screaming abuse at the government, the president, anyone in authority. Buildings were burned down and wrecked. Initially the city had set up some camps; soon they were unable to provide food and shelter to the swelling numbers coming in, so the camps were left to fend for themselves. The result was a dystopian vista of ruins and derelict buildings.

Five years later, all that was left was detritus, the flotsam from a wave of hopeless and despairing citizens abandoned by the government. Prior to the Collapse, Memphis had a population of around one million; now, it was barely a tenth of that. With no working infrastructure to support its residents, they relied on their wits, crime and the trickle of supplies that came from the West. It was a depressing sight; the group felt a growing sense of unease as they waited for Pat's return.

Finally, he rode back with a smile on his face.

"Managed to find the pastor. Had to convince him we didn't mean any harm, and that we'd share our supplies with him for his congregation. They have some lockups at the back of the chapel we can use. They're nothing fancy, but you can't see them from the road. I think we'll be pretty safe there."

"Well done," Roger said. "Let's get a move on before it's dark."

The group hurried to the chapel and were met by Pastor Michael, who directed them to the rear of the building. Everyone dismounted, unsaddled the horses, and put them in the large garage with feed and water. They made their way to the lockups to find a place to settle down and get comfortable.

Roger thanked the pastor for his hospitality and invited him to join them for dinner. Delighted at the company and the prospect of a hot meal, he agreed.

As Roger returned to the lockup, he heard the satellite phone beeping. He rushed to take the call. Jane had spoken to the coyotes. A meeting had been arranged for the next day at noon in one of the dockside bars. Two sisters, Jordan and Rachel Doobie, would be their contacts. Jane led the two women to assume she would be the one meeting them, with leavers in tow. Jane warned Roger that they would see through him with possibly deadly results if he didn't win their trust. It was up to Roger to put the next part of the plan into action and not get himself killed in the process. Jane confirmed she and Jay were OK, but not quite where they expected to be.

CHAPTER 29

Jane and Jay's flight had its own dramas, though not as life-threatening as the journey on the ground.

Jay had modified, then flight-tested numerous times, the two-seater version of the ultralight. Other mechanics in the village helped him meet Roger's tight deadline.

The first flight, flown solo, was exhilarating and frightening. The craft was extremely responsive and required only minor alterations to the flight control mechanisms. The main problem was the engine—they couldn't get it to run smoothly. It misfired, coughing and spluttering to such an extent that Jay's first flight lasted only a few minutes, reaching an altitude of just two hundred feet before he had to land. The engine misfire was finally diagnosed as dirty fuel blocking the carbs. Once the gas tank and lines were cleaned out, it purred like a contented cat.

Finding an adequate substitute for antifreeze posed another problem. Flying in the middle of Winter meant the likelihood of burst hoses as the craft was left overnight in freezing temperatures. This problem was only partially resolved by putting sugar and diluted molasses in the cooling system. Not ideal as a long-term substitute, but it seemed to work.

After Jay had completed a dozen solo flights, he suggested Jane join him. It was "safe as riding a bike," Jay said reassuringly. Jane was not convinced. She was petrified as she sat in the co-pilot seat for the first two-person flight. It had been installed right behind Jay's, reckoning it would offer better balance than a side-by-side arrangement. That had yet to be tested.

Jane knew she couldn't put it off any longer. Reluctantly she got in, fastened the harness and crossed her fingers. Her eyes closed as Jay opened up the throttle. The engine made an ear-shattering noise as Jay revved it up to the limit. She felt the craft bump alarmingly down the makeshift airstrip, and then they were airborne. After a few seconds, she opened her eyes to the sight of French Creek disappearing from view as they climbed, flying southwards over SR 90. To avoid flying over villages or towns, Jay banked left and gradually ascended to 2000 feet, cruising over swathes of forest between French Creek and Columbia. The majestic views soon pushed aside Jane's fear. She stared down in wonder at the stark beauty of the Kentucky countryside. Frost was still thick on the north-facing hollows, with splotches of evergreen trees breaking up the brown, leafless forest that stretched as far as the eye could see. It was a breathtaking sight, seeing nature in its raw mid-winter beauty. Relaxing a little, she settled back to enjoy the rest of the flight.

Jay tested a few maneuvers and pronounced himself happy with the ultralight's responsiveness. He intended to fly higher on the trip to Wilmington to avoid the attention of anyone on the ground. And the possibility someone might take a shot at them. Though they couldn't go too high, they would navigate using basic AAA tourist maps, following the main roads, rivers, and other landmarks.

After this brief flight, Jay turned for home and landed without incident. He checked how much fuel they used and calculated what they would need for the 250-mile trip there and back. The ultralight proved remarkably economical. Even so, they would need twelve gallons of fuel weighing nearly a hundred pounds. It was an amount the village could hardly spare. Still, no one complained as the fuel was carefully siphoned into the five-gallon containers.

Each of them could only take about twenty pounds of supplies. One change of clothes, some pre-packed MREs and water. Plus, a handgun each, one rifle and a limited amount of ammunition.

The weather was overcast on the day of departure and just above freezing. Most of the village lined up at the airstrip to wish them well. Jay started his takeoff run from the furthest end of the airstrip. With maximum throttle, the engine screaming at top revs, he coaxed the ultralight into the air. Jane's role was the navigator. For the first part of the journey, she directed Jay to follow SR 90 to Glasgow, then across to Bowling Green. Traveling at the most fuel-efficient speed (about sixty MPH), they reached 1-65 in under an hour and followed the interstate South over the Kentucky/Tennessee border. With the aid of a basic compass, they headed due West, intending to go north of Clarkesville. But as they passed by Paris, then Dresden, aiming for the Mississippi, the slate gray clouds started to thicken with snow. Jay had to drop to a thousand feet to keep the ground in sight. By early afternoon, the conditions became so murky he decided to abort the flight and find a place to land.

Landing would be risky in this weather and on an unknown landing ground. The ultralight needed only about 450 feet of reasonably flat ground to land. But they had to make sure it was far away from any houses or villages so as not to attract unwelcome attention. Luckily, as it was Winter, most places would have fires burning to keep them warm. The smoke from the chimneys would be a sign that people were around.

After circling and surveying the land beneath them, Jane spotted a deserted road south of SR 104 in some marshy flatlands. Jay dropped down and saw no signs of life. With the snow picking up, he decided this was as good a place as any and brought the ultralight down safely on the small country road. He taxied along until they discovered an old barn. With some effort, they opened the doors and managed to squeeze the craft inside. Relieved to be out of the freezing weather, they closed the barn doors up and took stock of their surroundings. It was far from weatherproof, fortunately, it was big enough that the worst of the wind and snow wouldn't affect them. It was filled with large round hay bales, which made for comfortable sitting and sleeping.

Jay suggested lighting a fire would be too risky. Unenthusiastically, they opened some MREs and settled down to eat a cold meal optimistically described as a beef stew but looked and tasted like mud.

"So far, so good," said the ever-taciturn Jay. "Not quite where we want to be, but under the circumstances, could be worse."

"I guess so," Jane replied, chewing on the beef stew and trying to ignore its god-awful taste. "Are we only about a couple of hours from Millington?"

"About that. Going nowhere until the weather clears, though. I suggest we try and get some sleep. Be ready to leave at dawn."

Jay spread out his sleeping bag on a bed of hay and settled down for the night. Jane was to wound up to sleep. There was a lot that could go wrong with this plan; convincing the smugglers that she had fulfilled her side of the bargain and finding her family would be the next hurdle. Would they be prepared to divulge that information before seeing the leavers? Her future was entirely in other people's hands. While she knew she could trust him, not having control was a challenge she found hard to accept.

Eventually, she settled in her sleeping bag on the soft hay listening to the scratching and rustling of unknown animals until finally falling asleep.

It was barely light when Jay shook her awake. "It's not looking too bad out there. Not ideal, but I don't want to stay here. Let's get the ultralight onto the road and ready for take-off."

Minutes later, they were manhandling the craft out of the hanger and pointing it into what little wind was coming from the South. They had just finished packing their gear and refueling when a voice startled them from behind.

"Hey mister. What's that machine called?"

They turned to see a couple of boys, one around twelve-years-old, the other a little younger, looking at the ultralight with puzzled expressions. They leaned on bicycles that had seen better days, as had their clothing which was torn and faded, barely covering their skinny bodies.

"Christ," Jane said. "You scared the shit out of us. Where did you come from?" Jane quickly noticed they had a couple of .22 air rifles strapped to their bikes. The guns wouldn't kill you but could be uncomfortable if they hit you in the wrong place.

"We're out rabbit hunting. We live a mile or so up the road. You can't see it from here because of the mist. Does that thing really fly?" One of the boys gently touched the wing with a mixture of awe and admiration.

"Yes, it does," Jay said. "And I'd be grateful if you didn't touch it. I don't want anything broken." Jay's tone was less than friendly.

"Just interested, that's all." The boy stood back and looked at them both. "Why don't you follow us back to the farm for some breakfast? Our Pops would be really interested to see this thing. He loves engines and stuff."

"That's mighty kind of you boys," Jay replied, trying to sound disappointed. "We wouldn't want to impose. Anyway, we have to get going." Jay tried to bring the conversation to an end, anxious that it might begin to unravel and become a confrontation. He certainly didn't want 'Pops' involved.

"Tell you what," Jane said. "Why don't you nip back home and get your Pops. Bring him back here and we can take him for a ride. Maybe you guys as well. How does that sound?" Jane's coaxing tone was a gentle attempt to get the boys to go along with her suggestion—and leave. It didn't work.

"Tell you what lady," one of the boys said. "I'll wait here with you, and my brother can ride back and get Pops and our uncle. They'll both be mighty keen to see this contraption." Clearly, the elder boy hadn't bought Jane's thinly-disguised diversion.

"Sounds fine," Jay said. "Let me give you some food to take back. We've got plenty." Jay turned, opened his backpack, and surprised them by turning back with his Glock pointed directly at them.

"We're in a bit of a hurry," Jay said by way of explanation. "Why don't you drop your rifles and skedaddle out of here back home?

Hate to be so rude, but it's time we left. Now do as I ask, and we'll all be fine."

The two boys looked at Jay, then at the gun. Without a word, they dropped their rifles and mounted their bikes in a panic.

"The bikes stay here," Jay said. "You're gonna have to walk back home guys. Now get going."

The boys dropped their bikes and ran off down the road.

"Fuck you two," one of the boys yelled. "Wait until my Pops hears about this. You're going to be in real trouble." He flicked a middle finger as the mist closed around them and they vanished.

"I reckon we've got about twenty minutes before they come back," Jay said. "Finish loading up and jump in. We've gotta get out of here."

"In this weather? Are you kidding me? You can't see more than one hundred feet." Jane shouted at Jay in astonishment. "Are you mad?"

"Probably, but I don't fancy meeting Pops and his uncle who'll be much better armed than those two boys. We haven't a choice. Unless you can think of a better idea?" Jay zipped his backpack and threw it in the ultralight.

"Not really," Jane admitted, still unsure about the safety of this takeoff into the mist and low clouds.

"Didn't think so. Quit whining and get in. We don't have time to argue."

Jay turned the engine over again and again. It just wouldn't fire.

"Come on baby, come on. Don't let me down now." Jay cooed to the engine like he was coaxing a reluctant dog to come inside. He continued to fiddle with the choke and throttle, trying to get the best fuel mixture without flooding the carbs. After a few minutes, the battery started to struggle to turn the engine over.

"What's the problem?" Jane asked, looking over her shoulder at the direction the boys had gone. "Those kids will be back soon."

"It might be flooded. Have to give it a minute. You're going to have to get out and turn the engine over by hand using the prop."

"How the hell do I do that?" Jane's voice rose an octave.

"Simple. You get out and when I say, grab the top edge of one of the props and pull down hard. Then immediately stand back, cause if it fires up, you'll lose a hand."

"Shit Jay," Jane said. "Isn't there a better way?"

"If I could think of one, I'd tell you. But I can't, so off you go and do as I say—exactly when I say."

Jane reluctantly clambered out of the seat, ducked under the wing, and positioned herself in front of the propeller. It was about six feet across and looked like a fearsome weapon from where she now stood.

"Turn it until it stops, then wait for my word. Trust me, I know what I'm doing."

"You might, but I don't," Jane said. "This is fucking crazy. It better work."

"Pull it clockwise, slowly. Until it stops—yes?"

Jane grabbed hold of the prop and pulled it down. It turned quite easily, then became much harder.

"Done. Now what?"

"When I say pull, you bust your gut and turn that prop as hard as you can. Ready…pull!"

Jane grabbed the prop and pulled down with all her strength. It moved about a third of a turn, and the engine spluttered to life. The prop spun for a second or two, then stopped as the engine died. Jane was already a yard back from the half-spinning prop as it stuttered to a halt.

"Nearly had it then. Try again," Jay yelled. "Put some real effort into it this time."

"Sure," Jane spat back. "I'm just taking it easy here. Just wanting to make sure I keep my arms attached to my body, if you don't mind."

It took three more attempts before the engine fired up and stayed running, the propeller turning just feet from Jane's face. Like a startled gazelle, she leaped back quickly into her seat as Jay increased the revs and lined up for takeoff. Suddenly bullets started to zip past their heads.

Jane turned to see three men and the two boys about two hundred yards away. Two had rifles and were running towards them, firing. Thankfully the distance made their shots ineffective, but not for long.

"Jay," Jane yelled over the engine. "Get this fucking thing going and in the air. Now!"

Jay needed no further encouragement as he gave the engine full throttle. The gap between the taxiing plane and the band of shooters remained the same for a few seconds, then gradually increased as they gained speed. More shots whistled by. One tore a hole in the wing fabric.

The ultralight only needed about a hundred and fifty yards for takeoff. Within seconds, they were airborne and heading for safety into the clouds. Jane looked down at the group and waved a goodbye as they disappeared from view.

Jane breathed a sigh of relief. Jay looked to the wing that sustained damage. Through the noise of the engine and the air rushing past, Jane shouted, "Is that serious? The hole in the wing?"

Jay shook his head and shouted back, "Should be OK to get us to Millington. I can repair it there. Set me a course, navigator!"

Jane had no clue about navigating blind. She did know Millington was almost directly one hundred miles south based on the AAA map she had looked at last night. She told Jay to head in that direction for an hour and a half. Then they'd drop down below the clouds to get their bearings from the land.

She tried to calm herself, controlling her breathing and closing her eyes. It wasn't the first time she'd been shot at, but it never became any easier. The threat of a sudden death is one she'd lived with for years. Now the possibility that she could be reunited with her family was making her more nervous about taking risks. Being shot by some random rednecks looking for something she didn't have would be a catastrophic way for this mission to fail.

After ninety minutes, a watery sun showed through the cloudy mist. The southward leg of their flight was nearly completed. They dropped down, to see the gray-green landscape beneath them. Jane finally picked out the I-365 that led into Millington from the East. The small town even had its own regional airport, though they didn't want to risk landing there. They had no idea the kind of welcome they'd receive. To the West was Meeman-Shelby State Park, which abutted the Mississippi. Jay flew over it several times. Seeing no signs of activity below, he decided to land in the parking lot next to Poplar Lake.

As they coasted to a halt and cut the engine, Jay told Jane to sit tight for a few minutes. If anyone appeared, they would have a chance to take off before any trouble could reach them. They sat in silence, listening and watching for any movement that might come from the surrounding woods. Eventually seeing no movement, they jumped from the ultralight and stretched their limbs. They still felt vulnerable in the open. They looked for a place to store the ultralight. The best option was a small hut on the edge of the car lot that contained a few pieces of ground care equipment and piles of salt for de-icing the roads. They pushed the ultralight over to the building managing to just fit it in and close the doors before snow started to fall. The only other building was a refreshment and concessions cabin, which looked promising as shelter for the night. Empty, looted of anything of value it did have a kitchen and back office that was sealed off from the weather. They moved in, dropped their backpacks onto the floor, and sat in the dusty office chairs.

"Think we can risk a fire here?" Jane asked, hopefully. A warm meal and a wash would do wonders for her mood.

"Maybe we can do something after dark, when the smoke won't be so visible and most folk will be inside," Jay answered." Let me have a quick look around and see if there's anything worth having. I'll collect some wood for the fire." He ventured off into the snow, now gently falling outside. Under different circumstances, this would be an idyllic getaway location for a quiet weekend, Jane thought. Those were the days.

While Jay was out, she rummaged through the cabin. There was a small kitchen, storeroom, and front counter where visitors would have bought refreshments in happier days. She found nothing to eat but plenty of burnable material to get a fire going. There were a few small tables and chairs in the eating area. The front windows had been smashed, allowing a freezing cold breeze and a few snowflakes to enter.

The porch leading from the back door was downwind from the snow and was a little warmer and drier. She dumped paper and cardboard onto the floor to prep for the fire.

About fifteen minutes later, Jay appeared carrying a metal trash container. "Bang a few holes in this and it'll make a good brazier, screen the fire from any prying eyes." He dropped it to the ground. With a hammer and rebar found in the hut, he created air holes around the bin's bottom. He grabbed his flint and magnesium lighter. In an impressively short time, he had a fire going.

"Let's both go and find more logs before it gets too dark," he said. "If they're too wet, we'll break up some of the furniture. Grab a bucket and go to the lake for some water as well."

"Yes sir!" said Jane, with a mock salute as she went off to do Jay's bidding.

Darkness descended early in the Winter evening. They had water boiling and the prospect of a warm MRE meal on its way. It was hot and tasted of something Jane couldn't immediately identify. However, it filled her up and brightened her mood. She fired up the satellite phone and finally built up the courage to call Jerome, the head coyote who was expecting to receive her and the 'goods' in Memphis.

"Jerome," she said. "Jane here. Just checking in to see what happens next. I'm near Memphis. I'll be there tomorrow."

"I was wondering where you'd got to." Jerome had an intimidating voice Jane feared and loathed. He had run and dictated her life for the past twelve months. She hated him with a vengeance, though she couldn't show it. He didn't waste any time getting to the point.

"You got the goods?"

"Yes."

"How many?"

"Eight."

"Eight? Good girl," he purred. "That makes me happy, very happy. Maybe you will be seeing the husband and the boy soon after all."

"You promised me. Once I'd delivered, I'd be free to go and meet my family. Promise me you'll keep your word?" Jane fought to hide the emotion in her voice. She tried to sound assertive, but knew he would always have the upper hand until she was reunited with her family. And honor didn't figure too highly in the coyote's attitude to doing business.

"Don't panic girlie," he said condescendingly. "Once we've seen the goods and got their money, you'll find out where your family is. When can you get them here?"

"Tomorrow."

"I'm out of town. My two assistants, Jordan and Rachel, will meet you at the Sluice Gate Bar on the docks. Be there at noon tomorrow. If you don't show, the deal's off. Remember to tell your people—it's five-thousand each, cash, gold, or diamonds. Have they got that with them?"

"As far as I know."

"They better have." Jerome hung up.

"Everything alright?" Jay asked as Jane slumped to the floor, staring at the silent phone. "All going to plan?"

"As well as a plan can go when the ass hole you're dealing with would slit his mother's throat if there was a profit in it."

CHAPTER 30

After the conversation with Jane, Roger pulled Pat aside for a private update.

"Jane and Jay are hiding out near Millington," he said. "They're okay. She's just spoken to her contact, a guy called Jerome. He's not going to be around so we're meeting his sidekicks tomorrow instead. A couple named Rachel and Jordan, around noon at the Sluice Gate Bar. So far, so good. Mind you that's the easy bit."

As they finished talking Pastor Michael arrived accompanied by a tall, heavily-built young man sporting a bushy beard and cowboy hat. The sleeves on his shirt could barely contain the impressive biceps bulging underneath. He walked with a lumbering gate two steps behind the Pastor. They made for an incongruous pair. The Pastor was no more than 5' 6", balding, and slightly stooped as though he had the weight of the world on his shoulders. Dressed simply in black, he bore the look of permanent sadness, a face that had seen too much suffering in its lifetime.

"Good evening, everyone," Pastor Michael said. "Thanks for the invitation to dinner. I hope you don't mind—I brought my son, Damian. He acts as my bodyguard and advisor."

Roger could see why. At over 6'5" and weighing close to three-hundred pounds, no one would pick an argument with this mobile mountain. Though, as he eased himself down into a chair by the fire, his easy-going demeanor and a smile that beamed through his beard made him seem anything but threatening.

As the group talked, the Pastor and his son began asking questions. Over their meal of heated MRE's Roger, Pat, and the others took turns to describe French Creek and their experiences since the Collapse.

Pat asked what Memphis had been like since the Collapse. The Pastor paused, stopped eating and stared thoughtfully into the fire. He paused for a few moments to gather the painful memories, and to control his emotions. When he finally replied his voice was barely above a whisper.

"It was a scene from Hades. God had forsaken this city. The very worst of mans' vices were to be seen once the government could no longer impose law, order, or provide food, and supplies. People faced with the worst choices often make the worst decisions, and so many did here in Memphis. The ill and infirm were left to fend for themselves. Most died. The strongest took control using unspeakable violence to achieve their evil ends."

He paused again, collecting himself. "My wife and I did our best to comfort the injured, sick and homeless, but we were overwhelmed. Not just by the numbers of dispossessed, but the lack of food and basic provisions needed to look after them. For over a year, it was as though the Devil himself had arrived from hell to take charge. Eventually, the thugs and their violence went away. People left for the countryside to survive outside the city. Then the smugglers and coyotes established their own brutal form of law and order."

Roger quietly interjected, "What happened to your wife, if I may ask?"

"She succumbed to an unknown virus and passed away two years ago. I was desolate for months. But my son and I had work to do, so we carried on offering what succor and support we could to our community as my wife would have wished."

"I am so sorry for your loss," Roger said. "You say the smugglers and coyotes are serving as some kind of quasi-police force?" He was keen to get some more background on the people he was due to meet tomorrow.

"Describing them as a police force may be putting it too strongly," the Pastor suggested. "It was in their interest that Memphis became a relatively safe place. After all, they want people coming here to cross to the West. If those people think they'll get robbed, injured, or even murdered by coming here…well, it's not good for business. With their connections in the West, they have a reasonable supply of food and other essentials that they exchange to local gangs who keep the peace. It's a warped setup, though it seems to work."

"That's a pretty screwed-up arrangement," Pat agreed.

For a few moments, no one said anything. Damian came back with an armful of wood and threw it on the flames, sending fireworks of sparks into the air, temporarily illuminating the scene around them. Only Roger, Pat, Landy, Pastor Michael, and Damian were now part of the discussion. The others had drifted off to their sleeping bags, their minds full of what trials tomorrow might bring.

Eventually, Damian asked the inevitable question. "So what brings you to Memphis? Hell on Earth, as I describe it. I'm sure it's not the weather or the scenery?"

Roger looked at Pat. Should he lie? Or did he trust these people enough to reveal the real reason they were sitting in a grimy lock-up in a city looking like a set for a post-apocalyptic movie? Roger's sixth sense told him he had little to lose by being honest. He explained why they were in Memphis. He did not reveal their plans for getting the group across the Mississippi, let alone anything about Jay, Jane, and the ultralight.

When he'd finished, the Pastor gave a slight, despairing shake of his head.

"We have heard of these particular coyotes. They are evil, dangerous, untrustworthy people, even by the abysmal standards the world has sunk to. I fear your son and the others will either be killed as they cross or suffer a terrible fate if they even get to the West."

"We don't have an alternative," Roger said, sensing that the Pastor might have a suggestion. While he was cautiously optimistic their plans would work, he was open to any other option. He still didn't mention Jane and her particular agenda.

With an avuncular tone, the Pastor replied thoughtfully, "There's always an alternative, my son. Maybe we could help each other and increase your chance of success as well? Everything is a risk with these coyotes, however we also have contacts across the river who are helping us."

The Pastor paused. "Before I propose anything, can you tell me the whole story of why you're here and what you intend to do? Something tells me you're not being completely forthright. I can't blame you for your mistrust. However, if you want us to work together, I need to know everything."

Roger looked at Pat, who shrugged. Landy, who had kept silent, encouraged his father. "Tell them everything, Dad. I reckon we need all the help we can get."

"Let's top up the coffee first," Roger suggested. Then he started; he explained about Jane's family detained in a small town in the West. The plan was for Jay and Jane to be on standby north of Memphis while Roger presented the group to the coyotes. He would ask them to honor their commitment and tell him where Jane's family was in Arkansas. If they did, Jay would fly them there, and Jane and her family would be united without any problem.

Meanwhile, Roger and his group of travelers would board the boat with concealed weapons, hijack it, then take it upriver where they could get away from the heavily-fortified areas. Jay and Jane were making reconnaissance flights up and down the river to find spots that might facilitate such a landing. They knew it wouldn't be easy, as the whole Western bank was guarded, patrolled, or had extensive electronic surveillance. But they heard the guards were getting lax and careless. The trick was to find those places. Roger expected to have a shortlist of such places within hours.

If the coyotes refused to reveal where Jane's family was, then they would fly over to Marion in Arkansas and try to find them.

Pastor Michael and Damian listened patiently while Roger, with additional information provided by Pat, laid out their plan of action. When they stopped, the Pastor looked concerned. He spelled out the problems as he saw them.

"You realize you'll be thoroughly searched before getting on the boat? How are you going to smuggle the weapons onboard?

Even if you do, what makes you think you will be able to overpower the coyotes? They are well-armed. Even if you do succeed and your friends in the ultralight find an unguarded landing point, what are you going to do once you land? The police are always on the look-out for undocumented arrivals. Get caught and it's a year in jail before being sent back to the East side."

"We're ex-military," Pat interrupted, feeling aggrieved that their plan was being so quickly torn apart. "We know how to handle ourselves."

Damian brushed aside Pat's show of bravado, "These smugglers have seen and dealt with military types before. You'll probably be zip-tied during the crossing to prevent any trouble. I can see what you're trying to do—the ultralight is certainly helpful—nevertheless I think your chances of success are very, very slim."

Roger stood up, mustering confidence he didn't feel. "I don't see we have a choice or many alternatives. We've come this far. We have to give it a try. There's too much at stake to go back. I know this plan has more holes in it than a Kentucky road sign, but with what we know, it's the best we could do. I appreciate your thoughts. Lacking any alternatives we'll run with it. Thanks again, for your time and hospitality. I'm off to sleep. Big day tomorrow."

He grabbed his sleeping roll and headed off to a far corner, annoyed his plans had been dismissed so casually. He tried to make himself comfortable, hoping sleep would overcome his worries. Instead, he began to doubt his abilities for the first time in many years. Maybe this whole idea was too full of holes to succeed? How could he forgive himself if anyone lost their lives, let alone Landy? He cursed the Collapse, the causes of it, the never-ending fight for survival that resulted from it. He was weary, tired of the struggle that had no end in sight. Maybe this could be his final swan song, successful or not, going down fighting with his fellow warriors?

With fatalistic resignation setting in, a strange comfort came over him. Damn the consequences; no more wavering, no more ifs and buts. He would do his best and hope to God it worked. If not, well, worry about that at the time. Within minutes Roger fell asleep content he was doing the right thing.

He woke suddenly with Pat shaking his shoulder. Excitement in his voice Pat whispered, "I need to talk to you, It's urgent." Roger struggled to process what was happening through the fog of his interrupted sleep.

"What's the time? Time to leave already?"

"No," Pat said. "I have some very interesting news. Come to the fire. Grab a coffee."

Roger stumbled across sleeping bodies as he made his way to the fire, surprised to see Damian in the same place he had left him hours earlier.

Pat handed him a steaming and extremely strong cup of coffee. They both sat down, facing Damian.

"What's the goddamn urgency?" Roger demanded grumpily. His attitude was frosty but the mug of coffee warmed him against the early morning chill.

Pat started to talk, barely concealing the excitement in his voice. "After you went to sleep last night, the Pastor, Damian, and I sat up talking. A few surprising things came out of the conversation... Maybe it's best if Damian explains."

Damian's quiet voice took over the conversation. He got straight to the point.

"I have some knowledge that could be of help to you—and us. For the last two years, my father and I have been smuggling in Bibles, food, ammunition, and supplies to help our community survive. Normally, I and a couple of friends go across to get what we need and come back. After all this time we know the unguarded places on the West bank, or where the patrols can be bribed to look the other way for a few hours."

Roger tried to control his surprise and excitement. "So, can you help us get across? What do you want in return?"

"We're not in this for profit. However, our funds are running precariously low. Most of our supplies are donated by friends in the West. Some we have to buy. What I'm suggesting is that whatever you were going to pay the smugglers—give us half instead. For that, we will take your group across, put them in touch with our church over there. They have a safe house where we normally store our supplies. It would only be for a day or two, then they would be on their own."

As Damian outlined his plan in more detail, Roger and Pat listened with a sense of excitement and relief. Maybe, just maybe, there was a safer alternative to using the coyotes?

"We haven't shipped people across before," Damian admitted, "My father is contacting the church by walkie-talkie to confirm if they can help. He should be back soon. We want to help your friends in the ultralight and their efforts to locate the lady's family. Give us a day or two, and we might be able to find them—especially if her husband is in the police force. In truth I'm not guaranteeing anything. We will try our best."

Pat turned to Roger. "What do you think?"

"This has a lot more going for it than our original course of action," Roger admitted. He reached over to shake Damian's hand, "You are a real Godsend. Let's make this work."

Roger suggested they get the rest of the group up to speed with the new plan.

CHAPTER 31

Jay and Jane awoke to another cold morning. The snow and ice had barely begun to melt. Jay managed to get the fire going again. Jane put a pot of water on for coffee. Breakfast was another MRE, euphemistically described as "bacon, eggs, and sausage stew."

"We need to get flying soon, see if we can spot any likely landing areas on the West bank," said Jay, as he washed down the last of his breakfast with a gulp of coffee.

He left Jane to tidy up as he went to check on the ultralight. Jane busied herself, cleaning their living area and packing her gear in case they needed to make a quick getaway. She left Jay's mess for him; she was not his housemaid. After a while, Jane realized she hadn't heard the ultralight's engine start. Looking outside, she saw Jay on all fours, crawling back, painfully, slowly towards the cabin. She ran to him, calling "What's happened? Are you badly hurt?". She knelt down beside him in the snow, ignoring the freezing cold on her knees and legs.

She caught a few struggling words. "Fell…Broken something…My arm I think...be careful it's very dangerous."

"No kidding? Christ, Jay, let's get you back inside and look at that arm." Gingerly, she helped him to his feet, trying to keep upright on the ice as they inched their way back to the cabin,

Once inside, she stoked the fire, put more water on to boil, and made Jay lie down while she looked at his right arm.

"This is going to hurt," she said. "I need to take your coat off and roll up your sleeve so I can see what the damage is."

"Get my flask out of my backpack," Jay said. "I have some brandy in there. Brought it along in case of emergencies. Now seems like a good time for a shot."

Jane dug the small container from the bottom of his backpack. She noticed an engraving on the side:

To my beloved husband on our 15th wedding anniversary, January 10th 2019

She handed it to Jay without comment. He took a slug, hoping to dull the pain.

If it was supposed to act as an analgesic, it didn't. Despite his best efforts, the pain remained excruciating as Jane cut her way through to his arm. Jane saw where the fracture was—below his right elbow. She was relieved to see no bones poking through the skin. It was a clean break as best she could tell. But without an X-ray, she had no idea if the bones had realigned themselves or if it would need an operation to do the job properly.

"I suggest you drink the rest of that," she said. "I'm going to try and reset it as best I can. This is going to really hurt."

"Gimme a second to chug this down and then just do it." In two swallows the flask was empty.

As Jane gripped his arm to reset the bones Jay howled in pain and then passed out. Doing so made it easier for her to maneuver the bones in his broken arm as best she could without an X-Ray. Feeling his arm, she guessed the two bones were roughly where they should be. She went to the pile of wood they used for the fire and found two pieces to act as splints. She bandaged Jay's arm tightly with some ripped-up towels.

Later, when Jay came round, Jane gave him a drink of water and three of her precious Tylenol.

"Where the hell did you find these?" Jay asked groggily, gratefully swallowing the painkillers.

"Helen brought them back from the Barter Fair. She gave me and Roger a few in case we needed them. Good she did, otherwise you'd be in agony."

"What makes you think I'm not?" said Jay, grimacing as he tried to get up.

"Whoa there," Jane said. "Just take it easy. Let the drugs do their job."

"We can't stay here any longer Jane. We're supposed to be scouting up the Mississippi for landing areas."

"That'll have to wait," Jane ordered.

Jay collapsed back onto the floor and stared at the ceiling, seemingly lost in thought or on the verge of sleep, Jane couldn't tell. After a few minutes, he turned to her and announced. "If I can't fly it, you'll have to."

"Me? Do you want to break your neck as well as your arm?" Jane scoffed at his suggestion. "I have no clue how to fly a kite, let alone that thing."

Mustering what patience he had as the pain pierced his arm, he explained. "We have no choice. Time's of the essence. We have to get up there and report back to Roger before he sees the coyotes. You've sat behind and watched me fly it; now I'll sit behind you and tell you how to do it. It's not that difficult—we have to make it happen."

"You have more faith in me than I do."

"No," Jay argued back, "I have a lot of faith in me to tell you how to do it. You'll get the hang of it. Give me an hour or two to get my act together, then we'll get it out of the shed, and I can start going over the basics. Then you can take a test flight."

Jane proved to be a quick learner. After an hour of theory on the ground she took her first flight. It was a little hair-raising, especially when landing on the ice-covered car lot. Then they did it again, and again. Jay bellowed instructions in her ear on how to climb, bank, control the throttle, and most difficult of all, set up the ultralight for a safe landing. They continued until the pain in Jay's arm became so unbearable he had to stop.

As they fell back into the cabin, cold and exhausted, Jay had to admit—Jane had done a good job.

"Don't sound so surprised," Jane replied, sounding offended.

"Don't get too ahead of yourself," Jay warned. "You haven't had to fly in bad weather, or at night, or land in the middle of a muddy field. Hey, that's for another day. Let's get some coffee going, have something to eat, and call Roger."

The call with Roger left them pleasantly shell shocked. He had delivered the news about the Pastor's involvement and the subsequent change of plans. They'd no longer need to fly up and down the Mississippi to find a safe crossing place. They would be staying where they were for a day or two, using it as a base to fly to wherever her family were-and back.

"This might prove easier than we expected," Jay said, relieved, painfully easing his thin frame onto the floor. "Give you a bit more time for some flying lessons. Any chance of a couple more Tylenol? My arm's killing me."

Jane rummaged in her kit and handed over two pills. Jay tried to get his arm in the most comfortable position as he lay down. Soon, he was asleep, allowing Jane to sit back, brew up some more coffee, and think. Things had certainly changed in the last twenty-four hours. Now, she was fractionally more optimistic that after twelve months she might finally get to see her family.

Her optimism was a little premature.

CHAPTER 32

Roger and Pat were heading to the meeting with Jordan and Rachel down at the docks. The day was a mean one with a cutting wind that went straight through their sheepskin jackets. The sky was a dull gray, not a patch of blue anywhere. Snow threatened, or rain if the temperature rose a little. The two riders ignored the elements as they walked their horses through the deserted streets of Memphis, mentally preparing themselves for what lay ahead. Occupied houses glowed with dull lights from candles or stoves. It must be a miserable existence, thought Roger. What does the future hold for these poor people? Five years after the Collapse and they aren't even close to getting back to normality. While just a few miles to the West was a lifestyle these people could only dream about.

How long will it take for the government to finally start regenerating the Eastern half of the country and rescue cities like Memphis from the pits of their current existence? Roger pondered. Surely they had the resources now? After five years? What was the delay? Or maybe, he thought, cynically, there wasn't the willpower or the money to take on such a momentous task.

"We're here, boss." Pat interrupted Roger's thoughts. He refocused on the job at hand. How to deal with these coyotes and get as much information as he could about Jane's family while using his group as leverage in the bargaining process. And how would they react when they discovered there was a delay?

As they entered Greenbelt Park, it was still morning. The noisy revelers they'd seen during their last visit were absent, making for safer passage to the bar where they were to meet the coyotes. Thankfully, no gunshots or fights broke out in the streets. Just a few drunken, homeless people asleep under sodden blankets and ripped tarps.

They stopped their horses in front of the Sluice Gate Bar. It was a shabby building, paint peeling off the brickwork. It had no windows, just a solid looking wooden door with bullet holes no doubt put there by some drunk customer. As if on cue as they dismounted, the door burst open and a woman unceremoniously dumped a man into the muddy street. He shouted an obscenity and staggered off.

"Same to you, asshole," she bellowed back, then turned her attention to Roger and Pat.

"Yes?" she demanded.

"Hi, we're looking for Rachel or Jordan," replied Pat.

"I'm Jordan. What do you want? Make it quick. I've got a bar to get ready for the lunchtime crowd."

"We were due to meet about a group of… travelers." Pat explained, not sure how forthcoming he should be in public.

"I was told to expect Jane," Jordan said. "Where's she at?"

"Can we come inside, we'll explain everything," Roger said, moving towards the door. "Is Rachel here as well? It would be good to talk to both of you at the same time. I think you'll want to hear what we have to say about Jane and the group."

Jordan motioned them to a booth at the back of the bar and asked if they wanted anything to drink.

"Two beers would be good, thanks," answered Pat, taking a seat so he could see the whole room

As they nursed their beers they appraised the surroundings. The room stank of stale tobacco, food and beer. Helpfully, the lighting was on full, allowing, Pat assumed, for cleaning up last night's debris. They could hear the hum of a generator providing the power. No shortage of gas here. As they took stock of the room, noting all the exits, the bare lighting showed the Sluice Gate for what it was—a rundown warehouse. The bar itself was made of pallets. Cobbled-together scraps of wood formed a countertop, behind which was a surprisingly good selection of beer and liquor, with brand names Roger and Pat had almost forgotten: Budweiser, Skol, Heineken, Johnnie Walker, Booth's Gin and numerous others. A selection worthy of pre-Collapse times. Obviously, there was a thriving trade across the Mississippi that kept the establishment well-stocked.

The tables and chairs were a collection of poorly made furniture, most of which in normal times would end up in a dumpster. It was a depressing place. Despite that it still had a drab, cozy familiarity that took Roger back to his days in the army. It reminded him of the dive bars he frequented in the less salubrious parts of the world he had visited. Dreary, dirty bars that somehow offered safety, companionship, and a place to relax. They had nearly finished their first cold beer (a pleasure they were savoring) when Jordan re-appeared from behind the bar.

She took her time reaching them, as she shouted instructions to the staff and organized the cleaning. Jordan was all business, brusque and to the point with everyone she spoke to. She was a striking woman, probably in her mid-thirties, her height further accentuated by the crocodile skin cowboy boots on her feet. Dressed head to toe in denim, she looked like a 1980s ad for Levi. Her long blonde hair was tied back into a ponytail. She grabbed a bottle of beer and strode over to the booth where Roger and Pat waited.

"Rachel's out back," Jordan said. "She'll be here in a minute. But you can start by giving me an explanation that proves you're not wasting our time. I don't have to tell you the consequences if Jane doesn't deliver the goods."

Keeping his voice calm, Roger replied, "We're well aware, thank you. That's why we're here. Jane doesn't trust you and your boss to deliver up her husband and son. She thinks you'll just take the money and our group and leave her with nothing. We've proved to you we're serious by being here. Now give us some proof you'll keep your end of the deal."

Jordan looked at Roger, surprised he was playing hardball with her. He was in her bar with her people all around him. Not, she thought, a position of great negotiating strength.

She took a swig from her beer. "Guess you'll just have to trust us, won't you? Not sure you've got much leverage here."

"I have no reason to trust you," Roger said. "And that's where you're wrong. We have more leverage than you can imagine. You won't want to put us in a position where we have to use it." Roger hoped his bravado would be enough to make her think twice before getting up and walking away. At that moment the door beside the bar swung open and a mirror image of Jordan walked across the room towards them. Rachel was Jordan's twin sister—same build, but with short dark hair, and without the proclivity for denim. Instead, she wore overalls.

"This here is Roger and Pat," Jordan said by way of introduction. "Seems like they're here to bargain on Jane's behalf. They claim they can make life difficult for us if we're not helpful." Jordan's sarcasm wasn't lost on them. They waited to see what Rachel would say.

"Daddy doesn't negotiate with travelers, does he Jordan?" Rachel looked at her sister, then back at Roger and Pat.

Jordan leant over the booth table and snarled a warning to the men, "I don't give a fuck whatever it is you're threatening. We had a deal with Jane. Bring us the goods then we'll tell her where her hubby and son are. Do that everyone lives happily ever after. Don't and it'll end in tears and it won't be ours. Stop jerking us around. Bring them here by this evening or the deal's off."

"Jerome is your father?" asked Pat, unable to keep the surprise out of his voice.

"Spot on, soldier," Rachel said. "You don't want him to find out Jane is fucking us around. You've got until the end of the day." She pulled a Glock from behind her back. She didn't point it at Roger or Pat but left it hanging by her side. "Just remember we have eyes and ears all over this city. We'll find out where you are, so make sure you deliver. Otherwise..." She raised the pistol and leveled it at Roger's head.

Roger tried to hold his temper. "Lady, your guns don't scare me. I've had more pointed at me than you've had hot dinners. After five years in Afghanistan, you're just kids with big toys. Secondly, you wouldn't want the group here at the moment anyway. So stop pointing guns at me. I'm not impressed."

"And why wouldn't we want our travelers here?" Rachel asked, ignoring Roger's slap down.

"Because three of them have the flu, Jane included," Pat explained, "If you want to risk catching it or giving it to anyone they meet, just say so. I'd be delighted to spread some pain and illness around this shit hole." Pat aimed his comment at Rachel, not bothering to conceal the disgust in his voice.

"Are you serious?" asked Jordan.

"As a pandemic. That's why we need another two or three days to make sure they're over it. We're here so you know Jane's not messing around. She wants to keep her side of the deal. Believe me, we're not here through choice. The group is only an hour's ride away. We can get them to you quickly once they are in the clear. Up to you. Take the risk now or wait 72 hours?"

Jordan looked at Rachel who nodded her head. She hesitated for a moment, "OK. You've got 72 hours. Daddy will be back by then, and he won't take any more bullshit delays, I can promise you that. Now finish your beers and get the fuck out of our bar." With that, Jordan and Rachel turned and left through one of the doors next to the bar.

Seconds later, the two women re-emerged. Rachel was now pointing a handgun directly at Roger, and Jordan had a sawn-off shotgun aimed at Pat.

"We've had second thoughts," Rachel said. "We're not convinced you're being straight with us. We need a little more insurance that you'll be back. So one of you will stay here until everything goes to plan."

"Don't even think about reaching for your guns," Jordan instructed as Pat moved his hands below the table. "We have back up." Jordan nodded towards the door where two men had appeared, also armed with shotguns. Roger and Pat knew they had no chance of shooting their way out. They rested their hands on the table to show they had no intention of trying anything suicidal.

Jordan nodded at one of the men. "Alfie here will relieve you of your weapons. Roger, you can go. Pat can stay and take advantage of our hospitality. We'll see you in three days."

Pat and Roger's guns were taken by Alfie, who threw them behind the bar. Roger moved slowly towards the door.

While he doubted threats would impress them, he couldn't resist a last word as he left, "Nothing better happen to Pat. If it does, you won't live to regret it. It will not end well for you."

Pat remained seated with an impassive look on his face and waved to Roger, "I'll be fine," Pat said, "Don't worry about me."

"It's entirely up to you if you'll see him again," Rachel answered. "Come back with the group, and it will all end hunky dory. Now get the fuck out of here and make sure you're back soon. Or…" She put the gun to Pat's temple and pretended to pull the trigger.

Roger slammed the bar door behind him. His anger and frustration made him urge his horse into a canter. His mind was reeling at the unexpected turn of events. They had walked into a trap, now he had one further complication to sort out.

The miserable weather and the dreary surroundings matched his depressed mood as he plodded back through the remains of this once great city. Known throughout the world for its music and culture, it now looked more like Aleppo in Syria or parts of Iraq after they had been bombed to smithereens. The silence was only broken by the echoes of his horses' hooves on the broken asphalt. Roger's mind was in overdrive, trying to untangle the complex web of problems this mission kept throwing at him.

CHAPTER 33

It was barely light when Jane heard the satellite phone ring. She grabbed it from her bag and went outside for better reception. Roger's voice came through tinny, faint, but clear enough to hear.

He avoided any preamble, knowing that both phones had a limited battery life and solar charging was slow-going.

"We met Jordan and Rachel," he said. "Told them you had the flu, that we needed another 72 hours to make sure you're in the clear. The good news is they agreed. The bad news is they've taken Pat hostage to make sure we turn up with you and the group. No news on your husband either. We'll know more later today."

"The bitches," Jane said. "I should have guessed they would try a stunt like that. What are you going to do now?"

"We'll figure out some way to extract him. I'm seeing Pastor Michael and his son in a few minutes. Maybe we can hatch some plan between us. Leave it with me. It's a distraction we don't need. We should have seen this coming. How's Jay, by the way?"

"He hasn't woken up yet," Jane said. "I gave him a few Tylenol, so he shouldn't be in too much pain. We did some flying lessons yesterday. I can just about handle that contraption." As Jane spoke, she heard the distant sound of shots and horses cantering through the woods on the far side of the lake.

"Roger, I gotta go," she said. "I think we may have company."

She switched off the satellite phone, collapsed the long antenna, and raced back into the cabin. Once inside, she grabbed the rifle, checked it was loaded, and ducked below the window. Carefully, she looked out across the lake to see three horseback riders coming from the woods. Jane estimated they were probably two hundred yards from the cabin. They would have to make their way around the lake to reach her, though it would only take a few minutes on horseback.

Jane grabbed Jay's binoculars to get a better look at the riders who were now looking in her direction. There were two women and a young man. They seemed an unlikely group to start trouble, but like the rest of the country, everybody was always on the lookout for free food and strangers to steal from. Thankfully, the fire they lit the night before had gone out. There was no smoke to give them away. Jane knew the cabin would be easy to see, though there was no reason for them to come this way except out of curiosity.

Jane heard Jay stir. He'd be of no use firing a weapon; his broken arm made that impossible. It would be all down to her. She waited until his eyes opened and quickly explained about the visitors.

"What are they doing now?" Jay asked.

Jane picked up the binoculars and peered out the cabin window. "Still just sitting there across the lake. No, wait, they're moving. The guy has a rifle. The women have bows and arrows. How quaint. They're coming around the lake. Shall I take the rifle guy out if they get closer?"

"If they find the ultralight, we're fucked," Jay said bluntly. "I don't want you to kill anyone though… Can we just scare them off? Talk to them? What do you think?"

"I don't want to kill anyone either," agreed Jane. "But if I have to, I will. Let's see what they do next."

The trio trotted around the lake, getting closer with every minute. As far as Jane could tell, the cabin didn't seem to be their objective, they were looking at something in the snow. She put the binoculars down, picked up the rifle, and used the scope to spy on them. They'd stopped; one of the women dismounted and appeared to be studying tracks. Jane knew they weren't theirs— they hadn't strayed that far from the cabin— the group crept closer, following whatever they had spotted in the snow.

Jane moved across the room to one of the broken windows and rested the rifle on the sill, tucking the stock into her shoulder. It gave her a better line of sight. She refocused on the man. He spoke to the woman on the ground while pointing to the cabin. After a further exchange of words, the woman remounted, and they continued toward where Jan and Jay were hiding.

"Go on, turn into the woods, please," Jane whispered to herself, willing them to not come any closer. She really didn't want to take a shot. If needed, Jane was confident she could hit the man. She slowed her breathing, held the rifle firm but not too tightly into her shoulder, and brought the scope's crosshairs to the man's chest. Her finger gradually increased pressure on the trigger. Time seemed to stand still. The horses trod through the snow and ice as the riders kept their eyes fixed on the ground. Any moment, they'd come close enough to the shed and see their footprints.

"Goddamn it, I'm sorry," she whispered, as she pulled the trigger.

The blast of the gun in the confined space of the cabin was ear-splittingly painful. For a second, Jane lost her hearing and balance. She dropped the rifle and looked out of the window. The man clutched his left arm as his frightened horse bucked and spun round in circles. The two women stared at the cabin, but neither came closer. Deciding discretion was the better part of valor, all three turned their horses around and galloped into the woods. Within seconds, they were out of sight. Jane loosed off another shot in their general direction for good measure. They wouldn't come back anytime soon.

"Did you hit one of them?" shouted Jay from the next room.

Jane stood up, slung the rifle over her shoulder. As a nurse, it went against every compassionate bone in her body to deliberately hurt someone. She hoped the man wasn't wounded too badly. These days even a small injury could be fatal. What was done, was done. Now they had to decide what to do and where to go next. There might be retaliation on the way all too soon.

"No, just wounded him," said Jane. "They've gone, though we have to assume they'll be back. We need to pack up and get out of here ASAP."

Jay struggled to his feet, groaning in pain. Jane put her nursing instincts aside and let him get on with it. They needed to move quickly. Jay, with his one good arm, slowly packed up their gear. They needed to get the ultralight out of the shed and ready for flying as soon as possible.

"How long will it take to get the ultralight prepped for takeoff?" Jane asked as she lugged the back pack onto her shoulders.

"With both my arms working, probably fifteen minutes. Who knows with this?" Jay pointed to his arm in the sling.

"We probably don't have much more time than that," Jane offered unhelpfully, "Let's get moving I'm getting tired of being shot at."

They hustled to the shed and maneuvered the ultralight into the car lot. Jay pushed with his back; Jane could see him blanch every time he knocked his arm on something. Soon, the ultralight was lined up on the asphalt. Jane strapped their backpacks behind the co-pilot's seat. Jay ran through the engine checks and set the choke. Jane filled the gas tank and tossed the empty container—they had just ten gallons left.

They still needed to prime the engine by turning the prop. Jane took up her position and went through the now familiar process. Infuriatingly a couple days in the cold meant the engine stubbornly refused to fire, despite Jane's exertions with the propeller. Jay fiddled with the controls, checked the fuel flow, prayed, swore, even kicked the engine as it failed to fire up. They were running out of time. Finally, the reluctant engine sputtered and then roared to life. Jay got in the rear seat; Jane ran round to take the pilot's seat.

"You remember what we did yesterday for takeoff," Jay said. "Check the flap and rudder are working. Then ease the throttle to start taxiing."

The engine noise made it hard for Jane to hear Jay's instructions, even as he leaned forward and shouted in her ear. She taxied the ultralight to the farthest end of the parking lot and turned around, ready for takeoff. There was little wind to help and the trees, just two hundred yards away, were disconcertingly close for Jane's comfort. Never mind, she reassured herself, you've done this before, you can do it again.

"You're ready," Jay bellowed. "When I tap your shoulder, ease back on the flaps and gradually turn on the power."

Jane did as instructed. Within seconds, they reached takeoff speed, and she felt Jay jab her on the shoulder. She pulled the lever controlling the flaps and felt the craft surge into the air. Despite the urgency of the situation, she couldn't help but feel elated and relieved. And not a moment too soon—looking down, she saw a group of ten riders cantering towards the lake.

They looked up and loosed off some shots. One shot found its mark, tearing a hole in the fabric of the wing. It was small, but could easily tear and make the craft unmanageable.

"Just what we need," Jay shouted. "Goddammit!"

He leaned forward and screamed into Jane's ear, "We're going to have to land to repair that. Throttle back to as slow as you can go without stalling. We'll fly low to spot a safe landing area."

Jane gave a thumbs up and decreased her altitude to two hundred feet and fifty miles per hour. They flew North, then West. They could see the Mississippi and steered clear. Eventually, they found a fenced pasture, no more than ten acres, with the nearest house a mile away.

Jay pointed to the landing area, and Jane waved in assent. She circled, lined up the ultralight with the wall at the nearest end of the field. Jay knew most beginners left it too late to touch down, allowing little room for landing and stopping. He urged her to bring the craft down earlier and more steeply than her instinct told her. On her first attempt, she overshot. Jane quickly pulled the control to ascend, turned around, and tried again. At the second attempt, she landed with a bone crunching thud on the frozen field, the ultralight bouncing precariously before settling and juddering to a halt.

"Well, that was fun," Jane said, as she took off her helmet. Jay looked decidedly gray.

"Yes, a real blast. Please don't give up your day job anytime soon."

Jane turned around and gave Jay short shrift, "Hey, I got us down in one piece. Be grateful for large mercies", she climbed out of the seat. "See what you can do about repairs. I need to touch base with Roger."

She grabbed the phone and called Roger. He picked up immediately.

"Long story short, we had to make a quick getaway. We've done an emergency landing to make a repair. I'm not sure what we should do next, or where we should go."

"Oh, Jesus. OK," said Roger, pausing. "Let's hope we can find you a place to stay on the other side of the river while we figure things out on our end?"

"That sounds a great idea, maybe a tad risky?"

"Got any other suggestions?" Roger shot back.

"None that come to mind at the moment. When do you expect to hear from the Pastor?"

"Soon. If his contacts have a place for you to land, you can hole up there until we know more about getting the group across. And getting Pat back."

"Fine," Jane agreed. "Call me back as soon as you know something. We'll hang here as long as we can. We can't keep flying around… haven't got a lot of fuel left. I hope to God we get some news about my family soon."

A note of concern came into Roger's voice, "We're too reliant on the Pastor for my liking. They better come through soon. We're running out of time and options. If we don't figure this out quickly, it's not going to end well, Jane." With that sobering comment, Roger hung up. She stared helplessly at the disconnected phone, wondering if this nightmare would ever end.

CHAPTER 34

It was late in the afternoon when Pastor Michael and Damian arrived back at the camp. Most of the group sat around the fire, making conversation as best they could. Things had taken a turn for the worse with Pat being taken hostage. An unexpected turn of events that put everyone on edge. They watched as their hosts—and possible saviors—approached them from the church. Roger came out of the lock up, his hands covered in oil from cleaning his guns. Wiping them on an old rag, he looked expectantly as the two men stood by the fire, warming their hands. The Pastor looked frazzled and tired. Damian was as impassive as ever. It seemed nothing fazed him, thought Roger.

"I have good news and not so good news," Pastor Michael announced. The good news is that we can get a boat organized for you to cross tomorrow night. Our contacts there have arranged for the guards to be otherwise engaged. Once you're across, you'll be taken to a nearby safe house for a day or two. After that, you will have to make your own way West."

Elation, relief, and excitement lit the faces of everyone there. They were finally leaving the East. A new and better future was within reach. Most importantly, in a way that didn't involve the coyotes. Jenny and Bryanna hugged each other in delight. The others were high fiving, smiling and looking like they had won the lottery.

Damian spoke. "The other piece of good news: one of our contacts has a large farm about twenty miles West of the river.

Your friends with the ultralight can land there. That's the best we can do. Finally, we haven't been able to find any information on her family. We're still working on that."

"Fantastic, that is truly wonderful news, thank you so much," said a delighted Roger. "So what's the bad news?"

"We don't have the resources to help extricate your friend Pat. I'm worried if we get involved, they will retaliate and make our work here even more difficult. We can't risk it." Damian looked genuinely sorry. Roger couldn't blame them for wanting to keep out of trouble with the coyotes and their gangster friends. They were risking enough by helping them cross—though getting handsomely rewarded for doing so. Jerome and his charming daughters wouldn't be able to automatically lay the blame on Damian and the Pastor. There were probably several other groups who could potentially do the same coyote work.

Damian put his hand on Roger's shoulder and quietly asked him if they could discuss the finer details of tomorrow's plans elsewhere? They went to the church and sat on the pews. The church was in poor condition, with many of the windows boarded up. Half the pews were missing. The floor was covered in dust. There was no heating—Roger could see his breath fogging before him.

"We need to discuss payment," Damian said, uncomfortably. "It's not that we don't trust you, but the men who'll be taking you across always demand it upfront. We need to see our share before we go any further. I hope you understand."

"Of course," Roger said. "I have the funds in a mixture of gold, silver, and gems. That should more than cover the cost. If you wait here, I'll get it."

Roger left and returned a few minutes later, carrying a small cloth bag, the banks used to transport cash. He placed it in front of Damian, who opened it and tipped the contents out onto the pew. Small ingots of gold and silver no bigger than matchboxes slid across the polished wood, along with some diamonds and rubies.

"This should cover whatever we owe you. To us in French Creek, they are worthless. We have hoarded them for years, imagining they would be worth something to someone one day. I hope that someone is you." Roger almost whispered, an automatic reaction to being in a church.

Damian picked up and scrutinized the ingots and gems. "These will be more than adequate. My father will be overwhelmed by your generosity." He scooped up the valuables and put them back in the bag. "Now that's done, let's go over what will happen tomorrow and where your friends can land their ultralight."

Later, Roger was on the phone, trying to connect with Jane, annoyingly, there was no answer. Herb should also be brought up to speed and given the information Jane and Jay needed, in case they called him. Herb answered, apprehension in his voice, expecting the worst. Roger succinctly explained what had happened since they had left French Creek almost two weeks ago. Herb listened and took notes on the conversation so he could explain them later to Jane. Roger gave him the precise details on where to land on the farm in Missouri. He then reassured Roger nothing of note or concern had occurred since their departure. On hearing this, Roger was relieved: that's one less thing to worry about. The conversation was over in a few minutes. Roger left Herb strict instructions to keep ringing Jane every hour until he got through. He had enough on his plate to keep playing telephone tag with her.

Back at the campfire, Roger saw Landy chatting with the others. The conversation stopped as Roger approached.

"How's it going," Roger asked. "Excited for tomorrow?"

Landy hesitated. "Yes. Well, I was… I've been thinking, I can't leave you to try and rescue Pat on your own. I want to help." He paused, gathering himself. "Before you tell me it's a stupid idea—"

Roger held up his hand, cutting Landy off mid-sentence, "It is. Don't even think about it son"

Undeterred by his father's negative reaction, he plowed on, "Listen to me Dad, please. You'll stand a better chance of success with the two of us going back for Pat. The Pastor and Damian, have given us a safe way to cross at any time. I can go later. Please let me help," Landy begged. "I know how to handle a gun. More importantly, the coyotes don't know me. Maybe I can get to Pat without them realizing I'm with you."

Roger couldn't deny the logic of the argument; two people did stand a better chance of getting Pat out. Landy being unknown to the coyotes could offer a distinct advantage. On the other hand, he'd finally found a safe way to get his son to the West; now he wanted to put himself in harm's way again. Bloody teenagers, always looking for trouble.

Roger sat down next to Landy, his hand on his shoulder, "I appreciate the offer, son. I really do. My immediate reaction is to say thanks but no thanks. However, let me think about it."

"I'm old enough to look after myself, you know," Landy added, still trying to change his father's mind.

Sure, thought Roger. Just like all those other eighteen-year-old "adults" he'd seen get killed in Afghanistan. They thought they knew how to look after themselves too.

Later that day, as Roger sipped a cup of coffee, he thought long and hard about his son's offer. It had sparked an alternative idea. He called Landy over and signaled for him to sit down.

"I've thought about your offer of help," Roger said. "I'd like to put that on the back burner for now. Your argument that having an unknown asset could help get Pat out, made me think we do need reinforcements. So here's what I want you to do..."

CHAPTER 35

The afternoon drifted into a cold, murky evening. The cloud cover would likely protect Jay and Jane from a frost, nevertheless they were still in for an uncomfortable night. Once they'd landed in the field, a quick walk around the perimeter assured them there were no houses close by. They returned to the ultralight to assess the damage and figure out how to repair it. After close inspection, Jay announced it wasn't too serious. They could do a working repair with some spare canvas and duct tape to cover the hole, then use strong twine to sew it in place.

"It won't hold forever," Jay observed. "We may have to fly slower until we see how it works. If I show you what to do, can you do the repair?"

"Woman's job, eh Jay?" Jane said, half-joking. "Sewing and mending?"

Jay smiled at her cheeky comment, "You're lucky I haven't got you washing my pants too."

Jane replied in mock anger, "In another time, in another place, that comment would get you whacked with a baseball bat. Under the circumstances, you're absolved. Let's get it done."

It was a rare moment of levity in what had been a fraught and dangerous day. Jane cut the canvas patch and set to work. Jay offered mostly unhelpful suggestions over her shoulder.

After an hour, they stood back and admired Jane's handiwork. They offered up a silent prayer for it to hold. The phone beeped and Jane ran to answer it.

"Roger," Jane said. "What's the news?

"It's not Roger. It's Herb. Good to hear your voice again Jane."

Hearing Herb flustered Jane for a second. "I'm—I'm fine, Herb. Did something happen? Are Roger and the rest okay?" A note of concern crept into her voice—or was it embarrassment at the memories hearing Herb stirred up?

"Don't panic," he said calmly. "All's well here. As far as I know, Roger is okay—at least he was when I spoke to him earlier. He said he'd be unable to call you for a while, so he left me with details on where and when to land in Missouri?"

"It's all been a bit scattered here," Jane said, regaining her composure. "Things have changed a bit. The original plan has gone out of the window. I'm still hopeful I'll see my family soon though." She immediately winced at bringing up the subject of her husband to Herb, of all people. It was too late to take it back now.

Herb stayed silent. Jane prayed for him to move past the tactless comment, which, thankfully, he did.

"Can you remember these directions if I read them over to you?"

Jane scribbled the coordinates on the back of the pilot seat, not sure if Jay had the ability to use such information. After another embarrassing silence, they each said hasty, uncomfortable goodbyes.

"We've got our instructions," she said. "They're expecting us tomorrow between seven and eight in the morning. Shit," she paused. "We're actually going over the Mississippi. Have you wondered what it's like over there? We'll finally find out. Christ, I haven't been this excited in years."

Hearing no answer, Jane ducked under the wing, and knelt in front of Jay. He seemed more than asleep—he was passed out. He look like death warmed up. She lifted his arm and unbandaged the wound. It had swelled and turned an ugly purplish color. It was hot to the touch. As hard as she'd tried, it still had gotten infected. She tried to keep calm as she mentally ran through her options, none of which were good. Jane could only re-bandage his arm and make him as comfortable as possible. Then she covered him with a sleeping bag and settled down next to him for what was going to be a long and disagreeable night.

She woke, stiff and cold, when it was barely light. Looking at her trusty movement-operated watch she realized they only had an hour to get the craft ready for takeoff. Just as she strapped in to his seat he opened his eyes.

With a confused look on his face, he asked, "What's happening? What time is it?" He wasn't completely lucid. A fever had started during the night and was making him slightly delirious. Jane tried to explain where they were going.

"We've got directions to the landing strip, and we need to get there within a couple of hours," Jane explained. "I'm gonna need you to stay with me and get the engine running. I can probably manage after that. Can you do that for me?" She stared at him, her face inches from his, willing him to acknowledge her. He was losing the plot and in considerable pain. She hoped he'd do what was needed to get them into the air.

"Take these Tylenol and see if you can manage the controls while I prime the prop." Jane grabbed three pills from her bag and stuffed them in his mouth. He swallowed them with effort, shook his head and tried to focus.

Jane grabbed the propeller and went through the now familiar routine, turning it once, then twice, and finally a third time before it sputtered into life, quickly settling into a smooth and reassuring putter.

Jane jumped into the pilot seat, belted herself in, and grabbed the map. To hell with coordinates. She was going to fly low enough to pick out landmarks, estimate distances with their maps, and hope to God she found the landing strip. She had no choice—Jay had already passed out again, his head lolling helplessly on his chest. She was on her own.

Jane surprised herself at how calm she felt—she was in control and focused, despite the dangers ahead. She increased the engine revs and began to taxi, readying for takeoff. Soon she was airborne and heading West. Her directions were brief and to the point. Fly West for fifty miles, then south for ten. Her destination was Bragg City (a slight exaggeration as it had a population of under two hundred). The inaptly named city was in the middle of vast farms with enormous fields about ten miles West of I-55. Once she'd found the interstate, she'd continue for another four miles South West until she saw a series of parallel canals adjacent to a small lake. According to her directions, immediately to the North would be the landing strip marked with smoke flares. They'd only be lit for a maximum of thirty minutes.

Jane climbed higher to avoid any interest from the guards or authorities along the Mississippi's West bank. The river looked like nothing more than a huge brown smudge, snaking its way from North to South as far as the eye could see. It was difficult to believe it could form such an impenetrable barrier between the two countries—one, thriving; the other, struggling to exist.

A patchy layer of cloud gave Jane all the cover she needed. It was freezing cold at that altitude; Jane knew she couldn't stay at that height for long. She needed to be lower to identify the motorway and lakes below and then see any smoke signals. With the Mississippi disappearing behind her, she began her descent. She flew for several minutes before seeing the black strip of the 1-55 beneath her—with cars and trucks speeding along. It was such an alien sight. She felt a strange rush of anger; how could life be so normal here? How could these people be so indifferent to what life was like just a few miles to the East? Jane stopped herself. There was no point in blaming them no matter how unjust it felt, that wouldn't solve anything. She just had to focus on identifying the landmarks below. Bragg City wasn't difficult to see—it was a collection of houses in the middle of a patchwork of huge brown fields.

Jane checked the compass and headed South West. She saw what looked like a series of canals flowing into a lake surrounded by trees and pasture. She descended to 500 feet as she approached the lake. With a flood of relief, adjacent to the lake she saw wisps of smoke rising lazily from a large field.

That was it! They were expecting her! Jane circled once, lined the plane up and to her delight landed without mishap. She was back in civilization after five long, frightening, miserable years. Overcome with emotion as she came to a halt, she burst into tears, sobbing uncontrollably with relief and happiness. It was all too much—the pent-up fears and frustrations rushed to the surface. She covered her face and wept tears of joy.

Soon, she realized she was no longer alone. Two men and a woman stood by the ultralight, looking at her concern and confusion on their faces.

"You okay, lady?" asked one of the men. "Are you hurt?". He was a short fellow with a bushy beard, grubby blue overalls, and a John Deere hat. "That guy behind you doesn't look too good," he added, pointing at Jay.

"Yes, sorry," Jane blubbered, wiping the tears from her eyes and trying to pull herself together, "Just a bit emotional at being back here after all this time." She slowly composed herself, jumped from the ultralight and turned to face her welcoming committee.

"I'm Jane and this is Jay," she said, pointing to his unresponsive body in the co-pilot seat. "He's in pretty poor condition. I think his arm is infected. You are?"

"I'm Bobby," the man said. "This is my brother, Tony, and his wife, Jamie Lee."

Tony was the polar opposite of Bobby—tall, skinny, with a gaunt face covered with days-old stubble, dressed in what looked like the family uniform of overalls and working boots—minus the John Deere hat. Jamie Lee was a plump woman with dirty blonde hair, probably in her mid-thirties. Her jeans were too tight. Over which she wore a black leather coat against the morning chill.

"Welcome to Missouri," said Jamie Lee. "You look like you could do with a bath, food, and some rest. Your friend looks like he needs a doctor. We'll get you back to the house and hide this thing before anyone gets suspicious."

"I've not heard a better suggestion in years," said Jane, wearily. "Lead the way."

CHAPTER 36

Fortune smiled on the group again, this time courtesy of Damian.

Roger had decided on a risky strategy. Landy would return to Jeff, the former Army officer, and ask for his assistance. Damian, on hearing the plan pulled Roger aside and suggested they go to a storage container down behind the church.

"How far away is this friend of yours?" Damian asked, as he fiddled with a huge padlock on the container's door.

"A good two or three-day ride," Roger said. "That's if Landy doesn't hit any problems. I know that's cutting it close with our 72-hour deadline, but there are no other options. We need back up."

"I thought that might be the case," Damian said. "Would this help?" He pulled the heavy door open to reveal a workshop full of engine parts. A workbench on one side had a large selection of tools and equipment. Propped against it was a motorbike of indeterminate make.

With a note of pride in his voice Damian explained, "I've been working on this for some time. It runs fine. I had to cannibalize parts from Harley's, Honda's, and Suzuki's to make it work, so it looks a bit strange. If your son thinks he can ride this, then it will be a lot quicker than going by horse to get your friend."

Roger looked at Damian, shocked. "This is incredible Damian. I'm sure Landy will get the hang of it. He'll have to—it'll save a valuable couple of days. Do you have enough gas?"

"If you know the right people, you can get a few gallons every now and then. Mainly from people you don't want to mess with. Then everyone assumes you're some kind of gangster when they see you riding and they leave you alone. Kind of win-win. Want to see this baby run?"

Damian powered up the bike. The pop-popping of the engine sounded remarkably like a Harley Davidson. He topped it up with fuel, checked the oil, and rode it to the camp. By the time Roger made it back on foot, an admiring and astonished crowd stood around the bike, interrogating Damian about how he had made it, from what, and a dozen other questions.

Roger drew Landy aside and explained the plan. To get to Jeff's in the time available he was going to take the bike-and get a crash course in how to ride it—now.

While Damian showed Landy how to start and change gears on a powerful 500cc motorbike. Roger dug into his backpack, pulled out an old map of Tennessee, and proceeded to mark the route to Jeff's. It was about 125 miles; he estimated Landy could make it there and back in one day max. This allowed another two days for Jeff to arrive, if he agreed to help. Roger decided to give Landy a personal letter to Jeff asking for his assistance. It wasn't exactly a begging letter, but close enough.

He watched as Landy learned how to handle the large machine, riding around in slow circles with a few initial wobbles. He stopped, dismounted, and cut the engine as Damian gave him more pointers. Landy practiced under Damian's tutoring the rest of the afternoon, eventually moving onto the street to get the feel of the bike at higher speeds. Locals peered out their windows to see what the noise was. One or two ventured outside, talking to Damian about the bike. Obviously, they had seen him before riding it down the street. None asked any questions about Landy or why he was learning to ride it. The less you knew, the less trouble you could get yourself in.

In the early evening, Roger pulled Landy and Damian aside, making sure they were out of earshot of the neighbors.

"You've got another few minutes to practice. Then I want you on your way. I know this is dropping you in the deep end Landy but we don't have much time. Here's a map to Jeff's place and a letter to give him. Keep it well-hidden. It should take you three, four hours to get there taking it easy. If Jeff is willing to help, give him the map so he knows how to find us. Then come straight back."

Bryanna came over unexpectedly and gave a package of food to Landy. "Thought you might need this," she offered generously. "We're all counting on you. Come back safely."

Landy looked terrified and excited at the prospect of making this journey by himself. It would be the first time in years he would actually be alone. He'd have to take care of himself, and make his own decisions. It was a rare slice of independence after the tiny, self-contained world of French Creek. Roger handed him a rifle and some ammunition. A solemn look on his face.

"I pray to God you won't need to use this. But it would be stupid not to take it. Now collect the rest of your stuff and be ready to leave in a half-hour. It'll be dark then."

Landy left as night enveloped the city. With no streetlights, he took care in negotiating the debris that still littered the road. Once out on the interstate, it would be quicker going. Roger had told him to steer clear of any inhabited areas and go West of Nashville to avoid meeting anyone. As the red rear light of the bike disappeared into the gloom and the noise of the engine faded, doubts about sending his son on such an important mission filled Roger's mind with dread. He could have asked one of the others to go, but Landy was the strongest—the one Roger trusted most to get the job done. There were so many risks—mechanical problems, navigation, bandits. After all that, what if Jeff declined to help? Sure, he offered—but did he really mean it? Roger would know for sure soon enough.

Roger reconciled with himself, believing once a decision had been made based on what he knew and what resources he had at his disposal, there could be no second guessing. Thinking like that, nothing ever got done. No one deliberately makes a bad decision, especially when it's a matter of life and death. You use your knowledge, and experience then act accordingly. Prepare for the worst and hope for the best.

Damian, watching Landy ride off, trying to inject a touch of levity into the moment, said, "Thankfully he won't get held up in traffic. Those semis can be dangerous on I-65!"

"Just bandits and murderers instead. I'll take the semis any time." Roger replied curtly then went for a late-night cup of strong coffee, still wondering if he'd regret this whole escapade.

CHAPTER 37

Jane was having a dream. She was in a warm bed with clean sheets and soft pillows, sleeping like a baby..

She slowly opened her eyes and struggled to process where she was. Hell! It wasn't a dream, she was in a comfortable bed—and it felt exquisite. Some dreams do come true she thought. Jane looked at the bedside clock and calculated she had slept for almost eighteen hours. Peaking over the thick comforter, she took in the comfortable, sparsely-decorated room. Yesterday came back to her—the flight, the welcome by Tony, Bobby and Jamie Lee, how they carried Jay into the farmhouse. She remembered eating a delicious breakfast of pancakes, bacon, sausages, and hot coffee before changing into an oversized shirt, falling into a real bed and collapsing into a deep sleep.

Jane swung her legs out of bed and padded to the bathroom. She turned on the shower and took her first hot, long soak in years. She was in heaven washing with beautifully-smelling soap and drying herself with soft fluffy towels. Walking back into the bedroom, she pulled back the drapes and looked across the farmyard. The cars, tractors, and machinery looked new and well-cared for. No aging, rusty vehicles held together with wire and hope. There was a pile of clothes on the chair: jeans, shirt, sweater, and new—new!—underwear. She dressed in a daze of euphoria and ran a brush quickly through her hair. Then headed out to find her generous hosts.

Tony was out feeding the cows. Jamie Lee put on some coffee and popped a couple of bagels in the toaster as Jane arrived in the kitchen. "How you feelin', hon?" she said. "You slept a good one there. We wondered if you were ever gonna wake up!"

"It was bliss. A clean, comfortable bed... It was like lying on clouds of cotton wool." Jane took a cup of steaming coffee and sipped it gently. "I can't thank you enough. I'm so, so grateful. I feel like a new person...glad to be alive. Speaking of which, how's Jay?"

Jamie Lee looked worried, "Not doing too well, unfortunately. We got a doc out, but he thinks the wound isn't the only problem. He says we need to take him to the hospital for some tests. Thinks there's a problem with his kidneys or something. Of course, since he's got no insurance or residency docs, any hospital will start asking questions. They might even report him to immigration."

Jane's fall from her morning high was abrupt. She put down her coffee and asked where Jay was. Jamie Lee pointed to a bedroom off the main living area. She went in quietly so as not to disturb him. Jay was awake, just. He looked dreadful; his skin had a jaundiced color and his eyes a yellowish tinge. It could be hepatitis, thought Jane. But how did he catch that?

"How are you doing, friend?"

"Feel like shit," he groaned. "My arm doesn't hurt too bad, but I have just fuck-all energy. I can barely get up for the bathroom. Seems I've got something else that's messing me up. They don't know what at the moment. How are you?" He struggled to sit up, unsuccessfully. He was so weak he just flopped back onto the pillows.

"I'm fine. Just worried about you," Jane replied. "You need a hospital, but Jamie Lee says that could cause problems. We're considered illegal here. How fucked up is that?"

Jay might have been drained of energy, it didn't stop him from being his usual obstinate self. "Don't let me hold you up. You got things to do. There isn't much of a choice, as I see it. Say I go to a hospital and get better. Then what? Send me back East? Bang me in jail for a few months? Or I die. Great choice, one you shouldn't have to make for me or you. I've got a brother-in-law somewhere in California. Maybe he can get me whatever papers I need. You can't stop here anyway," Jay said, shaking his head. "Go find your family. I'll be fine."

Jane was amazed at Jay's change of attitude. This once self-centered man had now become so considerate and thoughtful. What a transformation! She took his hand. It was warm and clammy. He barely had the energy to squeeze her's back.

"Let me go talk to Jamie Lee and Tony," Jane said. "See if we can't figure something out. Hang in there. Do you need anything?"

"A new arm would be good. Seriously, don't worry, I'll be alright." He said limply, lapsing back into sleep.

Jane went into the kitchen to finish her cup of coffee. She drank it gratefully, still unused to the strong bitter taste. It was a million miles better than she'd had over the last five years. Jamie Lee was on the phone, listening to someone who seemed to be imparting lousy news by the look on her face.

Jane contemplated her next move. She was stuck between two lousy options: stay, help Jay, and possibly be caught by the authorities—or strike out on her own with no support to find her family. She could take the ultralight. While she had made a few successful flights, negotiating solo to another state was a different matter entirely. She needed time to research, get on the internet, find and contact her husband. She had little time, under 48 hours.

Jamie Lee finished her call. "That was Tony," she said, looking serious. "His contact at the police station says the cops had reports about a ultralight flying near here. Immigration has apparently received the information as well. It'll take them a day or two to search all the farms. Tony said he saw you land a few miles away, which will send them in the wrong direction, not sure for how long. They're not as vigilant as they used to be, but they still have to put on a show of doing something."

"I'm guessing my stay here won't last long under those circumstances?" said Jane, hoping Jamie Lee would contradict her with some other plan. That wish was quickly squashed.

"You've got a couple of days, but no more. We can't take the risk of them finding you here. You can maybe fly to some place further away where you might not attract so much attention. Being so close to the border they get suspicious real quicken The question is, what do we do about Jay?"

Jane thought for a few moments. "If I was to fly out, and the people in town saw me leave, wouldn't that take the heat out of their search? Most would assume the plane's a single-seater. We could even remove the rear seat. They'll think I was the only illegal to have landed, that I've flown off someplace else?. Wouldn't they then call off the search then?"

Jamie Lee looked skeptical, then seemed to warm to the idea. "We don't have a lot of choices here. At the moment I can't think of a better one. If we take Jay to the hospital, he'll have to take his chances. We can say we found him by the road... Maybe this could work. Risky, but worth a shot."

"First of all I have to know where I'm going. I need to get in touch with my family... I'm rusty on using the internet. Can you help me get a location for them? I know roughly where my husband is and what he does."

"Honey, you are looking at the internet queen. What else have I got to do in this god forsaken place but play around online? Let's freshen the coffee and start. This should be fun."

Jamie Lee mesmerized Jane as she refined searches on Google, logged onto Facebook, and quickly found the website for the Marion police station. Jane's husband wasn't listed as a staff member. Some cops didn't want their names plastered all over the internet, Jamie Lee reassured her, for fear of reprisals. He didn't have a Facebook or any other social media either. She then went to the website of the local paper, the Marion Observer, and entered his name in the search box. After an agonizing few seconds, a list of articles and stories from the archives came up on the screen, all containing the keyword Davidson. Jamie Lee scrolled down soon finding one containing a brief story about a cop of the same name making an arrest of a local shoplifter two years ago.

"Is that him?" asked Jamie Lee, pointing to a grainy black and white photograph.

"Oh my God," Jane said, holding her hand up to her mouth in shock. "That's David. That's him. He looks so much thinner. But it's him." Jane felt tears welling. She wiped them away with the back of her hand. She stared at the man she hadn't seen for over five years. There he was, alive—at least two years ago.

"It's difficult to be invisible now," Jamie Lee explained. "Your coyote friends may be able to control many things, but a small-town newspaper reporter loves to write stories about people getting arrested. No way of stopping that."

"How far are we from Marion?"

Google Maps had the answer—one hundred miles, no more than a two-hour flight.

Jamie Lee then scouted out some remote landing spots within a few miles of Marion. "I've got a cousin down there," she said. "Let me text her and see if she knows the best place to land unseen. I haven't spoken to her in years. It'll be a strange request out of the blue. Hopefully she can help."

Jamie Lee tapped away on her iPhone and the message swooshed away.

"The internet has really come a long way since I last used it," Jane said. "It's incredible what you can find. That has saved so much time. Now that I know where David is, is there a way to warn him about what's going on?"

"You could just call him at the police station."

Jane had become so used to the lack of telephone access in the East she'd forgotten how easy it was to contact people here in the West. She wracked her mind for the best way to do it, then decided to just pick up the phone and call.

They looked up the number for the Marion Police Station and called on Jamie Lee's iPhone. A cheerful female voice with a strong southern accent answered. Jane breathed deeply. "Is Officer Davidson there, please?'

There was a pause as the receptionist referred to her computer.

"Sorry hon'," the voice came back on the line, "He no longer works here, as of a few days ago, I think. Is there another Officer who can help you?"

Jane stared at the red button on the phone, ended the call without saying another word, and burst into tears.

More coffee, plus a dose of whisky helped Jane steady her nerves. Before deciding what to do next about finding her husband, she realized she hadn't checked in with Roger recently. She found the satellite phone, now fully charged thanks to the electricity at the farm (another novelty!). Roger answered quickly. She explained where she was, Jay's poor health, that she had found and lost her husband. Despite this set back, she intended to keep searching and would, if necessary, fly herself to wherever he might be. Bad news was, she would need to leave her hiding place soon; the authorities were searching for her. It would probably mean leaving Jay behind.

"That's a real shame about Jay," Roger said. "Send him my best. If he ends up in the hands of the authorities, there's not much we can do to help. He knows that. As for your husband's disappearance, it doesn't feel like a coincidence."

He didn't fill her in on the current plan involving Landy and, hopefully Jeff's involvement. "We have to Pat back, find out where your family is, then get our group across to the West side—before the smugglers realize their pay day is not going to materialize."

"Any ideas how to make this work?" Jane said.

"Plenty, but none I'm confident in. You need to keep ahead of the authorities. I don't want to be rescuing you, too. Call that dipshit Jerome and tell him we'll bring the group down tomorrow."

"Sure," Jane said."

"Over and out." Roger cut the call without wishing Jane well, too preoccupied to bother with niceties.

CHAPTER 38

Roger was worried. He tried to quell the panic rising inside him. It had been over twelve hours since Landy left for Jeff's farmhouse. He'd estimated less than a day for the return trip; it was way past that now. Frustratingly, there was nothing he could do but wait. Roger quashed the urge to jump on his horse and head up the interstate. There could be any number of reasons for Landy's delayed return. Roger could think of none that were positive. So he waited and worried.

Late the next day, his worst fears were realized. The sound of horses barreled toward the church. It was Jeff and two friends—but no Landy. Clearly, he had reached Jeff. Something had happened to stop him from returning.

"Where's Landy?" Roger asked abruptly, in his frazzled state, forgetting to welcome his visitors. "He should have been back hours ago."

"Good news and bad news," Jeff replied. "He got to us, in pretty bad shape. He'd been shot twice, in the leg and shoulder. We left him with a doctor friend. She thinks he'll be okay. As we couldn't do much more to help him, and your need was more urgent, we got here as fast as we could. I bought a couple of friends who are pretty good in a scrap. They can shoot straight and take orders."

A string of emotions flooded Roger's mind. Shock, anger, relief, a demand for answers. Roger knew sending Landy had been dangerous, he had rationalized his choice and hoped for the best.

The news he had been injured horrified him, even if he was recovering. That didn't quell the anger Roger aimed at himself for putting his son in harm's way. He saved his real ire for the people who had done it. He asked Jeff, calmly as he could, what happened.

Jeff dismounted and put his arm around Roger's shoulder. They moved away from the others.

"Truth is, I don't really know what occurred," Jeff explained. "It happened just outside of Nashville. He told us he was only a few miles from the farmhouse when he stopped to fuel up. He said a couple of lowlifes came out of nowhere, demanding his bike. He managed to get away, but a couple of shots got him. Thankfully, he was only a half-hour from me. He made it before he lost too much blood. Passed out as he rode up to the front door. Our doctor's pretty confident he'll be okay, though she was insistent that he rest for a few days to get his strength back. Trust me; he's in good hands. The doc's an old medic from the Service. She knows how to treat gunshot wounds."

Roger calmed down, reassured a little that Landy would recover, though still shaken at the news. He didn't like relying on other people for his son's safe-keeping. Under the circumstances he had no choice. Reluctantly, Roger refocused on the present. There were more pressing matters that needed his attention.

He turned to Jeff, now back in 'officer' mode.

"Thank you for coming," Roger said. "And for bringing extra help. Who are these guys?"

"When I offer help, I mean it," Jeff said matter of factly. "Truth be told, this mission beats the hell out of plowing a field. Let me introduce you." He pointed to the two men behind him. "Meet Martin and Ben, both ex-marines, both bored, both good in a fight. They jumped at the chance to see some action and to help a fellow veteran."

Roger apprised the two men. Both looked to have led rough and tough lives. The word "grizzled" came to mind to describe them. Martin had dirty blonde hair, a scruffy beard to match, and faded army fatigues stretched over a muscled body. On his hip, he carried a whopping Magnum .44. in the rifle holster on his horse, an M4 Army-issued rifle. Ben was skinnier with cropped hair and a tattoo on his neck of the American Eagle with a gun in its claws. His choice of firearms were a Glock pistol and every fighter's favorite—an AK 47. Both looked to be in their late 30's, the grime and stubble of their beards making them look older. They were not the kind of guys to annoy, Roger thought. They exuded a potent physical menace, one he'd seen before among seasoned fighters. He was glad they were on his side.

"It's good to meet you both. I can't tell you how much I appreciate you being here to help us." Roger gestured toward the group of travelers behind him. "Let's get you some chow and your horses taken care of. I'll brief you on the situation in thirty."

Martin and Ben gave a couple of casual salutes, dismounted, and led their horses to the stalls.

Later, around the fire, Roger and Damian outlined their plan. They had to time everything so the group got away before Roger went to meet the coyotes and hopefully, extract Pat and Jane's family. Jeff, Martin, and Ben listened carefully, then made a few suggestions. By the end of the evening, Roger felt reasonably confident that most bases had been covered. However, there were still too many moving pieces for his liking. Tomorrow, they will find out just how good their plan was. In the meantime, Damian told the travelers to prepare themselves. They would leave under cover of darkness the next morning.

CHAPTER 39

Pat was philosophical. He had slept in worse places before, but only by choice, usually to keep out of harm's way. Being forced to spend time locked in a dimly lit, damp cellar wasn't too uncomfortable. The atmosphere was drenched with the smell of stale beer, stored there along with other bar supplies. He'd been loosely chained and well-fed. Armed guards arrived every few hours to allow him to use the restroom. Rachel and Jordan occasionally appeared, making sure he was still alive. They both sported machine guns to ensure he didn't try an escape. It wasn't comfortable by any means. For the moment, he didn't feel threatened.

Anyway, escape would cause more problems than it would solve. If the coyotes kept him as leverage, they wouldn't do anything stupid. If he got out, they would consider the deal off and possibly harm Jane's family. He didn't know about the developments with Jane's family or that Roger called in reinforcements. So he bided his time, knowing that Roger would come back for him sooner rather than later. He couldn't begin to guess how he would finesse his release while holding back the news that the group had already gone across the river. Despite his doubts, he had faith in Roger's abilities. He'd never let Pat down before. He knew this time would be no exception.

CHAPTER 40

It was early morning and still pitch black when the group of drowsy travelers readied for departure. They had been awake most of the night. The excitement, fear, and anticipation drove away any possibility of sleep. They stumbled around in the glow from the fire and a few candles, packing their meager belongings into backpacks. Damian warned them only to take the bare minimum.

Roger said his goodbyes. He'd known some of these people for years. He put aside his sorrow at losing friends and instead admired their pluck and determination to leave the safety of French Creek for the unknown promise of a better life in the West. Dick, Dwayne, and Bryan shook his hand, thanking him for everything he'd done for them. Austin hugged Roger, said he couldn't thank him enough for saving his life and giving him a second chance.

Bryanna and Jenny apologized. "We caused you a lot of grief in the beginning," Bryanna admitted. "We can't take it back. It's probably best we're going. French Creek is a great place, but I don't think we'll ever fit in, not after the way we arrived. So thanks for your help and understanding. We'll get out of your hair."

Roger wasn't the type to hold grudges, especially when it came to goodbyes, "Ladies, we live in desperate times. You did what you had to do. I can't forget, but I can forgive. It's understandable at times we have to look after ourselves first and others later. Not always a civilized way to behave, but needs must. I can't hold that against you. I wish you all the best in your new life."

They hugged and joined the rest of the group, who stood in a circle around Damian as he explained what would happen next.

"We're an hour's walk to the dock where our people are waiting. Then a trip upriver to our contacts on the other side. I'm not going to give you too many details. If any of you are caught by the authorities or other gangs, I don't want you giving any useful information away. We leave in five minutes. Double check that you have what you need. Then we'll go."

CHAPTER 41

Jane waited a few hours before calling Jerome to tell him the group would be there tomorrow. She wanted to learn more about her husband's whereabouts. When she asked Jerome, she was stunned.

"I'm on my way to see him right now," Jerome said. "I'll be back at the bar in a few hours. I expect to see him there. I figured getting a close-up might keep you from doing something stupid. And we have an extra layer of protection—your man Pat is safe and secure with us as well. It'll be quite the little gathering, won't it?"

"Where's my son?" Jane demanded.

"Oh, sorry. Did I forget to mention him?" Jerome said casually, "He's with his dad, in the firing line. I'm hoping we'll all have a happy ending here tomorrow, don't you?"

After five years of groveling to this overconfident bully, Jane could no longer contain her frustration and anger.

"You're a complete fucking asshole, you know that?" she yelled. "I'm going to do what I've promised. But if anything—anything—happens to my family, I will find you and kill you. Understand? If I can't find you, I'll go after your daughters. You've pushed me around long enough. Don't underestimate me, Jerome. You'll regret it."

After a brief pause, Jerome answered her outburst with an infuriatingly condescending tone. "The lady's grown some balls finally," he laughed. "Too late, I think. You'll do precisely what I say because you have no choice. You can threaten me all you like, but Memphis is my town. I can have you snuffed out before you cross the street. So don't threaten me. Bigger and better people than you have and they're no longer around to brag about it. So shut the fuck up, do as I say, and we all might get what we want out of this."

Then Jerome hung up, leaving Jane breathless and shaking. He got in the last word this time—but not for long.

Eventually, she pulled herself together and went back into the kitchen, where Jamie Lee prepared a mouthwateringly aromatic meal of fried chicken and cornbread. Even in Jane's fraught state of mind, the smell took her back to her mother's kitchen, comforting and calming her. She wondered why smells seemed to bring back more memories than any other sense. After five years of makeshift meals without any spices or taste, the smells were all the more noticeable. Shaking off her melancholy, she expressed her delight at the prospect of such a tasty meal.

"Wow, that smells amazing. I can't wait to try some good ol' fashioned fried chicken. Anything I can do to help?"

"I think it's you that needs some help, sister," Jamie Lee said. "I'm guessing that phone call didn't go the way you intended?"

"That obvious huh? You're right. That grade A asshole Jerome says he has my husband and son with him in Memphis. Added security, so the deal goes through. They'll be right in the line of fire when he learns the wheels have fallen off his very lucrative deal. I don't know what to do. Roger will have to figure it out.

Just when I thought I'd found him..." Jane slumped at the kitchen table, head in her hands.

If she expected any sympathy from Jamie Lee, none was forthcoming.

"That's a grand ole pity party you got going there girl. Feeling sorry won't get it done, now will it? Let's figure out what you can do. There's always an option. You've come too far to give up now."

Jane was initially shocked at Jamie Lee's unsympathetic attitude, though after a minute it did have the desired effect of shaking her out of her misery.

She decided that attack was the best form of defense. Sitting here feeling sorry for herself would achieve nothing. The obvious first step would be getting to Memphis.

"How easy is it to get from here to Memphis? And then getting across back East?"

"Not too difficult from what I understand and hear. All the security is aimed at people coming this way, not going back to the boondocks," Jamie Lee answered, dropping more chicken into the boiling fat. "Tony might know more. He'll be back soon for supper. We can ask him then."

The three of them discussed the options over dinner. Tony called a couple of connected friends; he discovered for a fee, Jane could hop a ride on one of the boats smuggling goods to the East. They decided it was better and safer to drive rather than fly to Memphis. Tony agreed to take her to meet his friend's contact, Wesley, in West Memphis. He would be leaving at three in the morning to cross the Mississippi. It would cost her $500. Jane offered the ultralight as collateral; Jamie Lee and Tony said they'd provide the cash. The journey was just over two hours by car—they would leave at midnight.

Jane held her breath as she called Roger. He'd just said his goodbyes to the travelers so was feeling a little down. She explained her plans to come to Memphis, how her family were soon to become hostages alongside Pat. Roger explained about Jeff, Martin and Ben's arrival. Both felt this was heading towards an unknown, possibly deadly conclusion. Neither had any bright suggestions on alternative ways to make it any safer.

"Jerome will be severely pissed when he realizes he's been shafted," Roger said. "But Jerome doesn't know our guys. I'm thinking we figure out how to get them inside to find Pat and your family. Jerome says they'll be on site; hopefully, it'll be easy to find them. More difficult to extract everyone without harm, particularly now's there's a youngster involved." Roger paused, clearly still doubting a good outcome.

"Maybe we can divide and conquer?" Jane thought. "Perhaps I can get Jerome out of the bar, tell him the leavers are waiting on the riverfront. Then your guys can deal with the sisters and find our hostages. They're not expecting trouble. If it starts to go pear-shaped, we have more manpower."

"True," Roger said. "I like your way of thinking. Let's rendezvous at ten tomorrow morning and discuss it further. We can go to the bar together, get the party started. Our guys can sniff around, see if they can figure out where hostages are being kept. But we have to be realistic—we are going in blind. Anything could happen. I'm not a fan of so many unknowns, however we're running out of time and options. Call me tomorrow morning and let me know where you are. Have you figured out how to get across?"

"Yes, Jane said. "I'm calling in a lot of favors."

"You're the master of that, "Roger said. "See you tomorrow. Safe travels."

She walked back into the house and sat down with Tony and Jamie Lee to prepare for their road trip. It didn't take long to get ready. Jane was taking only a backpack, some food, and a sawed-off shotgun with ten cartridges, courtesy of Tony.

Jane eyed the shotgun with surprise. She'd never had cause to use one. She asked him why it was better than a handgun.

He explained with a smile on his face, "It's an ideal weapon at close range. Plus just seeing it scares the shit out of most people."

Midnight soon came. Jane went in to see Jay. He wasn't looking any better—in fact, he looked worse. Jane felt awful leaving him.

"I've gotta go now," she said. "Things in Memphis have taken a turn for the worse. I'll explain it all when I see you again in a few days."

Jay looked up from his bed. His skin seemed almost gray, his eyes were bloodshot. His voice was barely a whisper, the words struggling to leave his mouth. "Jane, you know I'm not gonna see you again. You take care." he croaked. "Go get your family. Don't worry about me. These folks will get me to a hospital, then we'll just have to see what happens." He paused, "Make sure all this hard work pays off. Don't give up on the flying lessons!"

He slumped back onto his pillow, exhausted by talking and closed his eyes. Jane took his hand and kissed him gently on the forehead. He squeezed her hand as she eased away from him.

The journey to West Memphis was uneventful. Jane dozed a little. She'd forgotten the distances you could travel so quickly in a car. Before she realized it, they were crawling along a frontage road just off I-55. Wesley's directions turned out to be pretty accurate. They pulled into a car lot near some warehouses and waited, barely visible, under the dim street lighting. A few minutes later, next to the warehouse, they saw a flash of light blink three times.

"There's your signal," Tony said. "Time to go Jane. I wish you all the best. I hope you get your family back safely. If you need any help, you've got my number. Call any time." He counted out a stack of bills. "Here's $500. Make sure you only give it to him once you're on the boat. I'm not sure how trustworthy these guys are."

Jane didn't know what to say. This kind couple, who she'd never met before, had gone out of their way to take her in, look after her, then help get her across the Mississippi. She hadn't experienced such generosity in years.

She hugged Tony and pecked him on the cheek, "Thanks so much for everything. You and Jamie Lee have been so kind to me. I can never repay you. I really do hope we meet again under…less stressful circumstances."

Embarrassed, Tony didn't say another word as Jane climbed down from his truck. He lit her way across the car lot with headlights until she reached the warehouse. Then he powered up the engine and headed home.

Jane stumbled around the side of the warehouse, tripping over some old railroad ties. She came face to face with a huge man dressed in army fatigues. He was smoking a large cigar.

"Wesley?"

"Yes ma'am," he said, at the same time exhaling a powerful stream of smoke. "Good to meet you. Let's get going. Time and contraband wait for no man." His voice was a deep southern drawl, almost a growl. He took another long inhale on his cigar and turned in the darkness, walking towards the river, Jane followed the red burning tip of his cigar like a beacon. After a short walk he stopped then hopped aboard a golf buggy.

"Quiet and environmentally friendly," he said by way of explanation, as they hummed off silently into the night. A few minutes later, Jane could smell the Mississippi's distinct aroma—rotting vegetation, sewage, and fuel. They stopped at a wharf where a small barge was moored. Two men loaded boxes onto the deck, illuminated only by lights on their headbands.

"Nearly done boss," one of them said as Wesley walked towards them.

"You've got five minutes," he instructed. "Then we cast off. No delay." He turned to Jane. "Got your fare, madam?"

"I have," Jane said. "What are you taking across?"

He brushed her question aside, "I won't ask your business, so don't ask mine. Less we both know about each other, the better." He waved her onto the boat. "I don't normally take passengers, but your friend was most persuasive. Let's get this job done quickly."

Jane boarded the barge and made her way to the wheelhouse. There was nowhere to sit except the captain's chair, so she leaned back against the bulkhead and kept out of the way. A few minutes later, Wesley came in, fired up the diesel engines, and idled them while his crew cast off.

"How long will it take to cross?"

"Fifteen minutes."

Jane realized she'd seen no security guards, "Where's all the border patrols we keep hearing about?" Jane asked.

"Looking the other way," Wesley said. "Enjoying some of my finest whiskey and cigars. They don't care a damn about smuggling contraband to the East. Long as they get their cut. Smuggling people in the other direction? They are all over you like a measles rash. You see, if any get through and are caught, the authorities will figure out which stretch of the river they landed on. Then any guards on duty at that time get into some serious shit."

"Good to know," Jane said, and shrank back into the wheelhouse as the barge chugged across the Mississippi. A few sparse lights along the riverfront indicated Memphis wasn't far away.

Wesley slowed the engine to idle and drifted towards a dilapidated jetty. As they approached, a generator fired up and two halogen lights shattered the night's darkness, harshly illuminating the dock. Two men and a woman emerged from the deep shadows. They grabbed the ropes thrown by one of

Wesley's men and tied them to the dock, bringing the barge to a sudden halt.

"Where's Jerome?" shouted one of Wesley's men as he hefted the first boxes onto the dock. "He sent a girl to do a man's work?!"

Horrified, Jane realized the woman must be one of his daughters. What fucking lousy luck was this? Of all the places she could have landed, she ended up right into the enemy camp. Jane grabbed Wesley's arm and pulled him close. Deciding that she could trust him, she whispered, "Wesley. These people will kill me if they find me here. I'll hide until you've unloaded and then jump ashore. Don't say anything, I'm begging you."

"Your secret's safe," he said conspiratorially. "Just give me the cash, and my lips are sealed." He held out his hand. Jane gave him the money envelope, which disappeared into his pocket without being counted. He left her cowering in the shadows of the wheelhouse. He strode confidently down the deck and began helping unload the contraband.

"Let's get this done quickly so I can get myself a drink in your delightful establishment, Miss Rachel," he said amiably. Jane let out a sigh of relief. This unknown man had kept his word. So far.

"Sure thing, Danny," she said. "Be my guest. This is a good delivery run. We need this gear badly—business has been booming."

Hearing the woman's name, Jane knew she was in danger of blowing the whole operation if Rachel came on board and found her. She shrunk back further into the corner of the wheelhouse and listened as the group worked and joked, moving boxes off the dock and into the bar cellar.

Jane couldn't know her husband and son were just feet from where she was hiding.

A nail-biting twenty minutes later, Wesley (or was it Danny? Jane assumed he used fake names to avoid detection) lifted the last of the boxes on his massive shoulders. The group disappeared up the steps and into the bar. Rachel killed the lights and turned the generator off. In the silence and darkness, Jane relaxed a little. According to the clock screwed crookedly to the wheelhouse wall, it was four-thirty in the morning. She had five hours to wait and not get caught before meeting Roger. She groped around for a flashlight. She had seen one lying on a small shelf next to some tools. Once she'd found it, she crept off the barge, along the jetty, away from the bar. She would visit it again in just a few hours under much different circumstances.

Further along the dock, the beam of light picked out a set of stairs that ran up alongside another warehouse. Jane climbed them cautiously. At the top, she saw the main street where all the bars and other dockside businesses had storefronts. She knew a lone woman walking down this street would not go unnoticed by any early risers. The last thing she needed was someone taking an interest in her, asking questions, or even worse, trying to rob and assault her.

She scanned the alleyways between the buildings and saw a pile of trash and discarded boxes. Controlling her disgust and shivering in the cold, she burrowed beneath them, trying to get comfortable and wait until it was time to meet with Roger.

CHAPTER 42

Roger heard bells tolling, close by and loud. Waking up from a dead sleep, he tried to pinpoint the source of the persistent ringing before realizing it was from the church next door.

Sunday! What a fine day for a fight, he thought, as he pulled on his jacket and headed towards the smell of coffee. Jeff, Martin, and Ben were already up and preparing breakfast—MREs mixed with bacon and eggs from Jeff's farm, washed down with coffee that could double as paint stripper.

"Morning, gentlemen," Roger said with more enthusiasm than he felt, "Ready for action? I have an update which will make life a little more complicated. It appears they not only have Pat as hostage, but Jane's husband and son, too. They are all being held at the bar. Extraction is now three people. Jane is coming from Memphis to help, so we have five of us against an unknown number of hostiles."

"What's the plan now?" asked Jeff.

"We have the advantage they don't know you three. I propose you visit the bar when it's quiet this morning, scope the layout of the place. Hiding three people securely means either an upstairs room or a cellar I'm guessing. I can recon the outside before we go in, find any back entrances that we might need to use. We need to know how to get out of there alive and quickly. They'll be potentially eight of us. We can take a couple of extra horses, load them up with dummy gear to make them look like pack animals. Then get everyone on them and outta there after the extraction. Once we're back here, we need to be prepared to leave Memphis fast. Jerome won't take this lying down. He'll want revenge."

Martin, his hoodie partially obscuring his face, asked a question Roger knew was coming.

"What are the rules of engagement here, sir? These shitheads don't seem the type to give up without a fight. Are we extracting hostages with minimal collateral damage or do we want to reduce the chances of any trouble later on?"

"People who take kids hostage don't deserve a second chance in my book. Do what you feel is necessary. We leave in an hour." With that, Roger got up, checked his weapons, and packed them in his saddle bags.

Martin and Ben nodded their heads; they now understood the assignment too well. They took Roger's orders as carte blanche to do pretty much as they liked. This could turn out to be an exciting day. They started to check their guns and ammo one last time.

When the church bells finally stopped ringing, Pastor Michael came over from the church.

Smiling benevolently and making no excuse for waking up the entire community, he explained, "I like to call the local folk to prayer the old-fashioned way. The service will start in a few minutes. Can I tempt you to join us?"

"I appreciate the offer Pastor. I'm sure you can guess my answer. I'm not the churchgoing type. It would seem pretty hypocritical to pray then go kill someone. Maybe you say some prayers for the success of this mission instead? If you're willing to. We need all the assistance we can get. From anywhere", added Roger looking skywards.

"Of course, I will pray for a safe outcome to your mission. When do you leave?"

"Soon," Roger said. "We'll be gone within the hour. We may meet up here briefly afterwards to collect a few things then be on our way. We've already outstayed your welcome. If this all goes pear-shaped, you won't want us anywhere near here."

The Pastor's face showed little concern at Roger's warning. "We have faced worse foe than those criminals. We'll be fine. I trust in God, even if you don't." Changing the subject to less Godly matters, Roger asked, "Did our group get across safely to the West?"

"Yes," the Pastor confirmed. "Damian says it all went according to plan. They are now in a safe house, experiencing the joys of civilization again."

"Excellent. That's a huge weight off my mind. Thank you so much. I can never repay you."

"Not that a man of the cloth should say such things," the Pastor leaned in close to Roger. "But if Jerome and his crew were to meet an untimely end, not many in Memphis would shed a tear. And that would be enough payment for our help."

"Hopefully we can rustle up another miracle and do just that Pastor. I wish you and Damian all the best. You are true Christians and friends."

The men shook hands. Pastor Michael returned to the peace and quiet of the church. Roger double-checked the guns and ammo in his backpack.

Their respective mornings would each be very different.

They arrived at Greenbelt Park just before ten. The day was finally shedding the gloom and cold of the previous week and promised to be sunny, cool with a clear blue sky. A perfect day for a murderous showdown.

Roger had called Jane and arranged to meet near the Emigration Office, some distance from the bar where all the action would take place. It was still quiet, with only a few people out when they arrived. Roger spotted Jane sitting on a chair outside the offices. She walked over and hugged him.

Roger pulled back from her." Phew! You stink like you slept in the garbage,".

"You're not exactly smelling of Roses yourself. That's exactly where I've been for the last few hours. Excuse me if I look and smell a little ripe. I promise I'll scrub up next time I meet you, even put on a dab of Chanel."

Roger couldn't help but laugh. With a theatrical flourish, he picked some non-existent trash from her dirty blonde hair.

"Once we're through with all this, I'll book you into the Hilton for a spa and massage. Promise."

"I'll hold you to that," Jane said, then looked towards the rest of the party. "Are you going to introduce me to this fine trio of gentlemen?"

Roger made the introductions. They moved off the main street and into a small park. Once a quiet, pleasant oasis from the hustle of the city, it was now strewn with debris and trash. They tied their horses to the railings and sat down on some park benches that had seen better days.

Roger outlined the plan, such as it was: Jane would try to get Jerome out of the bar, telling him the group was in the park. Jeff, Ben, and Martin would go inside. Two would sit at a booth, while one sat at the bar. Roger would scope out the building's rear for exits and to see if there was any sign of the hostages. Then Martin and Ben would contrive a fight, the distraction caused by it would allow Jeff to get into the rest of the building to find Pat and Jane's family. All agreed that it was a flaky plan with so much potential to go wrong. They may have to improvise, never forgetting the only objective was to get the hostages out alive. Wherever else happened was up to good or bad luck.

When it came to making a getaway. The horses would be tied up a short distance away. Everyone was to grab the nearest and get the hell out of Dodge-assuming it all went to plan. They would reconvene briefly at the church then head for Jeff's farm. Jeff gave Jane a makeshift map with directions to his home should they get separated at any time.

A little after eleven, Martin and Jeff wandered into the bar and sat at a booth near the back of the room. There were no other customers to get in the way.

A tattoo-covered waitress came over to serve them. She had dirty bleach-blonde hair and a far from clean T-shirt emblazoned with AC/DC World Tour 2019.

"What can I get you guys?" she asked. "Do you want breakfast? Beer? Coffee? We had a delivery last night, so we have some Bud or Heineken."

"We'll take two coffees, please ma'am," Jeff replied. "Maybe some food in a minute."

"Sure thing, hon'." She turned on her heel. "Be right back."

As the waitress walked away, Jeff suggested, "Should one of us go to the restroom? See what's out back?"

"I'll go," Martin said. "I need a leak anyway." He headed for the door signposted RESTROOMS to the bar's left. While he was out of sight, Ben walked in, sat at the bar, and ordered a beer, not acknowledging Jeff's presence.

Both scoped out the room for exits or doors leading to other parts of the building. There wasn't much to see. One door appeared to go out the side of the building, into an alleyway. There were two others on either side of the bar, one behind it. They knew one went to the restrooms, so probably no exit there. Martin came back and sat down. They said nothing while the waitress came over with their coffees.

"Gimme a holler if you need anything else." She said breezily as she put their coffees on the table.

They feigned interest in their drinks. Ben supped on his beer and attempted to make conversation with the barmaid. Then Jane walked in, heading straight for the bar.

She spoke calmly to the barmaid, asking for Jerome. "He's expecting me. Tell him it's Jane."

The barmaid disappeared through the door at the back of the bar. Jane turned to glance at Martin, Ben and Jeff, her eyes revealing no recognition. Seconds later, the door beside the bar burst open and a tall, overweight man in his fifties blustered into the room. He was impeccably dressed in a jacket and pressed pants in an attempt to look like a successful businessman. He sported a huge, gray beard, though his head was bald. He reminded Jeff of Billy Gibbons from ZZ Top. For a man of his size, he moved with ease and grace, oozing a menacing confidence. This was a man used to getting his own way, thought Jeff.

He strode confidently to Jane and greeted her, arms outstretched, like a long-lost relative.

"Jane," he said. "So good you're here. So glad to see you after all this time. Can I get you some refreshment? You look like you could do with a drink—even a bath?"

"Very funny," Jane scowled. "I'm not in the mood for jokes, or refreshments, especially from you. Can we just cut the crap and get on with business?"

"Don't be so rude," Jerome said, smiling, or was it smirking? "After all we've been through? Thought you'd want to catch up on the last year. Seems like you had an interesting time an' all."

She ignored Jerome's fake bon homie, demanding, "Where's my husband and son?"

"Where's my consignment?" countered Jerome, his voice no longer quite so accommodating.

"They're all here, just up the road. You're not seeing them until I see my family. I figured you wouldn't want a troop of leavers wandering around here anyway. Could be bad for business if people realized what you were doing."

"I don't give a fuck what people think. "It's my bar. I do what I please. So quit this game of who goes first and show me the goods."

Jane moved closer to Jerome, her face just inches from his. She wasn't afraid of him any longer, knowing the room contained friends, ones who were quite happy to turn this into a bloodbath if necessary.

"You pompous, arrogant, murdering bastard. Bring my family here, now."

"Or what?"

"Or I'll blow your fucking head off," announced Ben, who had snuck behind Jerome and now held a gun, inches from the back of his bald head.

This was not part of the plan, thought Jane. Too late now—things were about to take off in who knows what direction.

Martin and Jeff remained seated, with hands on their weapons, watching the barmaid and the doors in case backup appeared.

The barmaid gradually inched towards the bar and put her hands beneath it.

"I really wouldn't do that," said Jeff as he moved from the booth to the bar in a few strides, all the while pointing the gun at her head. Reaching the bar, he leaned over and found her hand closing in on a baseball bat.

"I'll take that Babe Ruth. No home runs for you today. Now stand right there with your hands on the bar where I can see them. Jerome, you were about to say something?"

Jerome kept his composure as best he could with a gun at his head. He kept his voice calm and quiet.

"Oh Jane," he hissed. "What have you done? You really think I wasn't expecting some kind of game from you? I just knew you'd try something stupid. You haven't disappointed me. My girls are looking right at you through the mirror behind the bar. Neither of them are strangers to guns. I've got another downstairs with our guests. So what do you propose to do now?"

What happened in the next few seconds would forever remain a blur in Jane's memory.

Martin and Jeff opened fire. The two-way mirror behind the bar shattered, along with rows of liquor bottles lined up on shelves in front of it.
Caught by surprise, Rachel and Jordan ducked for cover as shards of glass exploded around their heads.

Before Jerome could react, Ben shot him twice, once in each leg. Jerome slumped to the floor like a felled cow, howling in agony.

"Jane, make sure he doesn't even attempt to get up," Ben commanded. "If he does, shoot him somewhere that will hurt even more." Ben ran for the side door next to the bar. Martin shouted, "There's stairs going to the basement on the right. Take a look down there."

Ben nodded and crashed through the door.

Jeff vaulted over the bar, pushing the stunned barmaid to the ground. He kicked open the door and charged into the back room to find Jerome's daughters picking themselves up from the floor. They were scrambling to find their guns from among the glass fragments that littered the room like confetti.

Jeff kicked their guns away, shouting, "Not so fast ladies. Or you'll get the same treatment as your pops." He pointed his gun at Jordan's face. "Face down on the floor, all of you and don't move."

Seeing Jeff had things under control. Hearing some shots from the basement Martin quickly followed where Ben had gone moments earlier, flying down the rickety wooden stairs. Once at the bottom, he saw three rooms off a dimly lit corridor. Ben had already crashed into one and been met with a barrage of shots, he backed off quickly.

From within a voice screamed, "Come in here and they die. I've got a gun to the boy's head. You move and he never sees his mother again. Now fuck off out that exit and don't come back."

Martin skidded to a halt behind Ben who knelt, gun in hand, inches from the door to the kidnapper's room.

"Take it easy in there," Ben said, trying to lower the panic level. "You know we'll take you out. Do you want to die? Be sensible—let them go and we let you live. If not, this will end badly for you. Don't be a fucking hero Jerome isn't paying you enough to die for him"

The response was immediate, "Go fuck yourself."

Martin tapped Ben on the shoulder and pulled out a stun grenade from his ammo belt. He waved it back and forth, like a child's flag on the fourth of July.

"Look what I got," he whispered, a wicked grin across his face. "Worth a try?"

"That's a bit extreme, don't you think?" Ben said.

"Got any other ideas?"

Ben didn't have one that came to mind immediately. All he knew was that something had to be done quickly: who knew when reinforcements might appear? Stun grenades were extremely effective in confined spaces though there could be damage to the hostage's hearing and sight. That, however, was the lesser of the two evils facing them. The other could result in some deadly collateral damage.

Ben nodded. "I'll shoot out the light in the hallway first. Then lob that in."

"Got it."

Ben's two deafening shots exploded the fluorescent light in the hallway. Simultaneously Martin threw in the stun grenade. For a moment, nothing happened. Then, a blinding flash. The explosion rocked the basement.

Both had crouched with hands over their ears for protection from the blast. Now they hurtled into the room searching for the guard, scouring through the smoke and dust.

Still chained to the wall, Pat waved them to the guard sprawled on the floor, trying to stand up and find his gun.

"Get that bastard's gun before he realizes what's happened," Pat shouted. Ben ran to the still disorientated guard and kneed him in the ribs. As he lay gasping on the floor, Ben dug in his pockets and found the keys to Pat's padlocked chains. He threw them to Pat who freed himself in double quick time. Pat crossed the small room to where David and his son cowered in the corner, hands over their ears. Not surprisingly, they looked bewildered and shocked by the sudden turn of events.

The guard tried to stand up, wobbling on unsteady legs and rubbing his eyes. Martin pushed him hard against the wall, his gun barrel pressed under his chin. The terrified guard held his hands up in surrender.

Martins' instructions left no room for misunderstanding, "You've got ten seconds to leave and never come back. If I see you again, you'll have a permanent cure for that headache." The dazed guard nodded his head groggily, then staggered across the cellar, bouncing off the walls as he stumbled out the door.

Martin and Ben ran over to Pat who was kneeling down in front of David and the boy.

"You guys OK?" asked Ben.

"I think so," answered David. "I guess, I hope. Bit deaf, we'll be OK. You're with Jane I hope?"

Ben confirmed he was friend, not foe, then ordered them to stay put. "We need to go back upstairs and assess the situation. Make sure it's all under control. Then get outta here asap. Go out the back entrance. Roger should be there to help you. If not, there's horses at the front. Get on one of those and get the hell out of here. We'll catch up later. Head for the church."

David momentarily ignored Ben's orders, asking anxiously, "Is my wife with you?"

"Yes, yes she is. Last I saw her, she was upstairs guarding Jerome."

"We need to see her," David said. "Please."

Martin thought for a moment, then nodded. "Gimme a couple of minutes to scope out what's happening. If I'm not back real soon, get the hell outta here." Martin left the cellar at a run, reloading his handgun as he went.

Upstairs, Jeff and Jane heard the gunshots and felt the floor vibrate when the stun grenade went off. They hoped it was their guys making the noise-a sign things might be going to plan

In the main bar area, Jerome laid on the floor, groaning in pain as Jane looked on, sawn off shotgun in hand, making sure he didn't try anything stupid. Jeff checked Rachel, Jordan, and the barmaid who he'd now bundled into the corner office behind the bar. He appeared unfazed by the commotion downstairs. He knew if a stun grenade had gone off, then it was done by one of his guys. It was likely things were reaching a noisy, successful conclusion.

Footsteps stomped up from the cellar. Martin appeared, looking grimy but happy.

"All good up here?"

"Hunky dory," said Jeff. "All good down there?"

"Hostages are safe and sound," Martin said. "The guard's gone and won't be back. If we're secure up here, there's some people wanting to meet the lady."

"Sure, be quick. Bring them up and let's get going," Jeff ordered.

Pat, Ben, David and the boy came bounding up the stairs. Jane took one look at her husband and son and ran towards them. The distraction was all Jerome needed—he reached inside his boot and pulled out a small revolver. In all the confusion, no one had thought to search him.

He raised himself onto one elbow, aiming the gun at Jane. A shot rang out—not from Jerome, but from Roger's gun as he crashed through the front door. The bullet tore into Jerome's neck, killing him instantly.

"Save the family celebrations for later," Roger shouted. "We have to get going, before too many people take an interest in what's happening here."

"What do you want to do with these three?" Jeff asked, pointing at the women on the floor. "Shall I finish the job? The less witnesses the better."

The three women looked up at Jeff, then Roger, horror and fear carved on their faces. "You can't kill us," Jordan begged. "We were just doing what Jerome told us to do. We won't come after you." Her eyes flashed tearfully at the men towering over her, guns at the ready. Her once confident voice now quivered with fear.

Roger walked over to them, his pistol aimed at their heads. The two daughters were as bad as their father, human traffickers of the worst kind. He raised his gun and put it against Jordan's forehead, "I'm not sure why I shouldn't shoot you both right now. But killing unarmed women is something I can't sink to even though you deserve it for all the pain and suffering you have caused. Martin, Ben—take these three down to the cellar and tie them up. Jeff, you stand guard at the door. We're leaving now. We'll regroup as planned."

Roger led Pat and Jane's family out into the street. Already, people gathered to see what all the commotion was about. Pat and Roger kept their guns in view as they mounted their horses and left the scene, trying to look composed and unhurried.

They were about a quarter of a mile down the street approaching the bridge when they heard three gunshots. Roger's heart skipped a beat; he stopped his horse and thought about turning back. Had the three women been executed? Could they really have done that? If so, it would be killing for the fun of it. There was no time to go back; he'd deal with it later. As they all turned onto the bridge, he looked over his shoulder and saw the three men riding away from the bar, smoke billowing from its front door.

These guys are maniacs, Roger thought, no more than freelance murderers. They brought an extreme level of violence to the rescue. Albeit one that ended successfully because of them. Did that end really justify the means? Infuriated and sickened, he kicked his horse into a trot, bellowing at the others to get a move on.

CHAPTER 43

Two days later, the group wearily reconvened at Jeff's farm. They had barely stopped for rest or food, wanting to distance themselves from the savagery of what happened in Memphis. Somewhere during the night, Martin and Ben dropped behind and disappeared in the darkness, leaving Roger unable to get their version of events at the bar. He'd have to talk to Jeff to get the full story. Nothing was said between the two of them on the journey. Roger wanted to keep the discussion between themselves.

Jane's reunion with her family was the high point of the trip. Her boy, Tom, had been just four years old when they were separated. He was now a young man of almost ten. He'd not seen his mother for half his lifetime; they had a lot of catching up to do. The three of them were inseparable, spilling out the details of their lives for hours on end as they plodded up I-65.

Roger phoned Herb to tell him all was well, except for Jay's illness, causing him to be left behind. He wondered if he'd ever find out what Jay's fate would be. Roger detected some mixed feelings in Herb's voice on hearing the news that Jane had been reunited with her family. No doubt he wanted Jane to return to French Creek for his own reasons.

They arrived at Jeff's farm late in the evening. Everyone collapsed into beds, on couches, or in chairs. They slept the sleep of the exhausted and happy. Breakfast the following morning was a communal and joyous affair. Roger sensed Jeff knew he was unhappy and wanted questions answered. He kept avoiding being alone with Roger all day.

The next day, Roger awoke early, hoping to catch Jeff by himself. Instead, he found an envelope addressed to him on the kitchen table, a brief letter inside:

Captain,

I guess you want to know what happened after you left the bar? To keep it brief, it didn't go quite to plan. I always knew Martin and Ben were a couple of hotheads, but they got carried away this time. I wish I could have stopped them. You know these kind of guys, you've seen them in Afghanistan. Once the killing starts, they can't stop until the dead bodies are piled high around them. I'll spare you the details of what happened. It wasn't pretty.

You're a decent man Roger who did nothing wrong here. Don't let a successful expedition be ruined by someone else's terrible actions. Let's leave it at that.

As always, it's been a pleasure working with you, fighting the bad guys, and winning. If there's a next time, I'll be there for you.

I have gone to Clarksville for supplies. It'll be a couple of days before I get back. I assume you'll be on your way before then?
As ever, it's been a real honor serving you, sir.

All the best for French Creek.

Mission, successfully, accomplished.

Jeff

Roger had to smile. Yet again, Jeff had watched his back for all the wrong reasons but with the best of intentions. He poured himself a coffee and sat in front of the fire, waiting for everyone to join him. Jeff's letter tacitly suggested they should be gone before he returned. Maybe he was right—no point having an acrimonious postmortem on the mission. After all, both objectives were achieved—Jane reunited with her family, and the group transported safely to the West.

Another day here and they'd hit the road for French Creek. He didn't know what Jane was planning; she'd no doubt update him when she knew herself. Future plans were not top of their family's agenda at the moment; they just wanted to enjoy the present.

Roger refilled his coffee and stared into the flames. Time to look after himself and his family. At that moment, what he cared for most came hobbling down the stairs—Landy, alive and well. He sat in the chair next to his father.

"How are you feeling, son?" Roger asked.

"Much better," Landy said. "Reckon I can ride a horse now." As he moved his leg, he tried to conceal a grunt of pain, "So. What happened in Memphis?"

Roger sighed. He really didn't want to recount the gory details right now, to anyone, let alone his son. He decided to save the conversation for another day.

"I'll tell you everything that happened in due time," Roger said. "I want to get home as quickly as possible. I'm getting too old for all this drama." He paused, fearing he'd get an answer he didn't want to hear. "What do you want to do son? Go back to Memphis and see if Pastor Michael can help you? Or what?"

Roger held his breath as Landy struggled for an answer. Finally, he looked at his father and simply said:

"Dad, I just want to go home."

CHAPTER 44

The safe house in which the French Creek group found themselves was a large cabin in the Wapanocca National Wildlife Refuge. Lacking any regular maintenance for five years it was shabby but comfortable. They didn't care. It had electricity and running hot water. The food in the fridge was a cornucopia of forgotten tastes and smells. For the first few days they were like children let loose in a candy store. However, they were still cut off from the rest of the World as the cabin had no cable or internet. Austin, Bryanna and Jenny were chomping at the bit to try and find their relatives and plan a route back home. The others were happy to be where they were and enjoying the largesse of the West.

Their guide, and safe house owner, Charlie made it clear they could stay for a few days and then have to move on. They'd each be given $500-and could add to it by exchanging any valuables for cash.

True to his word Charlie appeared on day three of their stay. He was a tall, gaunt man in his forties with a tuft of gray hair flopping across his shiny forehead. Painfully thin with a pronounced stoop it made him look much older than he was. He shuffled into the main room of the cabin early in the morning bearing donuts and pastries.

"OK everybody, here's what's happening today. I'm going to take you to St Louis and drop you off at the main Greyhound bus station. After that you're on your own. Don't think about trying to rent a car, book an airline ticket or even hitch a ride. The first two require a credit card and ID, the last one will probably get you arrested as a vagrant in this state. I've got two pay-as-you-go cell phones, sorry I can't afford any more. Once you're in the city you can use these to try and find friends and relatives to stay with. Any questions?"

"Do you know anyone who can get us some fake IDs?" asked Dwayne.

"I do, but it'll cost you about $2000. Remember these people want cash, not valuables for barter. Take those to a pawn shop if you have any with you. Again, some may want ID if it's a valuable item you're trying to get cash for. Since you've been gone the cashless society has practically taken over this side of the country. My suggestion? Just get to where you're going by keeping under the radar. Then you can explore your options for becoming legit Americans later. It sucks I know, but that's the way it is, Big Brother rules."

Four hours later, Charlie's van stopped and disgorged his awe-struck passengers on 15th street in St Louis, close to the Greyhound bus station. They all thanked him profusely for his help. Gathered up their meager belongings and watched with some apprehension as he turned up the ramp onto Highway 40 and left them to their own devices. They found a Cracker Barrel restaurant nearby. The novelty of ordering a full meal and hot drinks in air-conditioned comfort was overwhelming. Then realization descended on them like a heavy blanket. They were on their own. They had to start making decisions for themselves, and quickly.

Using the phone's internet service, Bryanna found an old friend living in Denver, working as a nurse. She called the hospital and after convincing her long lost friend it wasn't a prank call, secured a room in her apartment as and when she could get there.

Jenny went straight to Face Book and found her sister, Melanie, now living in Kansas of all places, just a few hours away! She messaged her. It was over an hour before she received a disbelieving reply from her sister, including a phone number. An emotional call followed, ending with a promise Jenny would be with her sister by the following day.

Austin had trouble locating his brother, Julian. With a last name of 'Smith' there were a lot of them, everywhere. Despairing he'd ever find him, he tried LinkedIn. Knowing his brother was a lifelong computer engineer and unlikely to have changed careers, he scoured the names that came up. After a few minutes, he spotted his brother's profile picture to discover he was working in Silicon Valley at Apple. He could not contact him, but now knowing his workplace, he was set and ready to head for San Francisco.

Dick, the youngest of the group, tracked down the Uncle Jack he was seeking. He discovered Jack had moved to Seattle-a long way from St Louis. However, like Austin, while he was unable to contact him that day he was happy and confident to head North West and chance his luck that a home awaited him.

Bryan had real trouble finding either of his two sisters. He guessed they had both got married and changed their last names. He didn't get along with his older brother, following a major business-related argument years ago. In the end had no option but to call him and ask for his sister's contact details. The conversation when they finally connected was brief and to the point. Obviously, whatever had happened in the past had not been forgotten. However, the animosity did not stop him from giving Bryan his sister's phone numbers. A call to one of them, and he was set to travel to Colorado.

Sadly, Dwayne had no relatives in the West he knew of and sat quietly listening to the whoops of joy as the others found their long-lost family members. As they all sat there pleased with their success at finding places to stay, they guiltily realized his predicament. To his delight they all suggested he could join one of them as they traveled to their respective destinations. He could stay as long as he liked while he figured out what to do next. Overcome and humbled by their generosity he chose to go with Austin to San Francisco where he thought his skills might be most in demand.

This whole relative finding process took hours to complete. By the time they had finished it was early evening. They walked down 15th St to the Greyhound Bus station and bought tickets to their different destinations. Some would take days to reach them, others just a few hours. They had to spend the night in the dirty bus station, not able, or willing, to try their luck at booking a hotel room. They didn't care. A few beers (heaven!) and a take-out McDonalds (bliss!) finished off their first day back in civilization.

They settled down on the hard bus station benches to try and sleep. They were still on cloud nine at the heady prospect of being on their way to see long-lost friends and relatives.

That all changed at 4.00am in the morning when the unsavory side of modern-day America appeared in the guise of five hooded youths carrying guns and knives.

Bryanna was the first to see them. She was waking up to catch her 5.00am bus departure. The five men, faces obscured by their filthy hoodies, stood in a semi-circle just feet from her. One waved a gun and demanded to know if she had any money.

"Just give it over now and you won't get hurt, bitch" he ordered menacingly. Bryanna had seen enough thugs traveling around the East in her time to not be easily intimidated. "Do I look like I've got money you asshole? If I had, I wouldn't be sitting here in a Greyhound bus station, would I?"

"Lady, watch your mouth, it could get you into trouble." threatened Thug One with the gun. He motioned to one of the others to wake up the rest of the group, which he did by going around kicking each of them. They all quickly opened their eyes and sat up half asleep, to be confronted by five youths pointing weapons at them. Dwayne struggled to wake up, his body still covered with a sleeping bag as he turned to look at the gang.

Thug Two, a large boy with his pants hanging halfway down his butt, swaggered over and pointed his gun at Jenny's head.

"OK, let's make this quick, all of you! Empty out your pockets and put your money and anythin' else of value on the floor. Now! C'mon people let's move it!" He put the gun inches from Jenny's ear. She looked petrified and quickly threw her pathetic few dollars on the ground. The others followed suit. The pile of cash amounted to no more than a few hundred dollars. The thugs were clearly disappointed in their haul. Thug One became agitated at seeing the paltry amount.

"For fuck sake's you assholes, is this all you got?" he jumped from one foot to the other, his anger boiling up. "Maybe if I shot one of you, I'd find some more? Who's it to be huh? How about this pretty lady here with the big mouth?" He swaggered over to Bryanna, the gun shaking in his hand.

Suddenly Dwayne announced in a confident voice waving a cell phone in the air. "Look guys, that's all we got, OK? Just take it and get outta here before the cops arrive. I called them when you first turned up. Should be here any minute".

"Like fuck you did, lying piece of shit. I should teach you a lesson." Thug Two threatened Dwayne, but a frisson of doubt had crept into his voice.

"Believe what you like; why'd do think I took so long to wake up?" Dwayne seemed unperturbed despite the threat leveled at him.

The gang looked at one another. By sheer coincidence, at that moment, a police siren wailed in the distance. The gang grabbed the cash off the floor and high-tailed it out of the waiting room into the coach parking lot, vanishing into the gray-blue dawn light.

"Fuck Dwayne, that was a bravado performance, I was practically shitting myself and you, cool as a cucumber. Did you really call the cops?" asked an awe-struck Austin.

"Nah. Last thing we want is a bunch of cops here? With no IDs we'd be in jail before those bunch of idiots. Let's just say I'm a mean poker player!" Dwayne smiled, delighted his deception had saved the group from further harm.

Their euphoria at avoiding injury was quickly replaced by annoyance and disappointment that their sparse cash reserves had been stolen. Three of them had managed to hide some from the gang. They generously divided it up, leaving each person with around $100 to get to their destination. Thankfully they had already bought their bus tickets. The tiny amount of money left over would have to be for food and drink.

For a final meal together, they wandered down to a scruffy 24hour cafe and ordered coffee and donuts. It would be the last time they'd see each other again. For Dwayne, Dick and Bryan, who'd lived together in French Creek for years, parting would be tough, after all they had been through, seen and survived.

It turned into an emotional morning as each member saw their bus arrive and said their tearful goodbyes. Jenny was the first to go, leaving a distraught Bryanna behind. They had been inseparable for nearly three years. They promised to stay in touch.

Then Austin and Dwayne left together. A few hours later, Dick boarded the bus for his long trip to Seattle. He was the youngest and had the furthest to travel. He kept his composure until the bus turned out of the station, then the tears flowed.

Finally, Bryan waited until the afternoon when the bus to Colorado arrived. He'd kept one of the cell phones, the other had been given to Jenny. They texted each other for a few hours as they traveled in opposite directions across the vastness of America.

Then Bryan's phone ran out of charge. That was it. All communication was over. Everyone was off on a new adventure, all hoping the West would provide a better life than the East. Some would find it so, others would discover it wasn't quite how they remembered it. One, unexpectedly, would return.

CHAPTER 45

French Creek was buzzing with the news about the group's trip and its successful conclusion. Herb had relayed the broad details at an impromptu village meeting.

Dick's parents were thrilled he had made it across safely to the West, even if they didn't know what his fate was thereafter.

Bryan's friends, likewise were relieved he had made it. A few close friends who knew Dwayne was gay had urged him to make the move so he could live life in a more understanding environment. They, too, were delighted he was safely on his way to a place where he could live openly.

Meanwhile, Herb had fallen into a deep depression upon hearing news Jane had been reunited with her family. He felt ashamed at being so selfish. He wanted Jane to come back alive but single, so they could plan a life together in French Creek. He knew that feeling so self-centered was wrong. He had lost someone he had fallen in love with, and it was driving him into despair.

After reporting the news to the villagers, he locked himself away, taking solace in too much drink and self-pity. He made for a pathetic sight on the rare occasion he was seen, usually on his porch, glass in hand, staring into the middle distance.

One person who understood how he felt was Denise. She had started a casual relationship with Austin soon after he was released from quarantine. While he had been part of Jane's group, he was ambivalent about their objectives, violence was something he despised. By nature, he was a wanderer. Happy to tag along with them to see if it took him somewhere that might offer any permanency. Managing to secure a home in French Creek initially suited him. He thought his peripatetic lifestyle was losing its appeal, French Creek seemed like a good place to put down roots.

Denise had been particularly attentive while he was in quarantine, and their friendship grew stronger over the subsequent weeks. He also found her daughter Sandra well-behaved and fun to be around. All seemed to be going well between them. Then the wanderlust kicked back in as Spring approached. He kept his distance from Denise once news of the group's planned trip West had been made public. He decided this was the only chance to get back with his relatives and put down some roots. His brother he knew had a good job and could probably help with a job.

He told a tearful Denise, and Sandra, of his plans just the day before the group left for Memphis. He felt bad about upsetting, even misleading them, but it was now or never.

As he rode off down French Creek with Roger and the other travelers he turned to wave Denise goodbye. She was nowhere to be seen.

A few days later, Denise was walking past Herb's house to collect some meat from the abattoir at the far end of the village. She spotted him despondently slouching in his chair on the porch, drink in hand.

She wandered over, announcing brightly, "Bit early for a drink Herb? Are you ill?""

"I'm fine Denise, just want to be by myself."

"Well, you don't look fine Herb, to be honest you look dreadful"

Herb gave a wan smile, "Say it like it is Denise, in my present mood you could call me anything and I really wouldn't care. Sorry, but that's how I feel. Mr Misery is in residence today, and has been for a while."

"Oh my what has caused all this? You're normally the life and soul of the party Herb. Want to tell me all your troubles, and I'll tell you mine?" asked Denise half-jokingly.

And that's just what they did.

After imbibing a lot more inhibition loosening alcohol, for the next hour both were in tears as they opened up their hearts and poured out their hurt feelings. It was a cathartic experience for both of them. Within the confines of French Creek such mutual 'therapy sessions' were unheard of. Everyone was too busy working or plain grateful for what they had to make public their 'feelings'. Talking about them to other villagers could be construed as a weakness and no one wanted to be labeled that way.

After the tears had subsided and the bottle of homemade brandy was empty, Denise and Herb felt an affinity, a bond that surprised them both. They both were trying to recover from a broken heart. They spent the rest of the morning talking about anything that came to mind. They were surprised that despite living in the same village for over seven years, they really knew little about each other. All that changed in a morning and a subtle transition from distant neighbor to close friend evolved between them that day.

In the weeks and months ahead they saw more and more of each other. Later that year Denise would suggest Herb might like to move in with her and Sandra, making it 'official' that they were an item. Herb would say 'yes'.

CHAPTER 46

The morning dawned bright and clear. One of these "good to be alive" days. The sun was piercingly bright, suspended in an azure blue sky. It was cool and invigorating. Roger and Landy wanted to make an early start. They were packed, provisioned, and saddled just after dawn. Pat would follow later.

A hundred yards away, cold and tired, two men lay submerged underneath camouflage netting and branches cut from a cedar tree. Joey and Allen may have been freezing, but they were on full alert as they had been for two bitterly cold days. Their patience was about to be rewarded. They were out for revenge. Their Dad, Jerome and sisters hadn't deserved to be murdered and their bar burnt down. Two hours after the attack, Joey and Allen had returned to discover the devastation and the charred bodies in the smoldering wreckage of the bar.

Inquiries among bystanders quickly provided them with reasonable descriptions of the group that had led the attack—particularly the man who commanded the operation. A combination of death threats and bribery among their underworld contacts led them to Pastor Michael's church. It hadn't taken long for them to learn all they needed to know about where the group was heading. They left him hanging by the neck from the large wooden cross inside the church. Without stopping for supplies, they rushed after the group. Anger fueled their energy as they pummeled their horses Northwards in pursuit.

Following their trail wasn't difficult. By the time Roger's group navigated around Nashville, Joey and Allen were within binocular distance of them. At Jeff's farm, they lay in wait for two days, scoping out who they should kill. Top of the list was the commander and they assumed his son. The other military type and the family, they'd deal with later.

Now, they saw Roger and his son leaving the farm. Going for good, by the way the horses were packed. It was now or never.

Both men lowered their heads and looked carefully through the telescopic lens on their rifles.

Putting their fingers on the triggers at the same time. Joey counted down: "Three, two, one."

THE END. OR IS IT?

About the Author

Paul H Rowney has spent most of his working life in magazine publishing. Born in England, he emigrated to America in 2004 and now lives nr Nashville, Tennessee on a farm with seven dogs and a menagerie of other two and four legged animals.

His interest in a post-apocalyptic world started when he read 'Alas Babylon' by Pat Frank. 'French Creek' is his first book inspired by living in rural Kentucky and the idea this would be a good place to survive in a post-apocalyptic society.

Each year on his birthday friends join him for a 'Apaulcalyptic Party' where they experiment for a day living without the conveniences of the 21st century. It isn't easy.

Preview of the sequel to French Creek

Here's a sneak preview of the sequel to French Creek...called '*Kentucky Rises*'.

Sacramento, California. *Office of Homeland Security. Eastern USA Division.*

Charles Kingston, Under Secretary for the Eastern USA Division, Homeland Security and senator for Western Kentucky, had a problem. Five, almost six years, after the Collapse little under his leadership had been achieved in bringing back a semblance of Federal Government control over the eastern half of the country.

Years of economic depression, plummeting tax revenues and supporting millions of migrants from the East, had kept the country almost bankrupt. What limited resources they had were used to prop up the economy of the Western USA. It left practically nothing to revive the fortunes of those back East.

However, the first Presidential elections since the Collapse were slated for next year and the Senator wanted to support his president's re-election chances by showing the voters they were finally doing something to reunite America.

He needed a big, bold, innovative and dramatic plan. A plan that would help the President, and by default, his own political future as well. He knew he'd been given a poisoned chalice, when offered this appointment. But his large corporate donors had urged him to take it as they saw big money coming their way when the East finally opened up again. He was getting uncomfortably squeezed from both sides: the president and those that lined his pockets.

It was time to make a name for himself. To go down in history as the man who made America whole again.

He'd asked his aides to come up with scenarios that would fit his grand scheme. Tasking them with thinking 'outside the box', to 'challenge every conventional idea', to be 'bold, 'creative and ambitious' with their ideas.

Unfortunately, Charles Kingston's inner circle had little time for his plans of self-aggrandizement. They'd heard it all before. Nothing ever came of it. Like most politicians he was all piss and wind.

Nevertheless, in spite of their doubts, if their revered Senator wanted some 'blue sky thinking', then they'd give him some 'off the wall' ideas to mull on. They all knew that the country was in no position to do anything except read the reports. Then wait for some unspecified time into the future when the country had the resources to implement a carefully constructed plan to gently meld America back together. That time was not now.

They also knew that the eastern and southern coastal cities were in a better position, economically and governmentally, than those in the interior. Reports coming in indicated that foreign imports had helped them create a partially viable economy. One still very much stuck in the early 20th century, but slowly improving. In terms of government, it was a mixed bag: Many areas were still run by gangs. Others had created councils or groups of powerful or wealthy individuals, who ran the cities in the form of a 'benevolent dictatorships'.

None of this, of course, bore any resemblance to what had been in place before the *Collapse*. However, it was a start. The belief in Sacramento was moving into these areas to re-establish a traditionally accepted form of State and Federal control would be a hard sell to those in charge. Indeed, after the corruption, toxic partisanship and ineptitude of the pre-Collapse government, Kingston's agents on the ground suggested he look for other areas to impose his ideas.

That meant considering states bordering the Mississippi. How ripe were they, Kingston asked his staff, for ReFederalization? (A phrase he had come up with and was now recommending be used in all reports. It had an authoritative ring to it he felt, a legitimate call to action).

The first problem his staff confronted was getting any concrete information from those areas of the country. Primarily rural states, their agents had difficulty mixing in with the local population. They were easily ousted as intruders. Getting up close and personal in these communities was a dangerous occupation. Nevertheless, keen to report something positive back to Sacramento, many of the agents disclosed that 'numerous' smaller communities were still struggling to move beyond a 19th century societal framework, and were 'desperate' for help.

They admitted the major cities on the Mississippi, like Memphis, New Orleans and Minneapolis were riddled with violence and corruption. In fact, it was so endemic with many gangs were making fortunes smuggling people westwards, and materials eastwards across the river. The agents believed they were hotbeds of subversion and potential lethal flashpoints for ReFederalization. Steer clear at all costs unless you want another civil war on your hands.

That left Charles Kingston with a Hobson's Choice. Play it safe, do nothing and wait another year or two to see if matters change.

Or, conceive a plan to ReFederalize some of the states bordering the Mississippi and use them as a 'beach head' (he didn't use that word out loud, it smacked of invasion. He saw his role as more rescuer and savior. Though it did encapsulate the approach he had in mind).

The task was enormous. How do you re-impose government at state and federal level? If the majority wanted it, then it wouldn't pose too many problems. But what if they didn't. How could you force them, without appearing as some heavy-handed colonial invasion?

Brushing aside the concerns of his staff, he produced and delivered his report to the President entitled:

The Refederalization of the Eastern USA

A proposal to rescue, revitalize and re-establish the economy and government of these states.

The proposal ran to 150 pages covering everything from persuading the Utility companies to start rebuilding their infrastructure, the availability of financial services, to healthcare, law enforcement and the creation of elections.

Every government department had its say. Six months later an inevitably watered-down version, now with the military heavily involved, was agreed upon. The revised plan focused on just one state being a test bed for how it could be rolled out across the country.

Even so it was a mammoth undertaking, one that had never been attempted before. The route to achieve Charles Kingston's lofty ambitions would take years or decades. With an election looming he couldn't wait that long. He wanted it completed in only two years.

To put it mildly, everyone involved had reservations. They could find a hundred reasons why the wheels could fall off this extraordinary scheme. Except Charles Kingston.

Brushing aside their concerns he ordered the plans for ReFederalization to be rolled out. He was looking forward to being the first senior government official to step foot in the eastern USA for six years.

The scene of his historic political triumph was to be, of course: Frankfort, Kentucky.

If you'd like advance notice and the chance to receive a free preview copy of 'Kentucky Rises', go to our Face Book page:

French Creek. The book

Thank you! Look forward to seeing you there.
Paul Rowney

Thank you! For reading *French Creek.*

I do hope you enjoyed the book. All authors crave feedback from readers, good or bad. It helps us create better books for future readers.

If you liked what you read their are two places you can go to leave a review-the lifeblood of a successful author and book.

-Join our Facebook Group where you can leave comments about French Creek and join in the discussion about post apocalyptic living in America.

-Go to the book's page on Amazon, here.

Read the sequel to *French Creek* before everyone else.

The follow up to *French Creek* will be published in 2023. It will reveal how the Government in the West finally starts to try and bring the East back into the 21st century. If you'd like advance notice of this book-and the chance to read a free copy, drop me an email at: paul@phrmedia.com and I'll make sure your the first to know when it's available.

Made in the USA
Monee, IL
25 February 2023